UP IN ONTARIO

UP IN ONTARIO

a novel by

JAMES SHERRETT

TURNSTONE PRESS

Turnstone Press
607-100 Arthur Street
Artspace Building
Winnipeg, MB
R3B 1H3 Canada
www.TurnstonePress.com

Turnstone Press gratefully acknowledges the assistance of The Canada Council for the Arts, the Manitoba Arts Council, the Government of Canada through the Book Publishing Industry Development Program and the Government of Manitoba through the Department of Culture, Heritage and Tourism, Arts Branch, for our publishing activities.

The Canada Council | Le Conseil des Arts
for the Arts | du Canada

MANITOBA arts COUNCIL
CONSEIL DES DU MANITOBA

Canada

Cover design: Tétro Design
Interior design: Sharon Caseburg
Printed and bound in Canada by Friesens for Turnstone Press.

National Library of Canada Cataloguing in Publication Data

Sherrett, James, 1975-

Up in Ontario / James Sherrett.

ISBN 0-88801-286-1

I. Title.

PS8587.H3945U6 2003   C813'.54   C2003-905319-9

Turnstone Press is committed to reducing the consumption of old growth forests in the books we publish. This book is printed on acid-free paper that is 100% ancient forest free.

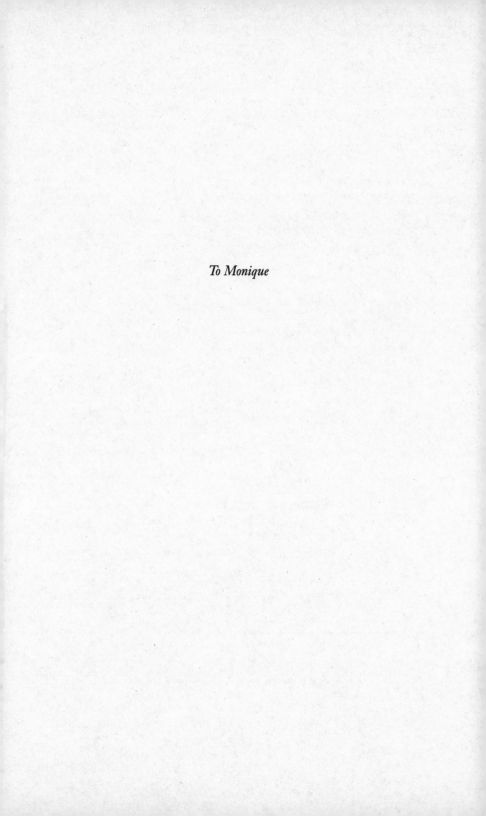

To Monique

ACKNOWLEDGEMENTS

For editorial advice, support, patience and excellence in partnership, I would like to thank Monique. For editorial and professional advice, through the many stages of the genesis of this story, I would like to thank Wayne Tefs. Thank you to Turnstone Press for publishing first books. Thank you also to David Arnason, Scott Montgomery, Jesse Simon, Stephen Osborne, Cassandra MacLean, Shannon Emmerson, David Jenkins, Julie Grundvig and Pat Buckna for contributing.

Finally, I would like to thank my family for all their varieties of support and caring. Mom, Scott, Dad, Linda, Nanny and Pa all had a hand in making the writing of this book possible. Hockey stars often thank their family for driving them to the rinks at six a.m. and freezing their toes off watching, and that sentiment seems apt to me now.

This story, like any story,
is true if you believe it to be.

—*J.S.*

FIRST

MANY YEARS LATER, AS SHE WALKED DOWN THE AISLE TO MARRY her second husband, Christine Johnson was to remember the first time she saw Gilbert Dubois. At the time, he smiled at her with what seemed like his whole body, held out his hand for hers, and helped her off the dock of Smith Camps into a small boat, where he taught her and her father how to read the maps and handle the engine through the choppy water. Christine was eighteen. In that small bay on the shore of Lake of the Woods, she felt the warm hand of Gilbert close over her own on the tiller of the twenty-horse Mercury outboard, and nudge her to apply the gas. The blond hair on his tanned arm brushed against her own arm as he said, "Just gently. Get the feel for it going slow first."

For the next two weeks, Christine watched Gilbert. From behind her sunglasses, in a beach chair beside her mother, she watched Gilbert load the guests and their boats with fishing gear

3

and coolers, watched his balance as he pushed the boats away from the dock and stepped in at once, ready to guide them around the lake. When Gilbert crouched down to untie a boat from the dock, Christine would lean forward in her two-piece and hold her breath watching the fine lines of muscle in the small of his back. When he looked back at her she didn't look away like she did when someone caught her staring in the city; she continued to watch him as he worked, as he returned from a day on the water and unloaded the boats, as his bare feet left footprints on the hot dock after he jumped into the lake to cool off.

One morning, Christine saw Gilbert on the dock showing a young boy how to jig a line down among the weeds to catch perch, and she walked up behind them to watch. She learned how to string a section of nightcrawler onto a hook and that Gilbert, who everyone called Gill, spoke with a slight lisp that made him pronounce her name in a way she repeated to herself over and over. Just before sunset, Gill showed up at the door of their rented cabin and asked if she would walk with him out to the point. He took her down a path along the shore to a quiet bay where a canoe rested on the rocks. They paddled out over the calm water and watched the setting sun turn the sky red and orange and purple. Christine told Gill how her mother Anne, who was twelve years younger than her father Spenser, had brought them to this place on the edge of nowhere so they could spend time together and see nature. Since her father had taken a promotion, her parents had been experiencing what her mother called "challenges." They were looking at a new house in a better neighbourhood, and her father spent most weekends travelling on business. Christine did not repeat to Gill how her mother had explained that a wife needed to have a good grasp of her husband's interests. Being on summer vacation, Christine wanted nothing but to be in the city with her friends, sitting around swimming pools and rubbing baby oil into her skin; instead, she had ended up on the shore of Lake of the Woods at Smith Camps with her parents.

The next night when Gill showed up at the cabin door Christine met him on the porch and they walked down to the canoe again, and the next night as well, though the third night was windier and they paddled further, to an island, where they got out and crept down to the shore to watch a pair of loons. They later spread a blanket and stripped out of their clothes and swam off the rocks together. Her legs clasped around his waist in the cool water, and she ran her hands through his wet hair while they kissed. At that moment, all Christine wanted was to stroke her hands over the blond hair on Gill's forearms, to hold on to the muscles in the small of his back and to pull his smile close to her.

When they tried to return the wind had picked up and the water was rolling and she remembered being terrified of tipping. She sat in the bottom of the canoe on the blanket while little droplets of spray cooled her face, and Gill paddled in the back. The lights shone through the windows of the rented cabin when they returned and Christine's mother waited at the kitchen table reading a paperback. She asked Christine to sit down, then she talked to her about being responsible and not getting herself into trouble like she had when she had been Christine's age. Christine remembered the smell of Jiffy Pop popcorn, which they made on the stovetop, and the way her mother cried when she hugged her and told her she didn't want her to make any mistakes with her life. At dawn, the sound of outboard motors woke Christine a moment before her father let the screen door slam behind him. Gill and her father fished all day and returned before dinner with a limit of pickerel. The last night of her stay at Smith Camps, Christine asked to see where Gill lived, and so he brought her to his campsite in a bay around the corner from Smith Camps, where his yellow tent and clothes line and fire pit all lay within a small clearing under a stand of white pine. When she asked, he told her he lived at the campsite because he didn't get along with his father, and it was better for him to be on his own, close to where he worked.

By the time Christine returned to the city, she and Gill had promised to keep in touch and to see each other when he came to Winnipeg. When Christine told her friend Cathy Dumont about Gill, she didn't get the reaction she was looking for. "He sounds like some kind of bushman. A voyageur like you hear about in those songs we used to have to sing." Cathy's family owned a jewelry store downtown and let the girls try on the rings after closing. Christine decided she did not care what Cathy thought, and she invited Gill to a play in Winnipeg where he could meet all her friends. When he arrived on time, in his canvas coat and corduroys, Christine felt awkward and ashamed, as she wore her best dress and had expected Gill to be dressed up in a shirt and tie, just as Bryan Richardson had dressed when he had taken her to see *West Side Story*. But she felt differently by the time the lights went down, and she leaned over in her seat to take his hand. They had walked through the lobby and her man had been the best looking in the room. Gill spent that night in the guest room of the Johnson house. Before bed, Christine's father Spenser invited him for a nightcap of port, and they discussed Gill's plans for the future and Spenser's interest in a proposed land development at Clearwater Bay on Lake of the Woods.

The fall stretched into winter and then on to spring with Christine busy in her first year of university. The next summer, after she had spoken to Gill on the phone a few times through the winter and had received a card and letter from him at Christmas, she hopped on the bus and he met her at the depot in Kenora. It was a week before her family arrived at Smith Camps and she took a room at the Inn of the Woods. Gill picked her up in a truck that smelled like old leather and they kissed on the bench seat as if he'd been away at war.

Every evening that week after his work at Smith Camps, Gill drove in to Kenora where Christine waited for him in the lobby of the Inn in a new sun dress, with her hair down over her tanned shoulders and her skin smelling of apples. Frantic with desire and laughing at once, they raced up the stairs, pulled their clothes off and slid into each other as soon as they closed the door, sometimes making it to the bed and other times ending up on the floor, wrestling for who would be on the top or who would end up with the carpet burns afterward. They used one of the queen-sized beds in the room for sleeping and the other for making love. When they were spent, they lay in the light of the setting sun and felt the breeze off the water cool the sweat from their skin. By dark they were so hungry they could barely speak. Gill took her to a different restaurant every night, and on the night before her family arrived, Christine chose a place on the waterfront where Gill suggested she order pickerel, caught fresh from the lake. Afterward, they ate ice cream and walked along the shore while the float planes landed in front of them. A thunder-shower rolled in and lit up the sky with great forks of lightning, and they found shelter under the awning of the Blue Heron gift shop. While they kissed, she felt his erection press against her thigh, and she smiled as a passing car honked and flashed its lights.

When they met Christine's family on the docks of Smith Camps the next morning they were late. They had played too long in the shower before setting out in the boat from Kenora. The severe look on her mother's face when they docked told Christine more than she needed to know; her mother had been young and reckless in the summer and remembered well what it was like to find yourself beyond the boundaries of youth. For the whole trip she kept her eye on Gill and Christine, as if her vigilance could keep her daughter from doing what she wanted to do. One night, she told Christine that she wished she had never changed her name when she had married, and she hoped Christine talked to her before she thought of marriage. That week ended up as Christine's last trip to Smith Camps with her mother and father. The next year Christine's father made the trip with two fellows he knew from the golf club, and Gill guided them further down the lake, past French Narrows to The Elbow, where they caught a limit in two hours and ate shore lunch on the rocks.

Once the fishing season closed in November, Gill moved to a one-bedroom apartment on Lanark Street in Winnipeg. He took a job with CN switching cars in the rail yard and waited for his acceptance to the winter term at University of Manitoba. Christine decorated the apartment in January when she moved in. They commuted to school together in her Datsun 510 and took turns packing lunch. The summer that followed, Christine and Gill married in a ceremony at St. Charles Golf Course, and they lived in the apartment on Lanark for three years until she had completed her law degree and was pregnant. Just before they learned they were to become parents, they signed the deed for a parcel of land in Storm Bay on the north shore of Lake of the Woods. The summer came and they camped out on the land every weekend and built their cabin. By the third trimester of the pregnancy Christine felt exhausted just thinking about commuting every weekend, and the cabin sat for the winter half-finished with the shingles on the roof but none of the windows in their frames. Wade Dubois was born on March 3rd, 1974, with a full head of fair hair and blue eyes and long fingers just like Christine. The next time Christine visited the cabin, Gill had finished most of the work except for the decorating, and he led her with Wade in her arms through the door to give them the grand tour of the place she knew he hoped would become their home.

And what happened then? As much as they thought and hoped being married and having a son would not change what they had, it did. Over time, they both changed and their relationship did not change along with them. Reconciliations and understandings became harder to achieve. For Christine, Gill remained a great guy, someone she loved to be with. But he was not ready to be a great husband or father, and Christine needed him to be both. She wanted to go back to work and she needed him to be there for her and for Wade. Over time, stubbornness and conflicted loyalties took hold of each of them, and their relationship stretched beyond its capacity to hold each of them to the idea of the other, and to the idea that they would be together always.

And so many years later, Christine arrived at the altar where her second husband waited, and she stopped remembering how the summer weeks used to fly by when she and Gill and Wade were together in their cabin on the shore of Lake of the Woods.

AT THE CABIN
—*July, 1977*—

AS HE ARRIVED AT THE END OF THE DOCK, GILL UNBUTTONED HIS pants and let them fall around his ankles, stepped out of them, skinned his chamois shirt over his head, and stared down at his trembling reflection in the flat water of Lake of the Woods. He dove in and the water closed around him in a rush. This early in the year the water still stung, providing a chilling headrush: sixteen is sixty-one. Gill surfaced. His arms swooped up—left, right, left, right—like paddlewheels pulling him back to the dock, up the ladder. He bent at the waist to a dish on a board, plucked the soap and lathered, sluicing himself for a second dive, this time no pulling strokes, no hands tracing a heart shape and then cutting it in two, only brisk rubbing: suds out of clefts, hair, wrinkles. He wore no swim trunks, no wet fabric to drip and carry water after he'd dried with the faded blue towel that curled around his waist and tucked under itself like a sleeping animal in

10

the cold. He slid his feet into his bathing thongs and slapped his way up the dock to the winding path, to the cabin, to get dressed. Things to do, a meeting to keep, and a rhythm to it all through the dipping waves out on the lake and the rustling leaves of the poplar above; a rhythm that included collecting his wife and son. But before that, there was the cabin to ready, wine to chill, dust to wipe, floors to sweep. Gill let the screen door bang shut behind him as his eyes adjusted to the darkness in the cabin, and he stopped in the middle where he could survey everything, check to make sure it was right, fit for his family. His books made neat piles row against row slumped onto the wall, blankets had been smoothed for sleep, sheets pulled tight underneath, photo collages squared and grinning back.

Gill let the towel unroll from its tuck around his waist and slipped into dry clothes. The towel, halved and wrinkled, hung on the railing of the stairs leading down to the path, to the dock, the lake. Gill felt a tightness in his chest as time crept up on him. Out the back door and up to the driveway, he turned and looked back at the cabin, at the first glimpse Christine and Wade would see. The ignition of the Land Cruiser fired and Gill caught the roll of tires with the clutch, reversed in a wince of gearing, and drove out along the gravel road followed by a ghost of dust. The bends of gravel led to more and better travelled roads, through the swamps and over creeks, and further, to the highway, where he turned into traffic speeding by and into town to the two he loved.

On the way to Dryden, Thunder Bay and Sault Ste Marie, the bus stopped once in Kenora at the Norman Hotel, where Christine and Gill had gone for dinner when first dating. Gill parked the Land Cruiser under the wide branches of the white pines, bought a *Winnipeg Free Press* at the hotel gift shop, then sat on the hood reading the news from the city and the world. The bus depot parking lot was in front of him, the sun high in the cloudless blue sky. He looked up when he heard the growl of gears from the bus as it downshifted at the top of the hill. A line of cars towing boats and campers with their windows open streamed past as the bus pulled off the highway: the Friday afternoon eastbound from Winnipeg, twenty minutes late. The first person off the bus when the door swung open was Christine, a black bag over one shoulder and Wade in her arms. She put Wade down and pointed to Gill who was walking towards them. When he saw Wade start to run towards him, Gill squatted on his heels to catch his son when he jumped into his arms.

"Make me fly, Daddy," Wade said after he had hugged his father. "Like Superman."

"You're getting too big," Gill said as he moved his hands to Wade's hips and lifted him up over his head, up to arms length, where Wade arched his back, straightened his legs, and thrust his arms out in front of him in perfect flying position. Gill held Wade as high as he could until his shoulders burned, then he pressed him up to balance him, and let him fall, never taking his hands off him, letting him fall straight down and feet first. Wade's blond hair flew up and his eyes grew wide as Gill caught him just above the ground. As they looked into each others' faces Gill felt an overpowering love for the little creature in front of him with its own name and eyes and voice. Then they started over to the bus to find Christine, who had just staggered free of the throng of passengers.

"Let's get out of here, Gill," she said.

Gill picked up the two bags and started whistling. "Ready as you are."

"Mom, did you see me?" Wade said.

"What were you doing, Wade?" Christine said and looked at Gill.

"Flying. Daddy makes me fly. Like Superman."

"I saw that. It was pretty good."

"We could show you. Right, Daddy? We could show her."

"We'll show your mom later, Wade," Gill said. "After we've practised."

Wade took his backpack from Christine and tried to whistle his own song. Christine held Wade's hand with her left and Gill's hand with her right and the three of them walked over to the green Land Cruiser where the windows were down. As Gill loaded Wade into the back seat, she got into the passenger seat, tilted her head back, and closed her eyes. Gill knew well the feeling of arriving where you wanted to be, of needing time to let all else melt away, making the space for what you wanted. He was sure the bus trip could not have been easy, it being hot, the bus being full and Wade being a bundle of energy. A few minutes later, they crossed the Winnipeg River, where the current was strong, swirling and eddying below them and the water pressed out of Lake of the Woods to the prairies in the west, and Gill said, "Wade, your great-grandfather, who came to this country from Dundee, Scotland with a hundred dollars on his pocket, he helped build this bridge when he came back from the war." He pointed at the bridge they were crossing with its high cement columns on the four corners shaped with sculptures of Indians fishing and netting and hunting. "A long time ago. When I was young like you."

Wade crawled into the front seat and stood on the floor between Christine's feet to look out the window. "Where is he now, Daddy?"

"He's gone," Gill said. "Up in the sky." Wade looked up at the clear sky and Gill wondered how to explain to him that his great-grandfather was dead, and his grandfather soon would be as well, and one day he himself would be. "Look, Wade," Gill said pointing out over the water at a big boat cruising by. "That's what we're going to be doing. Driving the boat on the water." Wade put his hand on the window sill and watched the boat run through the waves, parallel to where they drove on the highway. Christine placed her right hand on his stomach and held the back of his overall straps with her left. Gill drove on and watched the boat with Wade until the highway went up a hill and inland.

They passed through Kenora and out the far side with the lines of traffic. Gill played a game with Wade to spot license plates with different colours: Michigan, Indiana, Missouri, Alberta, Illinois, Wisconsin, Quebec, Minnesota, North Dakota, Iowa and Saskatchewan. By far the most other than Ontario were from Manitoba, and Gill told Wade that people called these the Tobans. The names and colours of the license plates occupied Wade until they were east of Kenora and up to highway speed. By the time they turned off the highway, Gill knew it was time for a swim in the lake and dinner. It was the start of the Canada Day long weekend, the weather was beautiful, and they were together. Once they turned onto the gravel road off the highway, Wade sat on Gill's lap, leaned on the rim of the black steering wheel and felt it pull left and right around the curves in the road and through his hands. The wind came in the windows as the road passed through a stand of ancient white pine and the fresh smell told Gill they were almost there. Two more turns, a right and then a left, off the logging road and onto the road leading to the cabin. Up a rise, the grass growing long and green through the moss, each tall blade tinkling the underside of the Land Cruiser, each one sounding out a distinct note between the twin tracks of gravel, and at the crest, there it was. The road went another twenty yards to a gravel clearing; then a path led down to the cabin, the brown roof visible over the brush and through the trees, and beyond, between tall pines on either side, past the stone chimney, to Lake of the Woods.

Once the bags had been brought in, Gill put Wade down for a nap. He spread a light flannel sheet over his sleeping son, covered his legs with a sleeping bag and kissed him on the forehead. In the quiet that followed he joined Christine on the porch and they looked out on the lake in silence. While Gill had been with Wade, Christine had given herself a tour of the cabin. It was her first visit since the previous September, and Gill had heard her talking to herself, noting details of the work that he had completed. He looked around at the cabin and felt proud of the work he had accomplished. The couch they sat on he had built himself in a difficult process, in which he assembled the oak pieces to finish it, then disassembled them to move it, then reassembled them to sit on. And the design he had done himself as well; rope netting woven into a pattern supported the cushions instead of springs which would rust, the sliding support beams extended out at the feet to re-lay the cushion and make a bed.

"This couch looks great in here," Christine said. "Now we need to get you on some chairs."

"There's lots still to do; the floors, the walls, the doors. The outside's done. And the windows and insulation. And all the electrical and plumbing, they're done too." Gill pointed with his hands and rolled his head around the cabin as he spoke. "What do you think about putting curtains up until the walls are done? Some heavy blankets on rods so they'll slide, for privacy. But the first thing we need in here is a table. Smiths have one for me they don't need anymore."

"It's oak, too?"

"Yep. Rough around the edges, a little chewed by use. But workable," Gill said, enjoying the regular rhythms of their small talk, when they got to know each other again. His job kept him here and her articling work kept her in the city. Wade sometimes stayed with Gill but mostly stayed with Christine.

"Do you have any work to do this weekend?" Christine asked.

Gill shook his head. He knew it was a busy weekend and a part of him felt he should have been working even though he knew he needed time off as much as anyone. Besides, most of his clients were from the States, and for them, next weekend was the big one; Fourth of July their celebration. Gill had done well all week guiding a few families from Wisconsin staying at Smith's, and they had tipped him generously.

"This weekend," Gill said, "my job is to see you and that son of ours."

Christine sipped from the glass of wine she'd poured herself, rubbed her body along the back of the couch to Gill and nestled her head onto his shoulder. She put her hand onto his leg and he laid his over it while stroking her hair with his other hand, smoothing it behind her ear and finding it smelled of apples. She told him about the hierarchy of the law firm, how partners ran the show even if they had no clue, how the pecking order was determined by how much each partner billed. Gill listened and let her roll over all of the things that she would have been telling him every night if they lived together. "I'm so glad to be here, Gill. The office is just hell before a long weekend. All the lawyers want to get out of there. The workload for the students goes through the roof. Some things for next week I couldn't get done."

"Are you going back early?"

"I brought them with me."

Gill's hand stopped in mid-stroke, cupping the back of her head. "I thought we said no work on our weekends."

"I know. What am I going to say? It has to get done. The lawyer I'm working with this month, Gordon, he needs it done." She sat up and looked at Gill. "What else am I supposed to do?"

"Tell him you can't do it."

"I can't not do it," Christine said loudly. Gill held his finger up to his lips to quiet her. "Oh, he sleeps fine," she continued. "Other than the secretaries, I'm the only woman in the office, how will it look if I'm the only one not done?"

Gill shrugged and didn't know what to say; he knew she was a hard and determined worker, if she could have had things done by Friday, they would have been done. "So you do it."

"I know, but how do you think I feel? I don't want to be working on a file when I'm at the lake with the husband I've seen only two days in the last month."

Gill stroked her hair and didn't say anything, thinking that he had learned that sometimes it was just best not to say anything, to let her work things out for herself. She took another sip of her wine and out in front of them the wind swept across the lake, the waves rolling in from the west and then away to the east. They looked out onto Storm Bay, to the small unnamed island in front of the cabin and the reef off the far end, to the rise of rocks on the shore to the east and the jack pines standing amidst the granite rubble, and to the distance, to thousands of separate islands and channels and reefs, like a huge mirror had folded in on itself to repeat a reflection over and over. Without a guide, anyone could get lost.

In 1949, after an eight-hour journey by boat from Kenora, Ken Smith arrived at the bottom of an unnamed bay to the east of Heenan Point on the shore of Lake of the Woods and built the first cabin of what was to become Smith Camps. At first, Ken and his wife Nancy rented the two extra rooms of that first cabin to guests who came to fish for pickerel, jackfish and bass during the hot summers. In the evenings, Ken set a fire on the beach and cooked the catch of the day in a cast-iron skillet the size of a truck tire. Nancy brought salads and breads from the kitchen and they sat with their guests on stumps cut from the clearing where a second cabin was being built. Gill had heard the stories about the early days so many times he could recite them himself, before they had the guest cabins, when guests and the Smiths lived together. Since he had started working at the camp fifteen years after it opened, and since he bought his lot from Ken Smith six years later, the Smiths were like family to Gill. For two summers, Gill worked double shifts to pay back what he owed Ken, and the fishermen who came a long way to fish at Smith's were good tippers, and Gill ended up making good money without his wage. The same fishermen came back year after year and Gill guided them to some of the same spots, and some new spots, and eventually, as the facilities at Smith's got more like home, the families of the fishermen started joining them.

And so Christine ended up at Smith Camps five years after Gill, with her mother and father, and their marital challenges and their shiny new Cadillac. When Gill first saw Christine he felt struck by the beauty of her skin as it played out along her long, tanned legs. He had never known a girl to wear sunglasses before and when she lifted them up to shake his hand upon first meeting him he felt like the ability to speak had slipped away. She still brought this speechlessness to him sometimes, if they had been apart for a long time, as they frequently were, or if she dressed up for a special occasion; she stunned him still. So it made him sad to see her tired from her job in the city, where he could not help her as much as he wanted to with their son.

The next afternoon, as Gill took Wade down to the lake so she could get her work done, he continued to think about the circumstances of their life and he wished they could always be together; that either Christine could find work in Kenora as a lawyer or he could bring himself to move back to Winnipeg. Wade and Gill swam from the dock around the shore to a rock a foot under the surface and rested. Wade slid and climbed all over the rocks and Gill's torso. The water in the shallows felt warm, the small green algae suspended throughout and floating on the surface. Wade laughed and crawled onto Gill's knee where he got shot out into the deeper water and then paddled back for more. When Wade tired, they swam back along the shore to the dock and Gill climbed up the swim ladder with Wade in his life jacket clinging to his back. Wade shivered and his teeth chattered while out in the water of the bay, beyond the small island, a pair of loons fished for ciscos and shiners. The loons dove and surfaced within a small area, looked around with their sleek heads, and dove again. As they fished and their prey schooled up in the shallows, the area they surfaced in came closer and closer to Wade and Gill, who were sitting on the end of the dock. With the calm lake and the sun low in the sky, the circles the loons made as they surfaced and dove rang outwards like a bull's eye. Gill leaned down over Wade's ear and whispered to him "Stay still. Just watch them." And right then, a loon surfaced in the dark water off the end of the dock and Wade pointed.

"Loon," Gill said to him, pointing as well.

"Loon," Wade said as the loon dove and its mate surfaced a little farther out. Gill could see the loon as it dove under the surface and he followed it with his eyes. The loon's wings spread out as it swam, steering and controlling its dive, its feet pumped under the tail-feathers and it knifed through the water. At the deepest point of its dive, the loon's neck coiled and then shot out, spearing a minnow. "Loon," Wade said again as the loon broke the calm of the water with the minnow. One flip of the loon's neck and the minnow went head-first down its throat. The loon dove again, out into deeper water, and soon the pair were out of sight behind the rocks. Wade shivered a little on Gill's lap, his lips bluish and some of his hair still matted from swimming.

"Ready to go warm up, partner?" Gill said.

Wade nodded and Gill gathered their clothes in his one arm and carried Wade up in the other. They did not disturb Christine who sat working in the front porch; they went around the cabin and in the back door. Gill helped Wade change into his sweat pants and then changed into his own, and they put a saucepan of milk on to make hot chocolate. The fridge in the cabin was an old white one with a silver pull handle and Wade's colourful magnetic alphabet stuck on the side. While the milk warmed, Gill showed Wade how to throw the letters at the fridge so they stuck. But as hard as he tried, Wade could not get them to stick as his father had. Once the milk was ready, Gill made three cups of hot chocolate and carried them out to the porch. Wade brought out the marshmallows that Gill handed him and they made Christine stop her work and sip with them from tea spoons. Gill and Christine talked and Wade ran around the porch pretending he was playing goalie for the Winnipeg Jets. In a few minutes the sugar from the hot chocolate wore off and he curled up on the couch between his parents and put his head down on Christine's lap. She shifted her work books to the floor and pushed them under the couch with her bare heels.

"How's it going?" Gill asked.

"Okay. I'm half-way. If you can take him," she said and pointed at Wade's back, "with you tomorrow morning, I'll be able to finish."

"Sure. I could do that," Gill said and thought of the hundreds of new things he could do with Wade, things he thought of all the time when he worked alone at the cabin. "I thought maybe we'd camp out one night, out on Oliver Island. Where you and I used to go. It won't be much different than before, only three of us now."

"One night?"

"Yep. We can try things. If we want to stay two, we can stay two." Gill saw her nod even though he could feel her skepticism. She ran her finger around the sides of her hot chocolate mug and licked the chocolate from her finger, then rubbed her eyes and sighed. "Is it that bad?"

"What?" she said and smiled, "Work? No, it just wears me out. I wish you were there with me."

"I do too, but you know I have to be here."

"I know, but I wish you didn't. I wish money wasn't such a thing, such a necessity. I like my work and the people there are great. But sometimes I wish I could just be at home with Wade and have you at work and be the way all my friends are. My old friends."

Gill laughed a short little breath of a laugh. "You wouldn't really be happy."

The loons out on Storm Bay had finished fishing and were calling to each other, the long, swelling cries carrying over the water to the cabin. Gill felt the familiar tones of the same conversation they had been having for years now start to settle in; a conversation that presented itself at every juncture of their life, at the point of every decision, but remained without a solution except the separation they lived with. "You and I both know it's not just the one thing. It's not just money."

"Yeah," she said and looked out at the lake. The breeze came up again and it was nice after the heat of the sun that lingered in the cabin. She let out a little laugh and turned to Gill. "The other day at work, Gordon, the partner I've been working with, who charges one-hundred and fifty dollars an hour, he told me that he doesn't know where his money goes. Can you imagine, a hundred and fifty an hour?"

Gill whistled and Wade stirred and tucked his hands up tighter under his chin.

"We were having a meeting and it had run late and we were waiting for a memo from another office. I was sitting in on the meeting because Gordon wanted me to. Before the others came back, Gordon told me about his trip to Hawaii. I told him I always wanted to go to Hawaii but never had the money. So he said I should see his pictures. He told me where to go, what to do and what not to do. You should have seen these photos, they were incredible." Gill nodded and watched the poplar leaves twist on their stems in the breeze. "And yesterday morning, Gordon came in and told me about the play he saw the night before. A British play from London. I asked him how much tickets were because I'd heard it was good and I wanted to go. But they were fifty dollars each. But he's got a really good sense of humour and told me about his date. She wanted to see how much she could get away with after the show since he was paying. They went to a nice restaurant and she ordered a bottle of the best wine. It cost over a hundred dollars. Gordon excused himself and got up to go to the bathroom and left her. He told me he wrote her a note for the waiter to give her. The note said what a wonderful time he'd had and that there would be a cab waiting for her outside to take her home, compliments of him, no matter how long she took to come out."

Christine laughed and Gill smiled and stretched his arm out across the back of the sofa. "So are you going to bill two-fifty an hour one day?" he said to his wife.

"One day. But I won't be like Gordon."

"No?"

"No," she said and looked out over the water. Gill swallowed the last sip of his hot chocolate and reached to collect the other two cups to take to the kitchen to rinse. "Do you not want me to tell you about work?"

"Sometimes I don't want to know. You never want to hear about my work," he said and put his hand on Wade's warm leg. "It's not a big deal, Christine. Sometimes I just want to concentrate on the here and now." Wade twitched his arms and leg in his sleep, like he was dreaming of chasing something or of being chased. Gill started to pick Wade up to carry him to the back bedroom for his nap.

"When he's in bed do you want to come back out?" Christine asked. "Sit with me while I read?"

Gill thought a second while he was sliding his arms under Wade's legs and back to cradle him when he picked him up. "I think it's time for me to have a nap too. Finish up out here and it'll be warm when you get in."

"I'll come now. This can wait."

Gill and Christine met in the bed and held each other in the place where he slept alone most nights. At some time they both drifted off to sleep. Wade woke them when he patted Christine's head with his hand. Gill dressed Wade in warmer clothes to take him out in the boat, his new boat, a eighteen-foot aluminum Sylvan he had bought from a guiding client from Illinois who had gotten cancer and been unable to return to fish. Wade followed Gill down the eight stairs to the path and the dock and the lake, and Gill carried their tackle, clothes and snacks in his brown backpack.

When they reached the dock, Gill strapped Wade into his life jacket, lifted him down and into the boat, untied the lines and stepped in himself. He pulled a paddle from a storage compartment and started to paddle them out into the lake. Wade watched him paddle for a few seconds, then climbed up on the driver's seat and looked into the deepening water, where Gill saw him watch the little whirlpools made by the strokes of the paddle. It was Wade's first time fishing. The quiet of the bay stretched out in front of them, calm like the water. A shining black cormorant flew low over the water from the western shore of Storm Bay to the east where the nose of the boat pointed. Gill planned to paddle around the corner, into the next inlet of Storm Bay, just out of sight of the cabin, where the shore grew marshy and the tops of the seaweed stuck up to the surface of the lake. Gill knew perch lived in the weeds, willing to strike anything put in front of them.

"Where are we going, Daddy?" Wade asked, looking up from the water.

"Just around the corner. To catch some fish."

"Fishing?"

"For perch. Your rod is right here, try and work it," Gill said and watched as Wade held the rod like he had seen done. Gill kept paddling, watching Wade concentrating on the rod, the line from the reel strung tight through the three eyes and tied to a swivel latched over the last eye. "Here, hold it like this, partner," Gill said, putting down the paddle and showing Wade to wrap his left hand around the cork handle. "This is the reel. This is the handle for the reel and you take it like this." Gill held the reel handle and gave it a small crank until the drag clicked on the tight line. "But don't turn it until we get you set up, okay?"

Wade nodded as Gill handed him the rod. He held it like he'd been shown, his left hand around the cork handle, his right on the handle of the reel. Gill picked up the paddle and moved them into the weed beds, saying, "Listen, Wade," and pointing to the floor of the boat where the tips of the weeds at the surface of the lake stroked across the aluminum hull with a ticking sound.

"What is it?" Wade said when he heard the weeds.

"Weeds. See them out there?" Gill asked and pointed to the water around them.

"Can't see," Wade said, standing on his tip toes against the gunnel. Gill lifted him and pointed again.

"See the tops of the green weeds?" Wade nodded. "They rub on the bottom of the boat when we go over them. You don't hear them now?" Wade shook his head. "That's because we're stopped. Listen when we paddle again." Gill took another stroke and the ticking started again, another stroke and it went faster. Wade got down on his hands and knees with his ear to the floorboard as the boat drifted out into the middle of the weed bed. Gill stepped over Wade, hoisted the anchor from the front storage compartment, secured the rope and threw it into the lake. The splash and a zip of the rope being pulled out startled Wade and he jumped up with a scared look on his face.

"You ready to fish, partner?"

Wade nodded and brought his rod up to the front of the boat. He sat beside Gill on the nose and they looked through the tackle box for a hook. In Gill's brown backpack were a Styrofoam cup of worms and some frozen minnows, which he unwrapped and crushed over the water. Wade peered down at the pieces of minnow floating on the water and held his nose as Gill splashed his hands in the lake. Perch started to collect just under the surface of the water with the aggressive ones darting up and hitting the pieces of minnow.

"Come here and see, Wade," Gill said and held out his arms. "Those are the perch."

"Perch," Wade said as Gill selected a hook from his tackle box, slipped the hook into the swivel of Wade's rod, pulled a worm from the Styrofoam cup, pinched it in two, pinched it in two again, and strung the shorter section onto Wade's hook. He lifted

Wade up to stand at the nose of the boat and see into the water.

Gill asked, "Do you want me to show you how?"

Wade nodded, excited by the darting shadows of perch he could see in the weeds. Gill pressed the release button on the reel and the hook and worm dropped to the water and slowly sunk. Right away, a perch about the size of Wade's hand streaked up out of the deeper water and hit the worm. Gill waited a second, let the end of the rod twitch twice and then jerked it up, pulling the wriggling perch out of the water to hang in the air. Wade clapped and watched the perch dance on the end of the taut line. Gill pulled the rod in and laid the perch on its side. He unhooked it and watched as Wade reached out to touch it. The perch gave a flip and Wade jerked back his hand, so Gill picked up the fish and held it while Wade touched it.

"Ooooo," Wade said stroking the scales one way and then the other.

"Let's put him back," Gill said.

"No. Keep him," Wade said, still touching the perch.

"We'll catch another. Watch, partner."

Gill dropped the perch back into the lake, picked up the rod, dropped the hook and worm in and pulled out another perch, bigger this time. He showed Wade how to unhook the perch and they threw it back. Then he handed the rod to Wade and it was his turn. Gill watched him concentrate on what he was doing, his little face frowning. The distance from the height of the rod above the water to where the perch struck the worm was so short there was no reeling involved in bringing the fish in. Gill sat next to Wade and talked to him and watched him concentrating. The perch were harder to catch than they looked, and Wade hooked only one about every fourth strike. Soon, they had to replace their bait with another section of worm but the appetite of the little fish never ended. Every time Wade lowered his bait down he got a strike. Gill felt sure they must have caught each fish twice, the odd perch bigger than the others, giving Wade a fight so that Gill had to watch the rod did not go overboard.

Wade and Gill fished through a light rain until they both felt hungry and could stay out no longer. Then Gill got the paddle back out and showed Wade how to paddle. When they got to the dock they tied up and Gill lifted Wade out of the boat, and they went up to the cabin to make grilled cheese sandwiches. Christine had left them a note saying she'd gone for a walk. As the rain fell into the water, Wade and Gill carried their grilled cheeses out to the porch and listened for the weather forecast on the radio. A bald eagle circled in the sky, wheeling around on the moving air and then returning to its nest in a crook of a wind-blown pine, whose limbs grew on only three sides, bent back by the prevailing winds. All of the white pines on the point at the entrance to Storm Bay grew stunted in the same way, formed by the wind. Wade went down for his afternoon nap while Gill washed up their dishes in the kitchen.

Christine returned just as Gill slid the frying pan away and they sat on the couch on the porch reading, as he had imagined they would do when he had chosen to build the couch seven feet long. He picked up a section of the newspaper from the previous Saturday, she pushed through the last pages of her brief. They made dinner together when they got hungry, they went to bed when the sun went down.

The next morning they packed the camping gear into the boat and set out for Oliver Island, where they found their favourite campsite unoccupied, and pitched the tent under a group of pine on a point. Oliver Island was a favourite place for people to camp on the lake and often canoe trips from the YMCA camp spent the night. All day long Gill and Christine and Wade swam off the rocks, lay in the sun and napped in the shade. At dusk, the bass came up to the shallows to feed on the crayfish and jump out of the water. Gill rigged up his fishing rod with a Red Devil spinner and caught two on consecutive casts while Wade watched

and cheered beside him. They let the fish go as soon as they
caught them and Gill kept casting the lure out, hearing the hum
of line as the hook arced down to the water.

Next morning, the Hibachi barbeque sat on the bare rock in
front of the tent where Gill had left it to cool the night before, a
rope stretched out from one pine trunk to another and towels
and swimsuits hung over it. Three stump sections stood upright
as stools around the fire pit where Wade and Gill and Christine
had sat. The skinned and whittled willow sticks they'd used for
roasting marshmallows and wieners leaned against one of the
stumps. All around the campsite the lake spread out in a mirrored surface. Inside the tent, Gill felt Wade stir beside him. The
night before Gill had told Wade that if he had to go during the
night he should wake Daddy and he would take him. Now the
sun was just starting to spread light around the rim of the horizon, the mist was starting to burn off, and Gill felt Wade curl his
body in the sleeping bag and roll forward onto his hands and
knees. The tent screen unzipped and then a second later Gill
heard the sound of Wade peeing. As long as he doesn't go too far
he'll be all right, Gill thought to himself. The sound of Wade
peeing died away and then there was nothing, no sound. Gill
waited a few seconds, then a few more, heard some water splashing, and then was seized by the sensation that something was not
right. He threw off his sleeping bag and pushed open the screen
zipper. Wade stood facing him, staring at something behind him.
Gill wheeled around and there was a bear; a small bear, like a dog
without a tail.

"Hey!" Gill yelled. "Ahhh!"

He waved his arms and shouted. He ran over to grab two willow branches at the fire pit and the air hummed as he swung
them and shouted. "Ahhh!" The bear dropped its body as soon
as Gill yelled and by the time he held the willow branches it let
out a low woof and ran into the bush. Gill swung the willow

branches against each other and they cracked. He swung them again and one broke, the end spinning away like a boomerang. It whipped through the air past Wade, and Gill leapt from rock to rock down to the shore and crouched and grabbed his son, lifting him onto his shoulder, wrapping him in his arms. He could feel Wade's heart beating against him.

"Jesus Christ, kid, that's a scare," Gill said to Wade. "Jesus Christ."

"What was it, Gill?" Christine said as she scrambled out of the tent.

"A little bear," Gill said.

"Oh shit. Is it gone?"

"Took off into the bush as soon as it heard the shouting."

Gill carried Wade back over to the tent. Wade had tears stretched in lines down his cheeks. Gill sat on one of the stump sections with Wade on his knee. "Wade," he said to him and held him around the arms, "I don't want you to go anywhere without me. That was a bear you just saw and they're dangerous. They can hurt you very badly. Do you understand?"

Wade nodded his head and looked at Gill. The tears were drying on his face and Gill wiped them with the pad of his thumb.

"So you won't do that again?"

Wade shook his head.

"He didn't know, Gill."

"He doesn't have to know."

Wade looked at Christine. "I had to pee," he said.

"And that's good, Wade," Gill said. "But if we tell you to not go out without one of us, you can't. You can't. You just can't. Okay?"

Wade nodded again.

"Don't be too hard on him, Gill. He's never seen a bear before."

"That's good. These bears aren't cartoons, Christine. They're real and can kill kids."

"But he's curious."

"Christine, I told him not to go out without one of us because there are bears on the island."

"Well, we shouldn't have come here then."

"No. He should have listened to me."

Gill and Christine stared at each other. Gill felt the adrenaline pumping through him.

"It's cold," Gill said. "We should all get some clothes on." He stood up with Wade in his arms and ducked into the tent to put on clothes. Christine stayed where she was and Gill changed Wade into his sweatsuit and put on his own sweatsuit.

Just as Gill poked his head back out from the tent, at the edge of the horizon, the top sliver of the sun came up. The water out in front of the campsite bloomed in streaks of sharp oranges ridges. Wade popped his head out and Gill sent him to sit with Christine while he ducked back inside the tent to get her some warmer clothes. When he touched her on the shoulder she turned and he offered her the sweat pants and sweater with a t-shirt inside, and then sat on the stump beside her, and beside Wade, and the three of them sat and watched the sun rise into the sky. The wind started to move the water as if a current pulled the waves to the distance. Christine put her bare feet up on Gill's knee and he closed his hand over her frigid toes to warm them. Wade asked questions about the sun and how it came up every morning and how it looked bigger this morning than when he looked at it in the sky. They sat on their logs and stared out at the lake and the waves coasting away, one after the other, until Wade was bored and hungry. Christine put together a breakfast and Gill prepared the boat to go fishing so that once they had eaten they climbed into the boat and cruised across some open water to the windward shore of an unnamed island. Gill set up Wade with the short ice-fishing rod again and Christine with her own rod.

Soon, Gill had them trolling along the shore trailing their

lines. The next minute, he snapped his wrist and the fishing rod in his hand came alive with a fish fighting him on the end of the line. He cranked the reel four turns to make sure the hook was well set, snapped his wrist again, and let the rod absorb the fight. Wade sat next to him on the edge of the transom, his feet on top of a red gas tank, watching everything his father was doing.

"You ready, partner?" Gill said and he could see Wade watching as the rod jerked in response to every movement the fish made; it straightened and then curved down at a sharp angle to the water.

Wade nodded, still watching.

"Come over here then," Gill said and lifted him over his leg to sit in his lap. Gill held the rod in one arm and hooked the other across Wade's chest. Wade reached out and held the rod and Gill closed his own hands over Wade's, strengthening the grip. "Now reel. Reel him in."

"It's hard," Wade said, struggling to get the handle of the reel in his hand. Gill looked at Christine and she was watching them, smiling, until she got a bite on her own line that surprised her, and she concentrated on what she was doing.

"Keep going, Wade," Gill said, knowing the fish they had hooked was only about a pound. With his hands, he only helped Wade as much as he needed so the rod stayed in the boat. "He's almost here."

"I am," Wade said in deep breaths, cranking for all he was worth.

"Get the net, Christine," Gill said and looked up to see she already had it poised at the edge of the gunnel.

"I lost my bait," she said and the boat leaned hard to the side where they all waited for the fish, the waves rocking them down close to the water and then up again. Wade kept cranking, the gears of the reel ticking out the time of the fight in bursts with Wade's pushing and pulling. The leader cut through the surface of the water and they saw the flash of light on the scales of the fish.

"It's a pickerel," Gill said as Wade cranked the reel and the fish came up, gave one last dive for the bottom, and then Christine scooped the net through the water. She lifted the wriggling fish into the boat, showering them all with drops of water. As soon as she put the fish down on the floor, Wade forgot about the rod and squirmed in Gill's arms but Gill would not let him go.

"Let me go," Wade said. "I want to see."

"Sit here, Wade. Hey. Just wait."

Wade stopped squirming for a second and Gill relaxed his hold on him. Then he jerked out of Gill's arms and half slid and half fell onto the floor of the boat with the pickerel and the net.

"Jesus," Gill said and dropped the rod in the transom. Wade was tangled in the net and the fish thrashed about. The golden hook with the gold spinner had come free from the fish and Gill could not see it in all the movement and then he heard Wade cry out.

"Stop!" Gill yelled and put his hands around Wade's back to still him. Everything stopped except the fish. It flopped up into the air and then landed with its gills flexing open and closed. Gill lifted Wade slowly and he saw the fishing line rising with his son and what he feared would happen had happened. When Wade had half slid and half fallen to the floor his knee had landed on the hook and it had looped through the loose skin over his kneecap.

"Gill, it's in him," Christine said.

"I know."

Wade trembled and tried to reach for the hurt on his knee. Gill's hands held his son's arms tight and lifted him to sit on his knee where he could have a look at the hook.

"Get that fish on a stringer, please," he said to Christine. "I'll see what we can do here."

A little blood slipped out of one of the holes punctured in Wade's knee. The skin under the surface started to turn purple where the hook entered and exited, which looked bad, but the depth of the hook was shallow, just through the skin. While it would take some effort to get out, Gill had seen much worse, like the time his brother William had reared back to cast and caught himself in the back of the head as he tried to throw a Five of Diamonds spoon for jackfish. Gill had taken too many hooks out of people before.

"Okay, Wade, just sit here," Gill said. "Christine, when you're done there can you go into my brown backpack and get out my filleting knife?"

"What for?"

"We have to get this hook out."

She looked at Gill for a second and it seemed like she was about to say something, and then she went to get the knife. She handed it to Gill and he could see Wade watch the knife pass in front of him. Gill felt him flinch as the knife slid out of its sheath and then Wade froze as the knife flashed in front of him, moving towards him.

"Daddy, what are you doing?"

"We have to get the hook out, Wade." Gill pulled the knife back behind Wade for a second. "Christine, can you get me some gauze padding from the first-aid kit?"

"In your backpack?"

Gill nodded. "This isn't bad, you know, Wade. I've seen much worse."

"It hurts, Daddy."

"I know, partner. You're going to have to be brave though. See those birds up there, and those over there." Gill pointed at some gulls circling over the end of a nearby island and over a reef. "I want you to watch them, they know where the fish are. If any of them dive down to the water I want you to tell me. Okay?" Wade nodded to Gill and squinted at the gulls. "I want you to watch them very close because I have to know if the fish are there. And you want to know too, right?" Another nod as Wade's hair blew in the wind.

Christine handed Gill the sterilized padding and he motioned for her to sit next to him and to take Wade. Then he slid his knife from the sheath again and laid it on floor. He kept talking to Wade about the gulls and the fish they knew about, making sure Wade was looking away from him and Christine was holding him.

"I have some things to do here, Wade, so keep watching for me, so we'll know where the fish are biting and can catch them." Gill picked up the knife and a loop of the slack fishing line leading to the hook in Wade's knee. He put the sterilized padding between his teeth to hold and followed the line to the hook. "What are the gulls doing, Wade?" he asked and grasped the hook gently. Wade opened his mouth to answer and Gill pulled the hook tight against the skin, slit the skin, and pulled the hook free. He dropped the knife away from him on the floor and pressed the sterilized padding against the cut, and it all happened so fast Wade did not have time to cry. The hook lay on the floor of the boat, ready to be baited and cast out into the water again. Only a small film of blood on its shank left a clue as to where it had been.

"You cut it," Wade said and looked at Gill.

"Be brave, Wade. I had to."

"But you cut it," Wade said and started to cry.

Gill looked at Wade and Christine and didn't know what to say. He tried to pull Wade to him to hug and Wade pushed against him and howled. Christine smiled at Gill and mouthed the words, "He's yours," as Wade yelled. Gill knew his son was mad at him and he could not think of anything to do.

"I hate you," Wade screamed. "You're not my dad. You don't live with us. You never come."

Gill loosened his arms and lifted Wade over the hook to a chair where he refused to sit, and instead slid to the floor of the boat. His tantrum would have to play itself out; the only thing to do was clean up the mess in the boat.

Gill picked up his filleting knife, leaned over the gunnel, washed it through the water, dried it on his shirt and slid it back into the sheath. The fishing rod in the transom rocked with the waves until Gill lifted it out, picked up the hook with the dried blood, and dropped it into the water to reel in the loose line. He put his knife back into his backpack, started the engine and turned the boat back to the campsite. There was lunch to eat and the tent to pack up and get back to the cabin. No one remembered the pickerel on the stringer over the side, and in the ride back to the campsite it broke free and either ended up dead floating in the open water and pecked at by gulls, or it slipped off the stringer and swam back down to the bottom to live on with a hole through its bottom lip.

When they broke camp, everything they had brought out to the campsite was packed away in the place where it came from: this was Gill's way, the way to keep track of all your tools and gear, which he had learned from other fishing guides and from the trial and error of losing things. They loaded the boat and he took it easy on the way back, with the wind gusting from the north-west kicking up whitecaps, and with Wade sleeping in the bow of the boat with his head resting against Gill's coat. The open stretch of water to Queer Island passed in silence as Christine relaxed and watched the waves and Gill piloted the boat. Once they entered the group of islands known as the Hades, the water calmed and Christine looked at Gill and said, "You could have told him you were going to cut it out."

"But I didn't want to have to fight him and cut him anyway."

"No, he would have just held still."

Gill thought about this for a second, and even though he disagreed, he didn't want to start a fight or continue to disagree. "Yeah, you might be right," Gill said. "You know him best." He wondered how much it affected Wade not to see his father regularly, and how much it affected Christine not to have her husband with her all the time. It must affect them; it affected him.

He knew that Wade was just a kid and did not really know what he was saying when he was hurt, but it had hurt Gill as well to hear that Wade knew his father was not always there for him. For the rest of the ride back to the cabin Gill wondered about how he could do a better job of being with his son, and of being with his wife, because they were not the same job at all.

As soon as they pulled into the dock and Gill shut off the engine, he heard the phone ringing. By the time he got to the first step leading up to the porch, the ringing stopped. He waited a second, leaning on the railing and catching his breath, and as soon as he turned to start back down to the dock the ringing started again. He picked up the receiver at the end of the third ring and it sounded as though a great commotion were taking place on the other end of the line.

"Is there a Gilbert Dubois at this number?"

"This is he."

"Is this the same Dubois that played left wing for Kenora in the Purolator Cup years ago? Gill Dubois?"

"Yes it is, who's calling?"

"Gill, this is Dr. Gauthier at Kenora Hospital. My son Justin played hockey with you. Your father's name is Lucien Dubois, correct?"

"Yes it is."

"I thought so. I've got some news for you. Your father was admitted this morning with abdominal pain." There was the sound of the hospital in the background, people moving and the intercom. "We've run some tests but nothing has come back conclusive. We should have a better idea of what's wrong with him by tonight."

"How did you get my number, Doctor?"

"In the phone book. Lucien listed you as his next of kin. I looked you up."

"Right."

"Anyway, what I'm getting at, Gill, is your father is not doing well. If I had to guess, I'd say he has a bleeding ulcer. Now, I don't want to scare you, son, but that's probably what's wrong with him." Gill looked out the front of the cabin to see Wade and Christine standing with their arms full. "But we'll know better tomorrow. By about noon. It's been one hell of a weekend."

"So I should come by then?"

"If you want to see him. You don't have to, just thought I'd call you to let you know. Oh, hold on a second." Gill could hear Dr. Gauthier cover the phone and have a muffled conversation with someone. Gill's legs trembled and he felt like he might fall through the floor of the cabin. He had not spoken to his father in nine years, since Gill had eulogized his mother and Lucien had shown up late and drunk. They had fought every day that Gill could remember them living together, before he had left home when he was twenty and moved out to Smith Camps. Gill remembered the day he left home as clearly as if it had been yesterday. May 3rd, 1968. It was a day just like any other day, just like all the days in all the years he remembered living with Lucien; they had argued with each other over who should park in the driveway; nothing worth arguing over. Gill's mother had pleaded with both of them to be nice to each other for once, for the last time they were together, but they both carried on, proud and stubborn and angry, and she ended up dying without seeing them reconciled. Gill had seen his mother alive for the last time on the day he had left home. Since then, there had been no family Christmas for Gill, no pictures of Wade with his grandfather, no invitation for Lucien to Gill and Christine's wedding. A year later Ken Smith had called him off the docks of Smiths and handed him the phone of the main lodge to hear that his mother had suffered a stroke in her home and the neighbours had found her dead.

"Sorry about that," Dr. Gauthier said as he came back on the line. "That's a long weekend for you."

"I can come tomorrow at noon?"

"Tomorrow, make it one. He'll be ready by then."

"Okay, I'll come in then." Gill paused and put his thoughts together. "Doctor, did he ask for me?"

"No. He said not to call you."

"But you did."

"Yes."

"Why?"

"Son, I'm a father too. Your dad's not doing too well. Now, it sounded like you and him weren't close. But if he went and you didn't at least have a chance to say goodbye to him, you know, to make things right between the two of you, then that would be worse than if you never knew." There was a scraping sound on the other end of the phone, like the doctor rubbing the phone over his stubbled face. "He may not be here for long, Gill. You should come and see him."

"I will. I will. One o'clock."

"Tomorrow. See you then."

The line clicked dead and Gill was left in his cabin holding the receiver in his hand. A knock at the window startled him and he looked over to see Christine looking in at him, seeing the look on his face and coming in.

"Who was it?"

"A doctor. Doctor Gauthier. From Kenora Hospital. My dad's there."

"Right now?"

Gill nodded. The door opened again and Wade came in. "He admitted himself. They think he has a bleeding ulcer."

"Who's bleeding?" Wade said.

"A friend of your dad's," Christine said to Wade; then to Gill, "Are you going to see him?"

"Tomorrow. One o'clock."

"Do you want me to stay?"

Gill shook his head and shrugged. "There's no reason for you to stay."

"To be with you."

"Who's bleeding?" Wade asked again.

"Nah. There's no reason. You have to get back. I'll be fine."

"Are you sure?"

Gill nodded and walked over to Wade. He picked him up and started to carry him to his bed against the wall.

"Who is it, Daddy?"

"A guy I used to know."

"A friend?"

"No just a guy I used to know. This guy doesn't have any friends."

Christine went out the back door and down to the boat to finish unloading their gear. Gill brought Wade in to have a nap in preparation for the ride into Kenora and the trip home with Christine on the bus. He set Wade down on the covers and sat beside him, helped him undo his shoes and tucked them under the bed. Then he pulled a sheet over Wade and kissed him on the forehead. The warm air blew through the cabin from the lake with the smell of pine and water and Gill smoothed the fair hair on Wade's head until his breathing was calm and even. Christine was on her way up from the dock and Gill met her and took the bags she carried. He and Christine finished unloading the boat, organized things in the cabin and packed her bags for Winnipeg. Then they loaded the Land Cruiser and went down to the lake to wash in the water, and to lie on the hot boards of the dock and let the sun dry their skin. As they lay and talked, they touched and held each other, and gradually their touches became more tender, and more intimate, and they made love under the sunlight on the wet wood.

An hour later, Gill stood on the asphalt and watched Wade and Christine waving through the tinted windows of the bus. The gears of the bus ground together and then it jerked into motion. The faces of Wade and Christine pulled away and Gill stayed behind as the bus groaned up the hill leaving black diesel exhaust. Every time they left he hated it. Starting a family and raising a son was not supposed to be this way. Gill knew they would be back or he would go and see them in the city; things would be good again like they could be, but the gap remained. He walked over to the Land Cruiser and opened the door, climbed up into the seat and put his hands on the spokes of the steering wheel. He knew they loved each other, but they were never with each other. He could enjoy the time they had together; he had told himself over and over to enjoy the time. But he could not escape the problems presented in thinking about the long run. How long could it be this way? It seemed that to be happy doing what he was doing Gill ended up giving up the most important people in his life. He started the Land Cruiser and pulled out of the lot, onto the highway and his own life, and the work that helped him through the time when he was on his own.

But in reality, not much remained to do after they left. Gill worked the next day but had no preparations to make, having already arranged to use the client's boat for the day, and all the equipment from Smith Camps. He could try to see his father at the hospital but he thought better of it. Friends of his lived in Kenora but he had no desire to see them. He drove back along the highway east out of Kenora, past the small, family-run industries. A float plane flew low overhead towards the lake where it dropped out of sight behind the trees. The two-lane highway twisted and turned and then around a corner a collection of flashing lights appeared where an Ontario Provincial Police officer flagged Gill down, and in the ditch he could see the wheels of a rolled car and its underbelly of piping and metal. A fire truck and ambulance lit up the scene with their lights while uniformed attendants rushed up and down the embankment from the shoulder of the highway to the flipped car with pieces of equipment in their arms. Gill crept past the collection of lights and activity and waved to the officer. He didn't recognize the flipped car and soon had accelerated back up to highway speed and continued with his own thoughts.

The gravel crunched under the Land Cruiser's tires as Gill pulled into the road to the cabin. He started to think about the things he had to do; there were always things to do. The Land Cruiser climbed the last rise on the road and he parked in the clearing. He sat without moving for a second and noticed in the back one of Wade's t-shirts crumpled in a ball. He leaned back, picked up the tiny shirt and unfolded it in front of him. He brought it to his face and smelled it and wondered if he had ever been as sad as he felt just then, as he pressed the thin fabric to his face and dried the tears welling up in his eyes. He opened the door to the Land Cruiser, carried the t-shirt in his hand and set out down the path to the cabin. The sun was dropping in the sky and the wind was blowing through the air. At the least, Gill knew, he could go out for a fish before it got too late. The sky was fair and the wind would give a good drift. There was at least that.

DUBOIS, Lucien Thomas—Passed away quietly and peacefully on July 8, 1977, at his home, after a brief illness. Widowed in 1969 by the early death of his beloved wife Chantal, Lucien was a devout member of the Kenora Legion and President from 1963-66. Lucien served his country as Gunnery Officer in the RCAF from 1940-44. He is survived by his two sons, Martin William and Gilbert James.

Lucien was born in Montreal, Canada, in 1928 and moved to Kenora with his new bride in 1952 to join the ClarkeWright Paper Mill, where he was employed in various capacities for twenty-five years before his death. In lieu of flowers, memorial contributions to the Heart and Stroke Foundation of Ontario or the charity of your choice would be gratefully acknowledged. The funeral service will be conducted on July 11 at 11:00 a.m. in the Harris Funeral Home.

CHANNEL MARKERS
—*July, 1981*—

THE COOL AIR OFF THE LAKE BLEW IN THROUGH THE BEDROOM screen and Wade stirred in his bed. He savoured the warmth trapped under the sheets, the heavy sleeping bag on his bed. Wade hardly moved when he slept at the lake; in part due to the weight of the sleeping bag and in part due to the fineness of the sleep, the air cool and fresh and moist, leaving dew on the grass that licked at his pant legs along the path down to the lake when he rose early and went fishing with his father. Sunlight crowded through the window above his bed, wedged out across Wade's sleeping bag, and he propped his pillow up against the head-board to read. Flat poplar leaves rustled and swayed through the streaming light, which flickered and trembled like reflections off waves. Wade held his hand up over his head and into the light's path; its shadow the only firm outline in the wavering patterns. The same air stirring the poplar leaves sifted into Wade's room with the damp feel of humidity. The smell of the pines in the forest felt heavy, the air almost carrying the sap.

Wade pulled the sleeping bag edge up to his chin and curled toward the door of the room. He and Christine had arrived the night before to spend the weekend with Gill. They had brought their things in from the car and fallen into bed. Wade had been looking forward to the weekend since school had ended in June a month earlier. He had not seen his father since the end of the hockey season, since his team had been playing in the city championship playoffs and his father had made every game, even the championship game they had lost. The team went out for a pizza party afterwards and Gill had not stayed for the awards presentations. At the party, Wade won the Most Outstanding Player award and had brought the trophy with him to the cabin to show his father. The engraved metal plate read *Wade Dubois—Most Outstanding Player—7-Year-Old Mighty Mites—City Championships 1980-81*. Wade's coach had called him "Sniper" and hugged him after he had scored his second goal. Wade had looked for Gill in the crowd but couldn't see him because everyone had been standing up. He hoped his father had not seen the hug.

Wade read until he heard the couch springs creak and his mother's bare feet pad across what he knew would be the cold floor. The bathroom door closed and Wade could feel his own bladder tell him it was time to get up. More footsteps sounded up the front stairs of the porch and Wade pulled back the curtain to his room as Gill came in through the porch, his empty coffee cup in his hand, the day ready to begin. Breakfast consisted of toast covered in peanut butter and slices of banana and sections of apple laid out on a plate. Gill refilled his coffee cup and went ahead of Wade and Christine to get the boat ready for a day on the lake. By the time Wade and Christine had packed their extra clothes, in case the weather turned worse, Gill had the boat loaded and the canvas top lying out on the dock to dry from the evening dew. Wade primed the bulb in the gas line and gave Gill a thumb-up sign. He wiped his face and collected black toast crumbs from the corners of his mouth. Gill turned the key and the Merc cranked over, fired twice and caught, the oil-rich blue exhaust steaming out the back as the revs climbed. Gill let the Merc slow to a fast idle and went to the back to stow the gear handed to him from the dock. Christine passed him the cooler, their bright beach towels, and Wade brought his mask and snorkel from the shed. They were ready to go. Gill untied the back and held the boat and Christine untied the front and stepped in. Gill pushed the boat off with one foot, stepped in to the console and steered the boat away from the dock and out into the small chop of Storm Bay.

"Wade, come here a second," Gill said, tapping the throttle down and then standing and steering the ploughing boat.

"What, Dad?"

"You're first mate. Take the wheel while I get us ready to go."

Gill busied himself at the back of the boat under the transom where the gas tanks were stowed and where the bilge pump needed some attention every now and then. Wade kneeled on the driver's seat, steering the boat out from the dock with both hands, but not touching the throttle. A fish jumped up between the waves out Wade's side and startled him. "A fish jumped!" he cried out, turning to his mother in the seat beside him and asking her if she had seen it.

"I think it was a pickerel," she said and fished for her sunglasses in her bag. "Just a little one." The wind blew her new hairdo back over her forehead and Wade watched her for a second.

"Can we stop and cast for it, Dad?"

"I thought you wanted to go out on the lake," Gill said, wiping the windshield with a rag.

"Yeah. Well, later then?"

"If there's time, sure."

Wade was satisfied at this and kept a sharp eye out for the glistening snap of light of another fish jumping or the rings in the water they left behind. Gill finished wiping the windshield.

"Out of the way, partner," he said to Wade.

"Can I drive, Dad?"

Wade saw his father give his mother a glance. Then he sat in the driver's chair and Wade sat between his legs and Gill let him steer while he pressed the throttle forward. The revs climbed and the sound of the Merc increased and the Sylvan slid up onto plane pushing white water off the side of the hull. Gill held the bottom of the steering wheel until they were steady on their way over the water. He showed Wade how to angle into the wind and adjust the wheel and course of the boat to the shape of the waves around them.

They passed across Storm Bay and Smith Camps on their way south through Eagle Pass and into Moore Bay. Wade knew Smith Camps was one of the best fishing camps on Lake of the Woods. It was not a big camp but it was well known. There were many people from a long way away who came to fish at Smith's: Americans and other Canadians and Europeans. Even a family from Peru came every year.

As they drove across the open water, Gill talked to Wade, telling him what islands they were passing, where the water was deep, where you had to watch for rocks and shoals when the water was low. He showed Wade how to read the waves, how to judge where they crested and how they reflected the structure on the bottom of the lake. The worst spots to watch for, he told Wade, were out in the middle of deep water, where you thought there was plenty of depth and then hit a reef at full speed. Christine looked out over the water and let her hair blow.

They cruised into Moore Bay, past Moore Bay Lodge on the southwest shore and through to the open water. Wade knew his father had never worked at Moore Bay Lodge but that it was still a good fishing camp. The forested islands, inlets, channels and peninsulas blended into one another but Gill had no problem finding the way. They passed Pipestone Peninsula where Gill trapped in the winter and he pointed out certain islands that would be good to have a camp on, their natural harbours on the leeward side and tall pine trees. Wade's hands only sparingly felt the gentle pull of the wheel as Gill turned it to guide the boat's course. As they exited Moore Bay they turned into the headwind again and Wade asked Gill where they were going.

"Down through French Narrows," Gill said. "There's an island with a beach and rock pit and picnic area. We'll stop there for awhile."

"It's a good place, Dad?"

"Yep. I take people there for shore lunch when we're down here fishing."

"Is this where we went that time?" Christine asked over the sound of the Merc, as her hair blew across in front of her face and she caught it and tucked it back behind her ear.

"You remember that?" Gill said.

"It's the only time I came with you. Of course I remember. Dominique Island."

Wade saw his father raise his eyebrows in surprise and he looked over at his mother.

"Did you like it, Mom?" Wade said, still steering the boat.

"I did. It was the best day I had at the lake that summer."

"Really? Did you catch any fish?" Wade asked.

"I can't really remember. I don't think I fished."

"You didn't," Gill said.

"Then how could it have been the best day? If you went fishing but didn't fish?" Wade said and turned away from steering the boat. Christine lifted her sunglasses onto her forehead and held them there in the wind. She kept looking forward, her other arm crossed in front of her holding her elbow.

"It just was."

"But how?" Wade asked again.

"I remember it that way. There was more to it than just fishing."

"Like what?" Wade asked.

Christine looked over and both Wade and Gill were listening. Gill adjusted the course of the boat around a small bald island in the middle of the open water and some gulls flew off the white rocks. The Sylvan rocked in the crosswind, the waves rolling under the hull.

"It was a beautiful day," Christine said. "I was a city girl and your dad was a handsome guy who made you feel comfortable. The lake was beautiful too."

Wade turned back to the steering wheel and adjusted their course to the port and back to starboard again. "But you didn't fish. And you were fishing."

"There's more to fishing than fishing, Wade," Christine said. "There's the lake and the nature and the people you're with. All of it makes it good. Not just catching fish."

"I still like to catch fish," Wade said.

"Me too, partner," said Gill. "But the other is good too. Now pay attention to your driving before we're on the wrong side of this buoy."

Wade elbowed Gill in the guts behind him and took the wheel with both hands. The boat headed right at a red buoy swaying in the waves. Wade turned the wheel a little to the port and knew Gill's hands were not holding it. He turned it back to straighten their course.

"Which way, Dad?"

"The reef's between the buoy and the island to the east."

"So right?"

"Yep. Starboard in the boat."

Wade nodded and concentrated on his driving. The buoy came closer and got bigger than Wade expected since he had only seen the buoys from a distance before. Its rusted base sat far below the surface of the lake, its top wobbled in the waves like

Wade's inflatable punching clown with the weighted base that always rebounded to its feet.

"Wade, are you on the right side?" Christine asked.

"The starboard, right, Dad?"

"Isn't he supposed to pass on the right, Gill?" Christine asked again.

"Wade, the starboard's the right," Gill said, not steering the wheel but pointing which direction he wanted Wade to turn. Wade pulled on the wheel and the boat banked and turned around the outside of the buoy. "There's lots of water on either side, Christine," Gill said. "And we only draw a few feet. We're fine. There has to be a wide tolerance for the markers because of the changing water levels all the time. As long as you're close you can get away with it."

The buoy passed them by ten feet off the port gunnel and Wade felt the tightness pass from his insides. He had almost felt like closing his eyes and letting go of the wheel and letting his father do it; but he had done it and now he felt good, like having the pressure in your ears ease away as you came back to the surface from a deep dive. It was done and he knew he could do it again if he had to.

The buoy bobbed and waved in the wake of the passing boat. The channel markers at the entrance of French Narrows were ahead and Gill slowed the boat to take the wheel. Wade switched over and sat between Christine's legs and she hugged her arms around his shoulders. They were almost at Dominique Island. The sun had risen higher into the sky so that to Wade it looked like it was about eleven o'clock. Gill slowed the boat and pointed at the island as they circled it, looking for the best place to moor in the wind that day. Wade went up to the nose of the boat to catch the landing as Gill eased the boat to shore. They set up their picnic on the rocks and Wade explored the island, finding a section of a dock with nails sticking out of it that had broken loose from somewhere and been carried either on the waves or in the ice to the calm shore of the island. In the fire pit on the bare rocks a few beer cans remained, half-buried by the dead coals. Christine assembled corned-beef sandwiches for them on rye bread and passed around a can of Pringles potato chips. After lunch, Wade found some blueberries growing on the island and all three of them spent the better part of the afternoon picking blueberries and putting the ones they did not eat into the emptied Pringles can for Christine to make a crisp when they got back to the cabin. Out from Dominique Island, a small reef stuck the tips of its black rocks above the water, and Wade and Christine and Gill swam to it to cool off once their Pringles can was full and their backs sore. Gill swam beside Wade while Christine had put her head down and raced out to be first to the reef. Wade made it all the way by himself, with no life-jacket, like he knew he could, since he had been enrolled in swimming lessons on Tuesdays at the Pan Am Pool for more than a year and could swim its length without stopping. All three of them sat on the reef, sunning themselves on the glistening rocks.

"I feel like we're seals," Christine said and Gill barked and slapped his hands together. Then Wade did the same and Christine called them the circus seals.

Clouds gathered in the sky to the west. In the distance, Wade saw darker and heavier clouds that Gill pointed out to him as they packed up the boat to go back to the cabin.

"We'll have to watch those, partner," Gill said while Christine changed out of her bathing suit in the bushes. "Looks like there might be lightning."

Wade did not understand why the clouds needed to be watched for lightning but he nodded to his father and told him he would keep an eye out. Once the boat was loaded up, Wade held the nose as his parents got in and Gill started the engine, then he pushed off from the rocks and jumped up on the nose like he had seen Gill do. He stepped down to the floor and his foot stung where he had stepped on a nail sticking out of the section of dock. He peeked at his parents to see if either one of them had noticed, and they had not, which was good; he did not want to tell them what happened because Marshall McFeetors, who sat beside him in French class, had stepped on a nail and had had to go to the hospital and get a needle, and Wade did not want to upset his mother or father when things were going so well, and he did not want to get a needle.

The trip back to the cabin passed, strung together with stories Gill told Wade and Christine about the islands and points and bays they passed, times he had guided people fishing, or seen something worth remembering, or heard a story about a place, so that by the time they came into sight of the dock it seemed like they had travelled through history to their time and place and knew everything about the lake. Rain had fallen on and off as they retraced their path and Gill had stopped the boat at the same buoy Wade had steered around to put the top up and bow curtain on so they stayed warm and dry. A cabin-cruiser had been moored for shelter at the bottom of Storm Bay and Wade said, "Hey, who's that? Do you know them, Dad?"

Gill shook his head and as they drew closer asked Wade if he could see the boat name and markings. The cabin-cruiser swung on its anchor rope in the wind, the name *Scotch and Water* visible on the stern. No one was above deck and Gill brought the boat in to the dock and he and Wade and Christine got out and carried their things from the boat to the cabin without seeing anyone aboard. They had been out on the water all day and the clouds that had poured so much rain down on the lake half an hour earlier were clearing to the south. As the sun dropped in the sky, the dark shadows around the rim of the lake stretched out over the water. Everything had the fresh, wet smell of life after a heavy rain. The colours of the trees and rocks and moss had a rich, deeper, shinier gloss to them. Wade walked up the path to the cabin behind his father when they were done putting things away. He looked down at the roots in the soil crossing the path and did not notice his father stop until he ran into him from behind.

"What is it, Dad?" Wade said.

"I thought I heard voices speaking from that boat. I wanted to hear what they were saying."

"What were they saying?"

"I can't hear now. It sounded like they weren't happy though."

Gill started up the path again and Wade followed. They hung their towels on the rope clothesline stretched between two trees behind the cabin and Wade took off Gill's Labatt's hat, which was too big but kept the sun off his face. Christine stood in the kitchen brushing out her hair when Wade and Gill let the screen porch door slam shut behind them.

"Are you guys hungry?"

"Yeah. Starved," Wade said and went towards his room to change. He pulled the curtain shut, stripped naked and slid under the covers to warm up. The cold clammy feel of his wet swim trunks started to fade as he held his privates cupped in his hand. Wade heard his mother say she thought she would make a roast chicken for dinner, then ask Gill if he had anything planned.

"Nope," Gill said. "Nothing as good as that sounds."

"Good. Why don't you guys get changed and I'll start making it." Christine started to bustle about the kitchen opening cupboards and asking Gill questions about where things were.

"You don't have to do this, Christine," Gill said. "I did have something planned."

"I don't mind," Christine answered and kept opening drawers looking for something. "It'll be fun. As long as you don't mind."

"It's not that."

"What is it then? We can make what you had planned."

"No, go ahead," Gill said. "I'm just not sure this is the way it should be."

"How? Me cooking? You're welcome to help with—"

"No. Making it like you guys aren't, well, my guests this weekend."

"I would want to help out and do this at anyone's cabin I was visiting," Christine said. "Not just yours. When we were out at the place of one of the girls I work with I made dinner too. Same thing here."

There was silence. Wade wondered what was going on, why were they talking about making dinner like it was important? Why did his father not want her to cook? Even though they did not still live together Wade knew they still liked each other, he could tell by the way they talked about each other.

"You're on the spot then," Gill said and Wade heard him walk towards his room. The next thing Wade knew his mother was shaking him to wake up and come to dinner.

After they had eaten, music started coming from the cabin-cruiser moored out of sight in the bottom of the bay. It was strange to hear the music over the water, sounding so close though it came from around the corner. Voices could also be heard, but none of the words understood as the sound of a 1950s-style big band played. Wade and Gill and Christine sat in the screened-in porch and ate their ice cream from bowls. In front of them, the lake looked calm and empty except for the occasional heron or gull winging by, or a fish surfacing to suck under a drowning insect. The dock stretched out into the water off the rocks, the boat rested against the tires on the leeward side. The sun had just set and its glow spread out across the sky and lit the clouds with shades of yellow, orange, red and purple.

"Great dinner, Christine," Gill said. "It's been years since I ate like that."

"Yeah, good dinner, Mom," Wade echoed.

"Like I said Gill, I was happy to do it."

"Well, it was good."

The plates were stacked and the utensils crowded on top with the bones. Gill picked them up and handed them to Wade, saying, "Here, partner. I've heard you're the dish jockey at home. Why don't you see how clean you can get these?" Wade looked up at him a second, then took the plates and went to the kitchen. He came back for the glasses and Gill told him the soap was under the sink.

The water ran in the sink, rattling at first, then bubbling as the suds built up. Gill came in to make sure he could find what he needed, then he returned to the porch and, once the sink was full and the water off, Wade could hear his parents talking, the big-band music still in the background. Gill offered Christine more wine and they talked about his new chairs for the porch, director's chairs they called them, which Gill had bought at a garage sale in town, all four for two dollars. The conversation stopped and the music stopped at the same time, and after a few minutes of quiet, Wade heard his parents talk about the sale of lakefront property on Lake of the Woods. He almost dropped a plate and it clinked against some others and he called out, "Everything's okay. Nothing broken."

Gill said, "Those dishes are so heavy I'm not sure he could break them. He's lucky to lift them."

"Garage sale as well?"

"Estate sale. No one I knew."

Wade took off his shirt to keep it dry and concentrated on doing a good job with the dishes while his parents kept talking about the things happening in their lives. He looked through the kitchen to put some of the dishes away and he had trouble finding where they went. A stack of clean plates and bowls and glasses grew on the counter until no room remained, and Wade went to ask Gill to help him. As he came to the door of the porch, he heard Christine say, "It sounds like a fight." And the voices from the boat on the bay were clear, a woman sounding angry, saying, "You always say that."

"That's the way it is," a man's voice said. "I never can win with you."

Wade saw Christine look at Gill just as something dropped

somewhere on the boat and shattered. Two solid objects slammed against each other, then a hollow knocking sound.

"Be careful," said the man's voice. "There's glass."

"Don't tell me what to do."

"Well, don't cut yourself."

"Don't tell me what to do," came the woman's voice, louder. "Are you going to help me?"

"With what?"

"This mess, you shit," said the woman. "Why do you always do this?"

"You dropped the glass."

"Do something."

"Fuck you, do it yourself," said the man's voice.

"No, fuck you," came the woman's voice, louder than before, spitting the words out. Then there was the sound of more glass breaking and she took a deep breath. "You fucked her! You fucked her! You fucked her!" Then another, quicker gasp for breath. "You fucked her in our house. In our bed. I didn't do anything."

"You're drunk. It was not in our bed."

"I don't care. You fucked her. You screwed her in our house. In my house. You fucking bastard, I wish I could kill you."

The was a grunt of exertion from the woman and a third shatter sound, smaller than the others. Christine and Gill looked at each other, not sure what to do as sounds of sobbing carried from the boat, lasted a few seconds, and then a scream of anger and pain and frustration and hate echoed around the bay.

"Go," the woman's voice said. "Just go, you bastard. Go! Take the dinghy and go." The sobbing stopped and her voice came out even and controlled, "I don't want you here. I don't want you near me." A few seconds later, a small outboard motor started and a low metallic sound rang out, a rope whipped against a metal railing, the rope wrapping around it in tightening coils until the hardened end dinged the railing. The sound of the small outboard got louder and then its roar was the only sound. The dinghy cut across the mirrored surface of the bay in an arc and then around the point. As the sound of the engine faded and the wake spread out over the water, the sobs of the woman returned, and she talked to herself, saying it wasn't her fault, over and over, it wasn't her fault.

Christine looked at Gill and then her eyes flicked past him, to where Wade stood in the doorway of the porch with the dishrag in his hands. Gill turned in his chair and also looked at Wade, and then got up.

"How are those dishes coming, partner?" he said to Wade, putting his arm around his bare shoulders, turning him back into the cabin to check on the job.

"Good, Dad," Wade said. "What happened there? With those people? They said a lot of bad words."

"I'm not sure what was going on. A fight, I guess."

"That man had done some bad things?"

"Yep. A very bad thing."

"But you and mom never fight like that," Wade said and twisted the dishrag in his hands. "And you aren't together. Is that why?"

"Why we don't fight like that? Or why we're not together?"

Wade nodded and whispered, "Both."

Gill laughed a short breathy laugh. "No, your mom and I never fight like that. Do you think we do?"

Wade thought about this for a second and then released the dishrag and shook his head. "No. I think you still like each other." Wade thought for another second. "But you're not together."

"No, we're not."

"Will you ever be?" Wade asked and Gill sat on the couch and Wade sat on the table in front of it. Late one night, when he was supposed to have been asleep, he had heard his mother talking to her friend Mrs. Dumont about Gill and how she knew they would not be together again. Wade had heard his mother say that she knew their separation had been for the best, for both of them, and that their divorce, when it came, would also be for the best.

"Well, Wade," Gill started. "You never know what will come tomorrow, or a year from now, or five. Sometimes you think you know, but you don't."

"So you and Mom might be together again?"

"No. I don't think we'll be together again."

"But you said you never know."

"I know. But some things you do know. Some things are a certain way because that's how they're best. That's the way they have to be. You wouldn't want your mom and me to fight, would you?"

"No. But you said you didn't."

"Yes, I did say that. But we don't fight because we're not together." He reached across and put his hand on Wade's knee. "Do you understand that?"

Wade shook his head.

"It's better this way," he said and took a deep breath. "Your mother and I are better apart than together. She wants her things and I want mine. We tried to have both and couldn't. You see?"

"Like what things, Dad?"

"Like she needs to be in the city and I need to be here," Gill said. "She needs her work at the law firm and I need mine. And hers is there and mine is here. There's more than that too." He squeezed his hand on Wade's knee. "But you see how it doesn't work?"

Wade nodded and put his hand on top of his father's. His head nodded and a tear dropped down his cheek and then onto his bare chest leaving a clear streak like glass. He saw his father's eyes fill with tears and his father reached out and wrapped his arms around him. They held each other for a while, crying silent tears. Then, they loosened their hug and looked at each other and smiled and sniffled. They went into the kitchen to put the dishes away in the cupboards. When the dishes were away, they went out to the porch and sat and enjoyed the loon calls and laughter. Later, after they had turned on the radio to hear the forecast and had made tea, they played crazy eights even though they were missing the seven of clubs, and then, right before bed, they went down to the dock and swam to cool off before bed. In the calm water they floated on their backs and touched each other underwater and looked up at the stars and the moon behind the shimmering northern lights.

In the morning, there was no sunlight on Wade's sleeping bag. The clouds had returned in the night and the feeling of rain hung in the air. The clouds jerked across the sky in layers over the water, low enough that Wade saw the greys and whites moving at different speeds. He got out of bed after he heard the door to Gill's bedroom open and then the bathroom door close. He didn't want to miss a minute of the last day at the lake. He walked across the the cold floor and stood outside the bathroom waiting. After a second of wiggling on the spot, he knocked at the door.

"Okay, okay," Christine said, coming out of the bathroom in her housecoat. "You won't spring a leak."

Wade rushed inside and pulled down his pajamas just in time. He stood there with the door open while Christine drew herself a glass of water from the kitchen faucet. Wade pulled up his pajama bottoms and was just about to ask for some water when Christine stopped him.

"Wash your hands, Wade," she said, pointing to the sink. Wade turned back and Christine continued. "Your dad said he was going to make breakfast. Do you want pancakes?"

"Yeah. With syrup and jam."

"If he's got it," she said and plunked the glass in the sink. "Why don't you get changed and we'll go for a wash in the lake while he gets things ready?"

Wade went to his room and stripped off his pajamas for his

swim trunks. It was cold in the cabin and he put on his sweat-shirt over top to stay warm. Then he pulled back the curtain and sat on the couch to wait for Christine. The sheets were cool under his bare legs and he shivered until she came out of the bathroom in her bathing suit. Gill came out of his bedroom and looked around the room.

"Am I missing the polar bear swim?" he said.

"You can come if you want, Dad."

"I think I'll stay here and get breakfast ready, partner. You go ahead."

Wade and Christine walked down to the water. Wade dared Christine to run to the end of the dock and jump in right away. He was just finished daring her when she dropped her towel, slid off her shoes and did it, her hair swinging side to side as she ran down the dock. She made a nice, clean shallow dive into the flat water and Wade stood there until she surfaced. He couldn't believe she had done it.

"Your turn," she called back to him, making rings around her as she treaded water.

Wade ran down the dock and cut into the water the same way as he had seen his mother do it, swimming underwater as far as he could. When he surfaced he shook his head and he and Christine smiled big smiles at each other. Wade wondered about his mother; to run and jump off the end of a dock into the chilly water was not normal for her.

By the time Wade and Christine returned to the cabin, Gill had the pancakes made and the eggs were waiting. He looked like he enjoyed being the short-order cook, asking Wade and Christine mother exactly how they wanted their eggs done. When the eggs were done as ordered, Christine grabbed napkins and they carried their steaming plates out onto the porch. Wade went to change into his sweat pants and shirt before eating in the cool air. When he came out onto the porch he wondered if the cabin-cruiser was gone. He asked Gill about it.

"I heard it in the night start up and head out," Gill said between mouthfuls. "I didn't hear another boat so it must have left alone."

"I think it did," Christine said.

Wade had nothing to say about this and so he ate his pancakes. When he was finished, he gulped his orange juice and wiped his mouth.

"What are we doing today?" he said to his parents. They looked at each other with questions in their eyes and raised brows, like the notion had only then occurred to them.

"What do you want to do?" Christine asked. "It's not really nice out."

"I don't know," Wade answered and looked up at the dark sky.

"We could go to town by boat," Gill offered, finishing his own pancakes and leaning on the table. "Get some lunch at the chip truck, see the lake."

"Yeah, the chip truck. I like that," Wade said.

Gill looked at Christine to see what she thought. She nodded and said, "Sure, we brought our raincoats."

The lake was starting to ripple as Wade and his parents followed the path down to the dock. The ripples spread out in furrowed arcs as the wind blew down through the trees behind them and in a curve over the bay. Gill removed the back and side curtains of the Sylvan top but left the bow closure on for protection. Wade ran back up to the cabin to get his raincoat and Gill started the Merc. By the time Wade was back at the dock, the Merc was warm and they were ready to go. Wade was on the dock ready to jump into the boat when he stopped.

"Hey Dad, can we bring out fishing rods?"

"I don't think we'll have time, Wade," Gill said. "Your mom wants to leave for the city by three. We better not this time."

"But just in case," Wade pushed, hoping to wet a line, hoping to do everything he wanted to do at the lake.

Gill looked over at Christine.

"Bring the rods," she said. "But we still have to leave by three, Wade. So if there's no time, we can't fish."

Wade barely heard the end of what his mother said. He was already at a run on his way to the shed to get his rod. Gill and Christine stayed in the boat and the Merc idled, the exhaust curling away from the ports on the back of the drive-shaft and over the lake. Wade walked fast back down the dock and handed his rod to Gill to stow away. The water on the boards made the dock slick but he didn't fall. He stepped into the boat and Gill pushed them away from the dock and drove out onto Storm Bay.

Wade sat between Christine's legs on the passenger seat and watched the dark water go by over the port gunnel. The little waves blurred together past the white water thrown from the boat's hull and Wade tried to watch one wave as it came into sight, crested beside the boat and then disappeared behind them. But the waves were always shifting and the wave he started to watch was never the same wave beside the boat or behind it where it melded with the water thrown from the hull or flattened out into other waves. Wade could only ever catch a glimpse of the wave before it disappeared or changed into a new wave.

Soon they were around the point of Storm Bay and heading west, past Smith Camps and onto the main channel to Kenora. Gill pointed out the channel markers to Wade and specified what each one meant and how they worked together. Some were reflectors marking the course to set and some were blinkers marking points of land and the red and black buoys marked the reefs. Wade watched and asked question sometimes. He was happy to be out on the lake with his mother and his father, and he looked forward to lunch at the chip truck. And maybe, if they were quick in Kenora, he could cast for the pickerel he had seen jumping the day before.

Gill nosed the boat in on the Kenora public docks and Wade jumped out with the rope. He watched Gill tie a loop knot with the front and back ropes to the cleats on the dock. Then they started up the hill to the chip truck.

Kenora was busy as it usually was on rainy days. The line-up at the chip truck stretched along the sidewalk and Wade volunteered to wait as Gill had to get some things at the Canadian Tire. Christine put up the hood on her jacket as the mist began to fall and waited with Wade in line.

Once Wade and Christine paid for the french fries, they turned and saw Gill on the far street corner talking to someone. Gill looked to the chip truck, gestured about something with his hands, patted the other man on the arm, and they both went on their way. Wade felt strange seeing his father in his normal setting and routine, like he was spying on him. Gill didn't wait for the light to change to cross the street. The strange feeling Wade felt continued as Gill walked across the concrete space to where he and Christine stood holding the three Styrofoam buckets of french fries. Gill rubbed his palms together when he got closer and it was amazing how his expression and eagerness made Wade feel like he was the best person to meet in the world.

"All right, how are they?" Gill asked.

Wade and Christine nodded and smiled with their mouths full of the french fries. Wade handed Gill a bucket and they started walking around Kenora, eating on the way.

"Thanks for the fries, Christine," Gill said.

"Welcome. These are the best, aren't they?"

"Yep," Gill said. "People talk about them all over."

"I remembered them from when we used to come in by boat."

"You and your family, or you and I?" Gill asked.

"You and I. Mom would never have wanted us eating french fries."

Gill nodded and shook his head. The falling mist collected in his hair and the three of them walked down and back along Kenora's main street, looking in the windows at the displays and the other people shopping. Gill greeted a few people he knew and introduced Wade as his son and Christine as "Christine." But they didn't stay to talk long.

At the top of the street, the lake was in front of them and they walked down the road and then the public dock back to the boat. They sat in the boat until they finished their french fries and then Wade took the three Styrofoam buckets to the trash can. He walked back to the boat licking the grease and salt from his fingers.

There was nothing else any of them wanted to do in Kenora, so Gill started the Merc and backed the boat out to the bay. The nose swung around and they did a slow troll of the Kenora waterfront, around Coney Island and the beach park, and through the narrows back down the channel to the cabin. It was relaxed and misty and cool. Gill pointed out the cabins on the shore, especially the huge one that was owned and built by John Wayne high up on a island outside Devil's Gap. As they left the tight passage and red and black buoys of Allen's Narrows and drove out into the open water, the wind got up. The waves were much larger than when they had gone to Kenora, the whitecaps foaming up and then disappearing across the grey lake. Gill slowed the Merc and angled the bow into the waves. Wade crawled up into the front of the boat under the bow cover. He lay down there on the cushions and looked back, his knees tucked up on the seat and his hands pressed together and under his head. He saw his mother's leg and tennis shoe and his father's leg, bare ankle and boat shoe. Past them, over the top of the transom, he saw the top of the Merc shaking and humming as it ran. And beyond, there was the wake of the boat closing together in a white rush of turbulence and the whitecaps reclaiming the grey water. One side of the wake turned over itself like a wave washing on a beach while the other tried to turn over but was fanned back by the wind, drops scattered into the air. Wade did not nap but felt warm and comfortable under his beach towel. The waves in the rough water popped him up and then let him crash down and his head bounced. The wet smell of the top and the cushions underneath him and the regular rise and fall of the boat contented him. They passed islands and mainland and the Anishnabe Indian reserve in the distance. Gill pointed out the YMCA camp, Camp Stephens, on a large island with painted rock faces. The only change the whole way home was when the Merc hesitated, missed, and then quit as it ran out of gas. The Sylvan glided into the waves and the propellor ticked as the momentum of the water pushed the blades against the gearing. Gill opened the sliding doors to the storage under the transom and switched tanks. Then he filled the drained gas-line by priming the bulb. The Merc started on the third crank and they were underway again, past Scottie's Beach and the entrance to the Hades Islands, out on the rolling waters of Bigstone Bay.

Wade slept most of the ride home in the car. As soon as Christine settled into traffic on the two-lane highway west of Kenora, Wade's head slumped onto his jacket against the window and his eyes closed. It had been hard to leave the cabin. Wade had given his father a long hug after his mother had said goodbye. He could see his father was holding back from crying the same way he was. He could smell the gasoline and soap and use in his father's shirt, and could feel the strength in the arms holding him. It had been very hard to see his father, standing at the end of the path between the road and his cabin, waving, and not coming with them. Wade had cried then.

By the time Wade and Christine arrived at the highway, he was looking out the window. And by the time they were in Kenora, he was hungry again and they stopped for sandwiches to take with them. They finished the sandwiches as they crossed back into Manitoba, and Wade fell asleep leaning against the window.

What Wade did not know was that Christine had stayed up late the night before reading for work, and Gill had come out to see her. He did not know how they had talked late, about him and themselves and their diverging lives; and then, by the faint whiff of kerosene from the lit lamp, they had made love in Gill's bed, where Christine had spent the night. These were things he felt in the rhythms of his parents, more than he knew, and more than he would ever know. His parents were still his parents and to him that was all.

Wade also didn't yet know that his parents' separation would be ending. Christine had told Gill the divorce would be coming, the papers had been filed and they would have to meet in court. She told him the process of the divorce, how things would change but really stay the same. He would be free to see Wade when he wanted. The rest they could agree upon. And as Wade slept in Christine's Volvo heading west on the Trans-Canada, he trusted things would be good, things would not be too different, and things were taken care of. The last thing he did not know was that Gill would be leaving Lake of the Woods. Not for good, but for a stable job, further west, in British Columbia's forestry industry. Wade did not know the weekend just finished was the last time he would see Gill for almost three years.

RINGER

YEARS AGO, A FAMILY OF AMERICANS CAME TO LAKE OF THE WOODS in July to celebrate their independence. They brought with them their sandals and barbecue and dog named Ringer, and passed into Canada late in the morning at International Falls. By the time they crossed the world's longest wooden bridge at Sioux Narrows, they were tired from being in the car under the hot sun. They had been on the road since sunup, when the father had packed them into the station wagon with their pillows and blankets. Ringer had whimpered the whole trip. The Canadian Customs officer had asked if the dog was all right and the father had smiled and said, "Yes, sir. He always does this." The father watched Ringer in the rear-view mirror because he often vomited, and, as the trees of the Canadian Shield blurred past, he cursed the damn dog and his own weakness for agreeing to let it come. While the rest of the family slept, the father listened to the whimpering the whole way. By the time he saw a sign for Rushing River Provincial Park, he could take no more and pulled in for a rest stop and to eat and to let Ringer out of the car.

The family fell onto the grass and picnic benches, and the mother unpacked the sandwiches. While everyone ate, the father walked Ringer along a gravel road that followed the bank of Rushing River. He threw a stick for the dog. By the time he returned, the family was waiting in the car. The mother tried to entertain the children with games like I Spy and questions about nature. The father wanted to sit on the bank of Rushing River, eat his sandwich and watch the white water and feel the cool air. He tied Ringer's leash to the hitch of the station wagon and ate his sandwich while his family waited in the car, trying to spy something that was pink. When the father had finished they were calling to him, tired of games and impatient to be going; they wanted to get to the beach and the swimming at the fishing camp. The father, who didn't like to be rushed, climbed into the driver's seat and they were quickly off again, out onto Highway 71.

The sound of the metal clasp and buckle bouncing off the pavement alerted the father and he slammed on the brakes. "Ringer!" he yelled and jumped out of the car. The only thing the father found of the dog was its leash tied to its collar and the hair that had pulled out. When he returned to his seat he was brushing dog hair from his pants. The family saw that he held Ringer's leash in his hand, and no more was said of beaches or swimming. A long and silent ride passed, retracing the route to Rushing River, the station wagon creeping along on the shoulder of the highway looking for a sign of Ringer. When they reached the place where they had parked for lunch, the boy asked the father why he had left Ringer behind; where was he now? The father said nothing to the boy. What could he tell the boy to explain what had happened: how Ringer must have suffered? He could think of nothing to tell the boy. Finally, the mother told the boy that Ringer had run away. For the rest of the trip the boy kept his eyes out the side window of the car whenever they travelled, looking for Ringer.

And years later, when the boy drove his own hot and tired family up through the Canadian Shield to Lake of the Woods, he was to remember what his mother had told him, and he watched out the window for Ringer, listened for the sound of metal on the pavement.

TRAPLINES
—*January, 1985*—

ONCE THE BEAVER WERE SKINNED AND THE PELTS STRETCHED OUT
in the shed Gill knocked the snow off his boots on the step and
entered his cabin on the shore of Lake of the Woods. He shivered
off the chill that had settled in his bones from standing out in the
shed and working so long, opened the stove door, threw a log on
the morning coals, spun the vents wide and heard the sap sing
out between the splits in the bark. Every few days of trapping
season he loaded the snow machine with supplies, the .243 rifle,
strapped the toboggan on the back, and headed out to the
Pipestone Peninsula to check his line. By the time he had the
shower running hot from the tank, the fire crackled in the stove
and he put the coffee pot on to boil. The water of the shower ran
hot on his cold feet, so hot at first he couldn't feel it, only pins
and needles, and he remembered the danger of burning when
you were cold, the way that heat tricked the body, a trick that

Gill and his brother William used to play with the American boys who came up from the States with their fathers to fish at Smith Camps, their license plates saying things like Illinois, Land of Lincoln, and Minnesota, Land of 10,000 Lakes. When Gill and William used to work as dock-boys at Smith Camps they would help the Americans and listen to their accents carry over the water, sounding like the men on the TV fishing shows with their "ain'ts" and sharp vowels. Gill's first job was to clean and package the fish the Americans caught. On brown butcher's paper with black writing he printed the code of contents, owner and date: 2-Walleye—J. Wilton—July 3. But when the men were out on the lake, fighting across the whitecaps that bounced their new bass boats and forced them to run at a quarter speed, and their families were on the beach, Gill and William used to have fun with the boys, catching frogs and heating them up until they burst and flipped upside-down, intestines popping out of their bellies, and joking that they were hungry for a good frog sandwich.

Gill remembered the whole scene and shook his head as a little grin caught at his mouth under the shower stream. In his mind he planned what he would say to his brother William that afternoon, when he saw him again after the years they had been apart. He dried and carefully pried the blood out from under his fingernails before he started his ritual of clipping and shaving: the hum of the electric shaver, the lather from the old-fashioned barber's brush, new razor blades each time, a small drop of the shaving lotion Wade had sent him last June for Father's Day. Gill's skin still felt warm and moist as he set off from the cabin and the cold air hit his face between the back door and the Land Cruiser. The usual errands that piled up over the course of a week had to get knocked off in town, then he planned to meet his friend Andrew Allen for lunch as he'd arranged earlier in the day when he'd been returning over the ice and had met him on the ice road. Since he had returned from BC, winter was the season when Gill liked Lake of the Woods best; when he trapped beaver out on the Pipestone Peninsula and then sold the pelts in town to the local taxidermist named MacLeod, who did a thriving business selling authentic souvenirs to tourists.

The only people on the road in the winter were the residents or the government workers. Gill turned onto the main road and tooted his horn at Jilly Barton in her Jeep going the other way. The Bartons lived on the second left turn in from the highway and Gill knew them, like he knew all the residents, by what they drove and by first name. He had done some work for the Bartons when he first settled back in Ontario after working in the logging camps of the Pacific coast. They had needed someone to put up a few more guest cabins and he had been available with his own tools. It was that simple, they hadn't even discussed a wage. The job was done on time, the right payment made, and they had become friends. Four or five times a year when a big fishing party came up from the States, Mr. Barton lent Gill one of their big boats for a week so he could accommodate the group and keep their lines mostly untangled.

The only people passing Gill on the Trans-Canada Highway were the truckers and the salesmen, all in transit between motels or homes and loved ones or loneliness. The old Land Cruiser was limited to eighty kilometres an hour with the hubs locked and Gill did not see much chance of unlocking them until March, so the drive to town was twenty-eight minutes of swap and shop on the radio interrupted by the hourly news from Toronto. Gill stopped at the bank, where he made a deposit of $2,000 cash to make sure the cheque to Christine cleared and Wade could make hockey registration dues. Then he went on to the Ministry of Natural Resources, where the whole office was on coffee and he saw himself past the front desk to find out if his friend Alan was in. He and Alan made plans to lift the dock once they had a clear day and the ice had thickened, and Gill made a mental note to get the jack from his garage.

Back in the Land Cruiser, Gill checked his list and then crossed the train tracks down into the valley, past the smell of the pulp and paper mill on the north wind, to the taxidermist's to check on a beautiful rainbow trout a client from Duluth was having mounted. He drove to the hardware store and then across to the lumber yard for a pick-up order. Once the lumber was loaded, Gill let the Land Cruiser idle in the lumber yard. The hand who had helped him stood at the gate and warmed himself over a pot-bellied stove until his gloves steamed from the palms.

Lists were what Gill used to keep his life in order when he had work to do. He looked down at his list on the passenger seat and knew the one thing he had to do, to check on his brother who had just arrived back in town, didn't show up on the list. He spun that Land Cruiser around in the yard and drove down over to Riverside, to the place his brother was renting on the edge of the Indian reserve. In the fresh snowfall, the only tracks visible left the garage, their Y-bend in the street starting to drift over as the wind got up. Gill stopped for a minute in front of the house to see if the lights were on inside and then carried on back up to the town, the main roads and the parking lot in front of the Kowloon Diner to meet Andrew.

More new snow started as Gill pulled in. The Land Cruiser belted out heat onto the inside of the front windshield making the cottony flakes melt as they touched the surface and the wipers smeared them away. Fresh snow, especially a light one like this looked to be, was always a good sign to Gill. It made the tracking in the bush easier and it make the trapping better since the animals stuck to the paths. He felt his stomach growl and realized it had been almost seven hours since breakfast. He was a little early to meet Andrew and sat in the Land Cruiser waiting. He did not like the prospect of walking into the restaurant alone as someone would be there he would know and he would end up having to sit with them. Gill switched the wipers off and let the snow melt onto the windshield and run down in bending rows to rest on the wiper blades. The engine fan started up and Gill listened and stared at the snow melting and running, and he felt sadness close in on him as he was reminded of sitting in the truck with Christine, towards the end, when things were never right and there had been many long, one-sided discussions heading down long, empty roads, with Wade in the back sleeping. Those times he did not remember as much as she seemed to. And when they talked now, when it was not about money or planning, and when it was not about their son Wade, too much remained unsaid and unresolved to do much other than wish each other well.

The engine fan finished its cycle and Gill made an effort to brighten up. If he tried he could laugh about it all, see the big picture, chalk it up to lessons learned. He thought how funny it was that so many things had happened to him in the Land Cruiser; good things and bad things and just other things he remembered. Dates at the movies and popcorn kernels ground into the seat covers under sprawled and searching young bodies. Trips up to the unmarked back lakes with friends to fish for trout. Fights and make-ups that made it worth the patience. Times driving into a summer sunset so bright you swore you could reach out and touch it and burn away. Trips to the hospital in the middle of the night. And many hunting trips, some where the snow was so deep it was coming over the hood and the only thing keeping Gill on the road was the knowledge of a thousand trips along the same track. Gill had put the old Land Cruiser up for sale before. It still was for sale if Gill got the right price, a price he knew to be too high for a fourteen-year-old truck on the road because he had built the dock of the insuring agent. Almost thirteen years it had been with him, the only thing he remembered buying that year; that and the wedding. As a tradition every spring, with his money from the traplines, Gill made himself a few purchases: new gear, or repairs to old gear that was still good, or a fly-in trip up north; something before the summer hustle. But that year it had been the marriage to Christine and the Land Cruiser, and only one of them was with him still.

Gill waited a couple more minutes until Andrew arrived and they went inside to enjoy a lunch of the kind the Kowloon sign promised: Canadian and Chinese food. After lunch, Gill carried on to his other errands, the part he had to order for the chain saw, the hose fitting he had to drop off for repair from the pump housing. He had dinner by himself at the diner of the Husky while the early sunset left the streets in darkness by the time he had settled the bill. A dim light pressed out from the front room of the house William had been renting for the last two months he'd been back in town. Gill had seen him twice during that time, both times at restaurants, and the only reason he knew where his brother lived was because he had sought it out and found it, two weeks after William had moved in and a week after he had started payment on a TV. Gill went to the front door, knocked and peered into a room without furniture, bathed in the bluish light thrown off by the TV. After a minute without an answer he knocked again and then set off through the drifts around to the back. The snow on the ground outside the back window glowed in the light cast from above. Gill stepped over to the window where the snow drift curled away from the house and peered in. Sitting at the kitchen table was William. Gill waved his hand up into the light and his brother jumped in his chair. He squinted then, creasing his brows, and motioned to the back door.

"Why didn't you just knock?"

"I did," Gill said looking into the room. "You didn't answer." An open mickey of whiskey grabbed his attention, the cap lying beside a glass poured half-full. He stepped to the table and drained the glass in two swallows, then turned to his brother. "I thought you went to the meeting."

"I did."

Gill stared at him but made no movement. "And this?"

"It's nothing. I haven't been drinking it. I didn't even have a sip, you can smell my breath. I was just sitting here."

Gill wiped the back of his hand across his mouth and stared. He measured out his words. "I don't get it. What are you doing?"

A dog barked somewhere in the night. Gill's boots squeaked on the linoleum as William stood dumb. Gill started to turn and put his toque back on, to walk out the back door.

"Waiting. I guess," William said. "Wait."

Gill looked over at William's face in the shadows under the single naked bulb and felt a flash of remembrance of an incident when he had been eight and shoplifting candy from the Chinese grocer with William and neither one had told on the other despite the lashings they'd received for their silence.

"I wasn't drinking it."

"What then? You buy a bottle, bring it home, get out a glass, open the bottle, pour the shit and you're not going to drink it?"

"I wasn't," his brother said and put his hands in his pockets. "I wasn't."

"Fucking right you were."

"I didn't want to." He took his hands out of his pockets and opened them. "I just wanted to sit here and be near it. Not touching it."

"What, like an old friend?" Gill said and spit while he spoke. "And you're on the wagon."

"I just wanted for something to change."

"What? What's going to change that you're not going to do?" Gill stomped to the back door. "Fuck it's hot in here." He took off his boots and then went to the sink and got a cloth to wipe up the melted snow. He wrung the water out of the cloth and it made a hollow echo in the stainless steel sink. "I don't understand you, big brother," Gill said, folding the dish cloth over the faucet and turning back to the table. "I came by to see how you were doing, if you wanted to talk or catch a movie. You know,

something nice. And you're in here playing shit-stick cowboy."
Gill ran his hand over his head feeling the stubble at the surface,
at a loss for what to do.

"Sit down, Gill."

"You want to go out for a drink? Maybe that would be better.
Dad used to go over to the Mill Town Lounge on Railway. It's
only a ten-minute ride. You could follow in his footsteps. Maybe
he's got a stool and mug there with his name on them."

William glanced up and he looked old. "Please, sit down."

Gill sat across the table from William, the bottle between
them, the light shining through the bottle of amber liquor making a dark stain on the wooden table. The empty glass sat beside
it. Gill picked up the glass, tilted it, ran his finger around the
base, then sucked the liquor from his skin. "I'm sitting. Now
what?"

"I thought we could talk. I haven't been away that long."

"Six years since I've seen you, William. Eighteen you've been
gone."

"Well, I wanted to come back. But things get so busy and hec-
tic. You lose track."

Gill searched his mind for something to say and nothing came
to him. He hated to hear the tone of defeat in his brother's voice
and the words he said, the excuses he used. The two sat at the
table and Gill stared at the bottle and his brother stared at the
window while in the front room the TV played "These Eyes" by
the Guess Who.

Gill started, "So what's new? How was the meeting?"

"Good. Good. You'd be surprised who was there. You'd know
half of them. It's depressing really. You get packed into the basement of the church, under the basketball net, on folding chairs.
They have coffee on a table at the front and cookies, not the real
Girl Guide ones but like them. The chairs are in a circle and
there's a meeting leader who starts things off with the feather. He
passes it on to someone and it's only their turn to talk because

they've got the feather. Eventually, it gets passed around the room and everybody gets a chance to go. They call everyone *members*. It's quite a little club."

"What did you talk about?"

"You introduce yourself and talk a little about yourself so people know you. What you do, when you started drinking, how old you are. Some people get emotional about it and I think they like that, it makes it real, tough. It's pretty routine though. You tell them what you tell people every day. 'My name is William Dubois, I'm thirty-eight years old, I worked for twelve years at the Inco smelter in Sudbury but I don't any more. I had a son there, and he's still there. I like camping and fishing.' Bullshit like that. Everyone has their story. You know yours, I know mine. We tell it every day." He paused with his hands clasped together on the table. "I went yesterday to the mill."

"To see Gabe?"

"Yeah. I need to do something. I can't live on my savings."

"And? What happened?" Gill asked.

"About the job?"

"Yes about the job. They said they weren't going to advertise it until next week. I told you to get your name in early. They'll have four hundred applications for something like that."

"He said he couldn't tell me until Monday. But I have a good feeling about it."

"That's good."

"It is good. It'll be good to have a job again. It was good." William got himself a glass from the cupboard and filled it from the sink, dumped it out the way he always did and filled it again once the water ran cold. "When was the last time you wrote a resumé?"

"Oh, three, four years ago. When I was out in BC. Why?"

"I touched up mine last week before I went. I took it in to Gabe and sat across the desk from him. He looked at it and I could see he read it close so it took some time. And while he was reading it I was thinking, because I knew what he was reading, I was thinking that my resumé, that piece of paper, is me. As far as the company is concerned, or cares, what's on that piece of paper is me. All of me they need to know. And it's crap, it's bullshit; not all, but a lot. To them, that's me. That's all. All me. And after, when Gabe was done with it, I looked at it. I looked at it close. And I felt like I couldn't find me in it. And that's just it. It's not only the mill. This has been my life, looking and applying for jobs, for weeks now, months. I haven't had a steady job since the smelter."

William started to relax as the story tumbled out of him. Zoe and he had split up and she'd taken their son Michael two years ago. Finally, he had gone to Toronto with enough money to survive a month. By his first week he was competing with high-school dropouts for jobs, and it was shit work but there was always someone desperate for it, willing to kick you in the balls to get it. He wanted something better, thought he deserved something better after twelve years on the line in Sudbury under the smokestack. By then the story had built up a momentum and kept tumbling out of William. He wanted a life he could get into and not have to worry about how he could not make monthly cheques clear from his account to pay for normal things like groceries and rent. He had no trouble getting his foot in the door with companies. He could lay it on thick, he was a great catch, he was organized and motivated and wanted to execute the company vision and mission. He had done it, made a perfect candidate for them to hire. Then, about six months into the job, the trouble would start when expense accounts were overdue and reports were waiting on someone else to be finished.

Gill poured himself a drink from the mickey. The newspaper on the chair between him and William was open to the classified section with some ads circled. Gill unzipped his jacket and laid it over the paper. He stood and dropped some ice in his glass and William did not move but continued to stare out the window at the snow pushed around by the wind in the darkness, or at the window and his own reflection. Gill could not tell which and he sat again and it startled his brother like he'd been absent.

"And I liked it too," William told Gill. He liked to be able to give them what they wanted, loved for them to want him. Jobs lasted for a while, the longest was eleven months and then he moved on and always made it seem good for him; he wouldn't become stagnant, could do better. He had all the lines to deal with being fired. He'd be in a new job soon enough. "It was all the same thing," William said, trying to put things into order. Gill sipped the drink he had poured himself and saw his brother watching him. Gill looked at his hands holding the glass and noticed some blood he'd missed under his fingernails.

"You always were the working man," William said and it reminded Gill of the way their dad Lucien had spoken to someone he did not like.

Lucien worked his job at the Kenora Pulp and Paper Mill and payed his taxes and he had felt that the combined burden of those two activities had entitled him to anything he wanted. He had fucked off to wherever when he was not working or sleeping and he had been lazy. Whenever their mom had wanted something done right, William or Gill had been charged with the job, and she had quickly learned that Gill was the better of the two for following through. When the time came after high school graduation, Gill had stayed in Kenora and worked away in his quiet way at his odd projects that he took satisfaction in seeing through, and William, who had been bright at school when he applied himself and had earned enough money to go away to school through summer jobs and a track scholarship in the 100 and 200, had left to pursue a business administration degree in Sudbury, which he quit three years later to work at the smelter and put together a down payment on a house for his expectant wife. In the bare light of William's rented kitchen, Gill knew there was no changing the things that had happened, there was only being less afraid of the things to come.

"And now what?" Gill said.

"And now?"

"Now what? What's changed?"

"What do you mean?"

"What's changed? Where are you now?"

"Where?" William pushed out his lower lip and shrugged like a man emptied of answers. He told Gill he was just trying to get back to something he knew, to what he called the "poor man's Betty Ford" with a line of credit at the bank and a job; to stay clean and off the booze. He licked his dry lips and took a sip from his water glass. He was not eating meat and he had started exercising, walking every day, faster and faster, he said, until he could run again, like he used to. He told Gill he felt like the ghost dog Ringer they used to warn the American kids about at Smith Camps: run until he could not run any more. William rubbed and stretched the skin on his cheek and Gill could hear each whisker's sound, could see an age spot behind William's left eye. "How did you get away, Gill? How did you not get caught in this?"

"I have to play the games too. I just try to keep it simple, that's all."

"You don't really have to play the games."

"I have to be a company man."

"How's that?"

"My company's me. But no one pays me. If the lake is polluted and the beaver all die and the fish move, I starve. No one wants a guide that can't lead them to the game. If the tourists move in and buy up all the land and come for a few weekends every year, I lose my business. No one wants to pay for what they think they can have for free. Just like you found out no one wants you if you're an unsafe Safety Supervisor." Gill met his brother's eyes and felt any number of things could happen: he and William could beat each other's heads in or cry in each other's arms. He did not mean to hurt his brother by bringing up old ghosts, but he did want to see his brother take charge of his own life, and the decisions he had made in it, and the consequences he kept having to live with every day.

"I've got to get going or I'll drink your mickey and won't be able to drive home." Gill picked his coat off the chair and the paper with the circled classified ads fell. He put his hand on his brother's shoulder and looked at their reflection in the window, a reflection that held him as he recognized it as the same gesture his father made to him when he was a boy and sitting at the kitchen table after some disappointment he could no longer remember. "Tomorrow's a new day, William. I'll call Gabe first thing. He should be able to put you on the floor at least."

"Thanks."

"You okay here tonight?"

"Yeah. But take the bottle."

"I'll call you tomorrow after I talk to Gabe," Gill said and put the bottle in his coat pocket to go.

They hugged at the door and didn't say much and Gill walked down the driveway to the road. The cool, sharp air pressed into his lungs and as he got to the end of the driveway William shouted to him from the doorway, "Gill, I'll call you. I don't have a phone." Gill flashed him a mitt thumb up and started the Land Cruiser.

The hubs were locked and the road felt slick and treacherous. As he drove out of Kenora, Gill could see cars in the ditches on both sides of the road, the flashing lights of tow trucks illuminating the tracks into the ditch of those that had lost control on the slippery streets. Thick clouds dumping snow made the night darker as the amber street lights lit the windshield in streaks. Gill stopped at the Safeway to pick up a few groceries in case the snow continued falling overnight. By the time he was on the highway out of Kenora only odd cars passed him, the beams of their headlights crossed his own and illuminated the falling snowflakes.

The Land Cruiser tracked well through the snow that fell over the land. In his mind, Gill kept hearing the voice of his brother and the story he had told Gill when he had first seen him at the restaurant in Kenora three weeks past. William had said he had a feeling like he was going to be the one giving the speech of remembrance at his own funeral. It was a strange thing to say and Gill had not thought much of it at the time. It was the kind of thing William said sometimes, melodramatic and fantastic and hard to take seriously. But it came to Gill then as he drove and it didn't seem as strange. The supply of cars passing Gill in the opposite direction was exhausted, the steady hum of the Land Cruiser's knobby tires the only sound. Gill flipped the lights to high beam and the snow fell faster, beginning to collect in loose shapes on the windshield outside the path of the wipers. A patch that had collected on the hood broke off and flew over the roof-line and Gill drove on. The hum of the tires gradually grew fainter as the snow grew deeper and the pavement disappeared. Gill turned off the Trans-Canada onto the Storm Bay Road and heard the speed of the fan change with the speed of the engine. The rear end slid out around the corner and the front wheels pulled the Land Cruiser back into line.

The new snow groaned and squeaked with each step Gill took down the path to the cabin. He set his groceries at the door and shoveled the path from the clearing where he parked to the back door of the cabin. He took his red toque off as he worked and hooked it on the bare branch of a young poplar. The bright colour stood out in the black and white world of the woods and the snow and the heavy clouds above, and the stubble on Gill's head was wet from the dust of flying snow. He lifted the last line of snow off the path and the walk was clear for a little while. He rubbed his hand over his head and sent water drops spinning. The snow kept on falling. The end of the path where Gill started had a light dusting of snow by the time he came to the cabin, but the job would do for now.

BLINDFOLD CREEK

ONE DAY WHEN HE WAS TEN, WADE SAT ON THE END OF THE Smith Camps dock waiting for Gill to return from guiding a party of Chicago businessmen. Nancy Smith sat down beside Wade and took off her shoes and rolled up the cuffs on her overalls and dangled her feet in the water to cool off. After a time, she asked Wade if he had ever heard the story of how they built the dam at Blindfold Lake, and Wade had not, so Nancy told it to him: how the channel where the government chose to build the dam used to be the Blindfold Creek, which joined Blindfold in a series of beaver ponds and streams to Lake of the Woods. Like all the lakes in the area, Blindfold drained into Lake of the Woods, which drained west through the Winnipeg River to Lake Winnipeg, and then north through Nelson River to Hudson's Bay. Back then, Blindfold used to be a great wild-rice producing lake, before they built the dam and the fishing camps that brought in the tourists. Because of the cover from the paddies, Blindfold held crappie, bluegill and pumpkinseed, panfish that Americans are used to catching and like to eat at shore lunch.

To build the Blindfold dam, the channel between Lake of the Woods and Blindfold had to be dynamited and dredged. The whole project started so that a retired senator, who had built his cabin on Blindfold, could pass his big boat through to fish on Lake of the Woods. The senator was a religious man and wanted to be present when they lit the fuse, so they had to set the charges off on a Sunday after church let out. It made one hell of a noise; no one had ever seen so many dead fish at once. People came from all over to watch the explosion. The water shot a hundred feet in the air.

A day later, the dead fish started smelling and the bears started coming. Jones McCabe, who was probably hungover from being tight the night before, found four bears sleeping under his cabin when he went out to do his morning business. The bears could hardly move. Jones shot the first three, reloaded his twelve gauge, and shot the fourth before it made the edge of the clearing. Once they put in the dam, the senator made the trip across every day for six years until he died of cancer.

GONE TWO DAYS
—*October, 1986*—

IT WAS A WEDNESDAY IN THE FALL, AND WADE EXPECTED IT TO turn out like any other Wednesday, with him going to school and then coming home, not doing his homework until later, helping Christine make dinner, going to hockey practice, and stopping for a drink at the 7-Eleven on the way home. But in the morning Gill came and the routine was broken. Three knocks on the door and Gill's face appeared in the window, his hunting coat on, the green Land Cruiser parked on the street facing the wrong way. Christine was dressed in her business clothes, getting ready for work and adjusting one earring, when she answered the door. "Well, shit," she said, seeing him and calling out for Wade to come and see. Gill smiled and even though he had a wary look on his face, like he could jump back from the door and disappear again, he didn't wait to hug her.

"It's been awhile," he said and slid out of the hug to look for

Wade. "Wade," he said, "the birds are in the potholes. They're waiting for us." He turned back to Christine, looked out to the Land Cruiser on the street and looked back at her. "We'll only be gone two days, southwest of here, towards Mariapolis."

Christine stood frozen in place; one knee was bent, all her weight on the other leg. "This is not happening Gill," she said and straightened her neck and hair. "He has school today."

"Nice to see you. I know he has school. He can miss a day. You look great. Win any big cases lately?"

"Hey, Dad," Wade said as he came down the stairs in his school clothes, "I thought I heard your voice. It was hard though because I had the blow-dryer going."

"Hey, pal."

"Are you going hunting?"

"He is," Christine said.

"Can I go too?"

"Sure," said Gill, bending over and untying his boots. "C'mon. Let's go get some clothes together for you."

"Whoa," said Christine. "Let's just hold on a second."

"Two days, Christine," said Gill. "I haven't seen him in two months."

"You make that sound like it's my fault."

"No," said Gill pulling together the seam and thread of his ripped cuff, "just the way things worked out. I had the chance to make some money and I took it. Things have been sporadic since I've been back. You never missed a cheque, did you?" He looked at her again, as if she were trying on a new outfit and had asked him to assess it. "You really do look good, too. I'm going to go and help him get his things now."

"That's not it, Gill."

"Come on. He needs his dad. You heard him. He wants to go. What's he going to miss in school?"

"That's not the point, Gill."

"Christine, I know that's not the point. The point is that I can't just come here and do this. I've got to let you know. We've got to talk about it. I just didn't plan this far in advance. I was in town to get some things done and didn't know if I would have time to see you guys, so I didn't let you know I'd be coming."

Wade stood for a few seconds and listened to his parents. As soon as they started calling each other by their first names, he started back upstairs to get his hunting clothes together. He could still hear them talking when he got to his room. His mother had not said no and he knew she didn't mind him being out of school for a day or two on special occasions. Gill came into Wade's room and looked around like he had never seen it before. Wade asked questions about what to bring, what they were doing, where they were going. They had talked about having a fishing weekend just the two of them but had run out of time to make it happen. Gill promised Wade they would do it next summer, when Wade was thirteen and they could have a whole weekend together.

On the way out the door Gill held out a business card to Christine. "Here's where we'll be staying." he said, "As long as they have a room. If not we'll go to the next town."

"All you have to do next time is call ahead, Gill."

"I will. But I didn't know myself."

"And I don't mind him going with you. I just want to know."

"Yeah. You're right. I didn't plan it though."

"You were going by yourself?"

Gill nodded and there was a long look held between him and Christine. Then it seemed like neither of them had anything more to say about the subject. Christine walked to the door and asked if they wanted to take any food and Gill told her they would get some on the way. Wade wore his old winter jacket and a camouflage shirt Gill had given him for his birthday and they were leaving. Gill carried Wade's duffle bag and his rubber boots out to the Land Cruiser while Wade turned to Christine.

"Don't worry, Mom. I'll take care of him."

Christine laughed out loud and pulled him towards her to hug. She opened her arms and Wade could see her eyes were shiny and bright, like she was going to cry. He hugged her and ran down the drive to the truck where Gill was waiting, and they were off. The truck smelled like gun powder and mud from the sloughs and all the old clothes that were worn only for hunting. They stopped at the 7-Eleven on the way out of town and Gill let Wade pick out a few things he wanted to eat, including the variety pack of sugary cereals. Wade tore into the Corn Pops before they left the city and ate them dry from the package. Gill stopped to fill up with gas and bought himself a coffee in a small town with a grain elevator you could see for miles around, and a tall church steeple rising up above the trees, and a motor hotel with a beer vendor and restaurant that looked dark while the sign read OPEN. Over the flat, straight roads they travelled to the south, then to the west, on right angles along the edges of ditches bordering the harvested fields. Gill talked to Wade about the work he had been doing out in BC, in a town called Tofino, where a big protest had shut down the logging operations as people chained themselves to the axles of trucks and camped in the tops of trees to stop them being cut. After almost two hours they pulled onto a gravel section road and Gill pointed out the windshield at the geese flying in the distance, specks of black against the clear, blue sky. They drove a little further and pulled off into a field of stubble.

The springs of the Land Cruiser creaked as Gill sat next to Wade on the tailgate; the calls of thousands of geese rang clear through the cool air as they got ready. Wade looked up and the flock was barely visible in the air above the vapour of his breath. Gill stood, ready to go and looked back at Wade.

"Have you got your boots on yet?"

"My socks keep bunching up and leaving lines."

"Pull them tight, then pull your boots. Here, I'll help you."

Wade held his socks up at the top and Gill pulled the boots

onto his foot with a clunk as they slid into place. Wade stood up
and gave them a test walk around the Land Cruiser. Gill reached
into the back and pulled out two gun cases while Wade waited
behind him like a relaxed soldier.

"Which guns did you bring, Dad?"

"The twenty gauge single for you and the 101 over-and-under
for me."

"Is it a twelve gauge?"

"Yep," said Gill as he untied his homemade gun cases and
grasped the recoil pad to slide the shotgun out. "Here, son. Hold
this for a second. Check it though."

"This switch?" Wade asked balancing the shotgun in his
hands. He remembered seeing his father push the metal lever to
the side with his thumb and so he did as well. The shotgun broke
in his hands like a firm cattail stem.

"That's it, Wade," said Gill. "See where the shells go?"

"Yeah," Wade said as he looked down the stacked barrels at
the circling reflections of light. He blew into the barrels and
lipped his fingers around the perfect metal openings where the
brass casings of the shells sat. The oil from the barrel had a smell
he remembered and placed immediately: the smell of his father's
shed at the lake. Every time you went into it, the sweet smell of
gun oil surrounded you and got into your clothes and hair. Gill
didn't store the guns in the shed but it was where he cleaned and
oiled them and where they lived during hunting season, when
they had to be cleaned after every use. Gill took the over-and-
under from Wade and handed him the single-shot twenty gauge.
It broke more easily than the over-and-under when Wade
checked it. Gill reminded him how to click the safety on and off
and left it on. The number-four shells rattled in Wade's pocket
where he put them and Gill closed up the Land Cruiser, then
they walked over the field and down the slope to a stand of trees.
Wade replayed in his mind the times he had been target shooting with his father; the way you called "pull" and then the clay

pigeon flew spinning out into the air; the way you had to brace and lean into the shot and then swing with the target and get out in front of it before you fired. Wade remembered his father's advice and the way the clay pigeons exploded when they caught a full charge of lead.

From the road, the ducks had been wheeling in the sky from the bluff to the south and back. From the knowledge of past hunts, Gill told Wade which field the ducks were stubbling in. A regular trade of teal and mallards flew between the field to the south and the slough in the bluff.

The wind started to blow into Wade's face as they crossed the field heading south. Wade could feel a change in his father as soon as they left the truck. Neither one said a word across the field. They held the barbed wires of the fence apart for each other at the edge of the field, handed each other in turn their gun, and slipped through. The grass grew tall and uncut. Gill crouched down to one knee and watched the sky. Wade did the same as the flights of ducks continued trading back and forth.

"See how they land into the wind, Wade?"

"Yeah," Wade said and watched just what his father was talking about.

"That's how they get up too. When they take off, be ready for them to jump into the wind."

Gill broke the over-and-under and rested it on the angle of his knee. He picked two red Imperial number four shells out of his pocket and slid them into the barrels up to the ridge of the brass. Wade did the same with a single number four shell into his single barrel. The safety was on and he closed the gun slowly, like Gill did, hearing only the short click of the gun locking shut.

Gill cinched Wade's shoulder strap tighter and Wade slung the gun over his shoulder. The wind flattened out the tall grass around them like waves across the lake. Wade was anxious to get going but didn't move. Gill watched the flights of birds rise up and wheel against the wind in the sky. He pulled the bill of his cap down over his eyes and looked over at Wade.

"It's still early. They haven't been hunted yet this year, I'd say," he said in a whisper. "A lot of young ones. We'll go around to that stand of willows," he pointed his finger in a deliberate motion, "and they should come right over. I'll go down and through the brush. You go parallel to me through the grass. Keep low and if birds come over, crouch and stay still. Let them see your back and your hat but don't move the gun or they'll flare off. Keep the muzzle pointed into the air."

Wade felt his feet tingle in his boots. He felt calm but excited, ready to go but not in a hurry. It was good; there was no need to rush it. Gill looked over at him, smiled and reached into his shirt pocket and pulled out a whistle on a string to put around his neck.

"This whistle, Wade," he said, putting it into his mouth. "I'll blow it when I see the birds coming so keep an ear out." He blew a short, flat note that was different from any whistle Wade had heard and its sound blended into the wind.

Wade listened and nodded to every word of instruction. He pulled his own cap down around his eyes and waited for Gill to start out. They sat still as a twitching flight of teal went right over them. Then Gill put his hand on Wade's knee. "Ready?" he said and smiled and Wade nodded. Gill took a last look at the sky and then crouched to his feet and started towards the brush. Wade waited until he could not see his father and then started to the willows. The long grass felt wet against his pants and Wade felt the moisture absorbed by his gloves, softening the leather. He crept along for a minute and then sat and rested. The brush his father had entered looked thick and tangled by branches, not an easy pathway, but if there was anything Wade knew, it was that his father could do it. He crept along again, almost to the willows before he stopped. The cool wetness of the grass soaked into his pants on the knee he had planted for support. A blackbird skitted through the brush above where Wade guessed his father would be. The time stretched out into minutes and Wade shifted his weight on his knee. Flecks of sunlight reflected off the water of the slough through the brush and the blackbirds swooped past in random patterns.

The grass brushed against Wade's face and curled around the back of his neck in the bending wind. The sound of everything around him became noticeable, like he had been forgotten by the world and only now saw what went on when he was not there. He heard the loud quacking of ducks coming from the brush and beyond the willows. A flight of six mallards flew right over him and made a wide circle to the south, quacking down to the slough below. Wade's heart beat so he felt it in his chest and arms. The mallards kept quacking and descending in tighter and tighter circles, their wings cupped to the air as they glided into the wind. Then, their descent trajectories changed, and they beat their wings hard and fast, straining up into the air. Wade watched the six mallards climb hard into the stiff wind and then things happened all at once. Three short blasts of the whistle sounded and then it was as if a charge had been set off under the water and everything burst into the air: the sound of the ducks getting up. The quacks and splashing and the beating of the air was something Wade had never expected. The ducks took off as if the charges were timed; one hundred leapt here, a hundred and fifty there. Through the trees the reflection of the sunlight off the water disappeared and Wade could see the flapping of thousands of wings at once, the horizon dark with ducks angling into the sky.

Wade crouched and held his gun in his tight hands facing the mass of quacking, peeping ducks. Once they were up, the ducks wheeled off in every direction; all their voices and bodies like one animal to begin, peeping and flapping, and then fractured and spreading out into the air. Wade stayed crouched and breathed. He heard the whistle again, then he heard his father's shots: One, two, a relaxed heartbeat apart. The air seemed to be pulled out from under three ducks heading straight towards him as they folded in the air and spiralled to the ground. Wade raised his gun to his shoulder. He concentrated on the bead at the end of the barrel but there were so many ducks flying by before he had a chance. He swung on a group of four and let them go. Then two more went by before he knew it and he waited. He clicked the safety off and stayed with the birds pouring over not twenty yards up when a loud quacking caught his attention. A lone drake was steaming down the trough of the slough. It had been one of the last birds into the air and was flapping hard to catch the safety of the flock. Wade brought his gun up in line with the drake and started to swing. The drake flared suddenly in a sharp arc and Wade stayed with him, leading him off the tip of the beak. The motion was smooth and fluid and Wade squeezed the trigger. The recoil of the gun popped him on the cheekbone as it jumped in his hands and he watched the pellets hit the drake and spin it down to the ground. It landed about twelve feet from Wade with a light sound in the tall grass. Wade cried out and jumped up. He knew his shot had been true but he didn't want to lose his first drake.

When he got to the spot where he had seen it fall the drake was lying with its head bent back against its body on a lifeless neck. Wade stood over it for a second looking at the ruffles in the breast feathers where the pellets had hit. There were tremors up and down and inside his legs. He reached out to pick up the drake but was shaking and could only touch it. It was still warm as he cupped his hand around its breast and the head flopped over, the blood on his hand warm and sticky between his fingers, the silver down feathers of the drake stuck to the blood. The blades of grass surrounding Wade waved in the wind, bending and flexing around the stillness of the duck.

"Hey, son," Gill called out to him, "did you get him?"

"Yeah," Wade said, his leg still shaking. "A drake."

"Good shot. I saw him fall."

Wade looked up and at his father coming out of the brush smiling. Wade noticed the three birds his father carried by their orange webbed feet, their wings fanned out in the wind. He had his shotgun slung over his shoulder and looked big as the wind inflated his coat.

"Nice bird, Wade," Gill said, laying his own ducks in the grass next to Wade's duck. "He's a nice one."

"Yeah. You too."

"Where's the gun?"

Wade looked at his father like he wondered what gun he asked about.

"I must have left it over where I shot from," Wade said and started back to find it. In the nest of trampled grass where he had knelt, the gun was lying where it fell. He broke it to eject the empty shell and walked back to where Gill kneeled with the ducks. He carried the gun broken and balanced on his bent elbow like he saw Gill do.

"Stay down and load up again, Wade. The birds will keep going over. If they don't see us we may get a few."

"Okay," Wade said and kneeled next to Gill to look at the ducks. He broke his gun again, checked the safety and fed in another shell. Two of the dead ducks' thin grey eyelids had closed over the black round eyes. Wade stroked his hand through the pin-feathers on the stretched wing of his mallard drake. Depending on the reflection of the light, the green head of the drake looked navy in places and purple around the edges and dark green through the middle. Wade looked up at Gill who was watching the sky and the clouds moving across it.

"Hey Dad, how did you get three with only two shots?"

"They were out at the far end of range so there was a good spread in the pattern. Some pellets hit one bird and some hit the next."

"You think I could do it?"

"Two with one shot? Sure." Gill smiled at Wade. The quacking of a mallard caught his attention and he twisted his head up to the sky. A pair went over out of range and wheeled back to the south and the field they stubbled in. "But two in one shot Wade, you have to be lucky too."

"Yeah?"

Gill nodded. It was a great starting to the day; three shots, four birds. Wade helped him put the ducks into the game pouch on the back of his jacket to carry. The sky was low, the clouds moving very fast but with no feeling of rain. The wind blew across the field and they started out around the slough to wait for the birds to come back. Gill talked to Wade about how they would both fire shots that missed, shots that clipped birds they would never find on the ground, shots that would drop ducks into water where they would dive down and hold onto reeds and drown themselves. With their shotguns slung on their shoulders, Wade and Gill walked down further, into the cattails surrounding the slough, to wait for the birds they could see circling on the wind above to drop into range.

The shower shut off and a minute later Gill opened the door and the steam crept out across the stucco ceiling of the motel room. Wade lay on his stomach across one of the beds and watched TV while Gill pulled his bag to the foot of the other bed and sat down with the white towel around his waist.

"What are you watching, Wade?"

"Nothing. There's a football game on but I don't recognize the teams. I think it's college."

The marching band was on the field for the halftime show. From the distance of the camera, the band spelled out the letters of the school in big moving shapes against the green artificial turf.

"Does your mother still go to the university games?"

"Not any more."

"Do you remember? We used to go all the time, the three of us."

"Yeah. I remember going to meet the players after one game."

"Oh yeah. And you got all their autographs. Do you still have them?"

"The sheet's framed on the wall in my room. You saw it, remember?"

"Right. Right, I remember."

Gill pulled socks and underwear out of his bag and put them on. Wade felt his face, hot against his hands from being out in the wind all day. Gill finished getting dressed and smoothed his hair out in the mirror as Wade watched him.

"I'm about starved. Are you hungry, Wade?"

"Yeah. There's a coupon on the table for a pizza restaurant."

"You ready to go?"

"Yeah," said Wade and rolled over on the bed to turn the TV volume off. "I don't think I'll get dressed up if that's okay."

"Fine. But you never know who you'll meet. I met your mom with a bucket of fish guts in my hands. The first time. She was a guest at the camp I was working at." Gill looked at Wade standing in front of him in the camouflage shirt. "Has she ever told you this story?"

Wade shook his head and sat on the edge of the bed.

"Well, that's really the whole story. I was going down the dock to a boat to dump the guts and she was coming up the dock from a day on the lake. I think her family had been at the camp before. But I never noticed her until then." Gill sat back down on the edge of the bed and started to put on his boots to go out.

Wade asked, "So then what happened, Dad?"

"I started seeing her around the camp. We went out at night with friends. I was lucky her family had just arrived. They stayed for a few weeks."

"And then they left?"

"Went back to the city. I called her when I went there for winter work."

Wade nodded and stayed on the edge of his bed. It seemed to him the only way his parents could have met, at the lake. He had heard in various ways before about his father as a camp guide where his mother visited, but never the whole story.

"C'mon, son. Get your shoes on and let's get some food."

Wade yawned and stretched and put his shoes on as Gill went out the door ahead of him. Gill's extra camouflage hat was a little big on him but he liked the way it matched his shirt. The carefulness, the wariness he always felt when he first saw his father again was gone now. He put the room key in his pocket, heard the door lock when it closed behind him, and ran to catch up to Gill. They walked out the front door of the motel and a block down the street to Luigi's Pizza where they ordered a Hawaiian and Wade picked off the pineapples. The dying minutes of the football game ticked off the clock as Wade and Gill returned to their room, the country music from the band in the hotel bar loud enough to hear through the walls. Wade took off his shoes, the camouflage hunting hat, shirt, under-clothes and crawled into bed. He propped his pillows against the headboard to watch the end of the football game and Gill went into the bathroom to wash up before bed. Wade heard Gill's toothbrush and the water running in the sink. The water ran a final stronger burst and there was a drawn out "Ahhh."

"What time do you want to get up, Wade?"

"I don't know. When can we hunt?"

"At first light," said Gill as he emptied his pockets and stripped his belt from the loops. "We should be out in the field by then."

"Should we call for a wake up?"

"Sure," Gill said and watched Wade pick up the phone. "What is it?"

"There's no dial tone."

Wade shrugged and handed Gill the receiver. They checked to make sure the the cord fit into the jack and the connections were all good. Gill stood and relaced his belt into his pants.

"I'll go and see about this," he said and went out, his unlaced hunting boots over his pant cuffs.

The door clicked shut again and Wade leaned back to watch the football game end. The next thing he knew, the game was over and a cowboy was riding a bucking bull around a rodeo ring. Somehow he had fallen asleep and as he looked over he could see Gill's bed still made in the flicker of the screen. Wade got up to pee and when he tried to get back into bed an uneasy feeling held him. After the fourth bull had spun off the rider, he put on his pants and shirt and slid his bare feet into his shoes. Out in the parking lot, the Land Cruiser sat exactly where they had left it, under the trees and locked, the gun cases still hidden under the blankets, the shell cases undisturbed. Nothing moved on the streets of Mariapolis except a silent cat crossing the road. Wade walked around to the back of the motel where the only light shining was a red exit sign in front of a steel fire-door. Back around the front, the desk was closed off by sliding bars. Two vending machines illuminated the lobby and the refrigeration cycle clicked on in one. The country music grew louder from behind a black fire-door and Wade went over to it and put his hand flat against the cold surface, which vibrated to the twang of the music. A soft scream of grinding metal came from the door as Wade put his shoulder into it, pulling it until it jerked open and the music and smoke rushed out. About thirty people were in the bar, all looking the same to him; most sat around the wooden tables, a few danced in jerky movement around a floor of wood paneling, more sat on stools with their elbows on the bar itself or swivelled sideways facing each other. The people at the tables closest to the door looked up at Wade when he burst in but went back to their business when they saw it was no one they knew.

Wade swept his eyes back over the room and saw a man at the bar with his unlaced boots over his pant cuffs. Wade had to look hard to recognize his father. Next to him, a woman in a black sleeveless shirt with a big mouth laughed and looked like she might swallow something. Her hair was red and curled around her face and mouth. Wade could see the line between her breasts down the front of her shirt when she fell forward and put her hand on Gill's knee. The same bull-riding rodeo he had been watching in his room played here on a big screen beside the bar. He could hear the woman next to his father laugh again in a high pitch and he looked over as she straightened herself on her stool, took a sip through the straw in her drink and crossed her legs in her denim skirt. Wade walked closer, pretending to be watching the rodeo, and then he could hear what they were saying.

"Are you here with the boys then, sugar?" the woman said.

"You could say that."

"You're with the boys? Then where are they?"

"I'm with my boy."

She said, "You mean your son?" and Gill nodded and took a sip of beer from the bottle in front of him. He was facing the bar and turning his head to talk. Wade saw the front of his hair standing up where he pushed it with his hand.

"Where is the little man?" the woman asked.

"In the room asleep," Gill answered and it hit Wade that his father was talking about him. He felt like he should not be there, listening and watching; he should be in the room sleeping. He felt his face hot in the smoky air, his eyes stinging. Why did he have to come here? Why couldn't he have stayed in the room? Any second his father was going to turn around and look his way and see him there. He had to get out of there, back to bed, to sleep. The last thing he heard was the woman ask his father why he was not in the room. "I buy you one drink and then," she said and Wade could not hear them any more. He walked with his head down around the perimeter of the tables towards the black door, past the rows of tables and chairs and the TV in the corner of the ceiling, to the door where he pinched his fingers on the latch as he slipped out into the cool and clear night air. People had been looking at him, he had felt it in his back. As he made his way along the hallway back to the room he sucked on his throbbing fingertips and felt like he might cry. The music started again and a tear leaked out of his eye and down his cheek. He walked away from the black door, the music, and where his father was; down the hall to the room and the bed and his things. At the door to the room he fished in his pocket for the key, could not find it, changed hands and pockets and then, with a surge of knowledge, knew he had forgotten the key and had no way in.

With his back against the peeling wall, Wade sat on the floor of the hallway of the only motel in Mariapolis until his bottom got numb. He thought about going back to the bar to get his father or just the key to open the room. He had gone halfway to the end of the hall when Gill came around the corner towards him. Wade stopped under a light and Gill kept walking towards him.

"What are you doing out here, Wade?"

"I locked myself out," he said and looked up at his father.

"Okay. I've got it."

Gill put his arm around him and Wade could smell smoke and beer as they walked back to the room, opened the door and went inside. Gill went to the bathroom, ran the water and returned with a wet wash cloth in his hand. He sat on the edge of Wade's bed and wiped the smeared grime from his face. When he had finished he took the cloth to the bathroom, slipped into bed, leaned over and reached to the lamp to switch it off.

"That's a nice watch, Wade."

"We can see what time it is."

"Yeah. I'll get us up. I have a built-in clock."

"What does it say right now?" Wade asked, checking his watch.

"Time for bed."

Wade smiled a little back at Gill under the light of the lamp. Gill tapped his forehead and clicked off the lamp. In the dark, the groaning of the hotel and the music of the bar sounded louder. Wade lay on his back and closed his eyes. The dark closed over him and he thought about the recoil of the gun against his shoulder when it fired. He relived each shot he had taken in the day, each miss he had made and each bird crumpling and spinning to the ground. The springs in Gill's bed creaked as he moved.

"We sure had a good day, Wade."

"Yeah."

"And tomorrow'll be better. Promise."

"Yeah." Wade said and tucked the covers under his chin. "I hope so."

The watch next to Wade's bed ticked out the seconds and the music in the bar played on. The air moved through the ducts of the hotel and somewhere water jerked pipes as it ran. Wade imagined the ducks rising from the water in a thick cloud, like a mist rising into a cold wind from a hot spring, and he could follow their peeping, along to the next slough or the next one or the next, touching down whenever he wanted.

First thing the next morning Wade heard the chirp of the bed springs as Gill coughed once on his way to the bathroom to get a drink. Wade remembered the motel and where he was the second the springs chirped, and he inhaled the dry air and coughed. Pressure felt trapped in his head in a numb, insulated way and his nose was stuffed.

"Daylight in the swamp, Wade."

Gill stood in the yellow light pushed out of the bathroom in his underwear. The smell of the slough lingered about the room from their boots and coats. It was dark outside except for the dull red glow of the exit sign. Water ran out of the tub faucet in a heavy stream and then stopped and the smaller streams of the showerhead rang against the bottom of the tub. Wade sat on the edge of his bed and blew his nose into his dirty sock from the day before. The pressure in his ears crackled and he checked the clothes he had hung the night before to dry. The knees of his pants were muddy but dry and stiff over the heater.

"Wade?" he heard his father call from the bathroom.

"Yeah?" he answered, walking across the room.

"Do you want to get in and get cleaned up?"

"Sure."

Gill pulled back the curtain and stepped out onto a towel spread on the floor. Wade stripped off his underwear and bent to pick them up. He looked at his father's penis and was conscious of his own with its first few pubic hairs. He stepped into the shower and stood under the hot water for a minute before starting to clean himself. The water smelled in a funny way and a rust teardrop stained the tub under the faucet where it dripped. Wade dried himself and got dressed as Gill pulled on his coat, and they cleaned the room of their things and checked under the beds and through the blankets for missing items.

The coffee shop in the motel was still closed tight, no light yet under the stars in the east when they left. The Land Cruiser was started and packed, and then Wade and Gill left Mariapolis, driving south along a main road as the stars began to disappear. Gill stopped at a twenty-four-hour gas station at the crossroads and filled the thermos with coffee. Wade bought two Oh Henry! bars with some money Christine had given him and ate dry Froot Loops from the box. Dawn was a time of day he never saw. The air was fresh and he saw his breath. He looked out the window at the fields and the sky as the Land Cruiser's off-road tires hummed along the pavement. Gill slowed the Land Cruiser next to a bluff twenty minutes after they left the gas station.

"This is the McManes slough," he said as they crossed the ditch and drove onto the field, parked under some trees in a bluff and got out.

The quilted jacket sleeves Wade slid his arms into were cold from sitting out all night, the air felt crisp. The sound of geese surrounded them; the closer ones louder and clearer, easy to locate, the further ones blurred and muted, seeming to come from everywhere. The geese moved and their calls slid over the fields, and while Wade looked up into the sky and expected to see them against the dark, he knew they could be a mile away.

"Not quite daylight in the swamp," Gill said and smiled at Wade. "That's good. We should be in before they come back."

"The birds?"

"Yep. They'll be out in the fields feeding until sun-up. Then they go to water."

Wade pulled his gun out of its case and checked it. He put his toque on and was ready to go as Gill checked the over-and-under. Gill closed the back of the Land Cruiser quietly and they walked close together along the edge of the bluff through the receding dark down toward the slough. The grass was tall, hollow and stiff, crackling underfoot in the cold. Wade curled his hands together to keep them warm inside his gloves. He looked up at where he thought he would see geese migrating south but there were only stars and the sliver moon.

"You warm enough, Wade?"

"Yeah. It is chilly though," Wade said as he struggled through the grass. The walking was tough and he almost fell forward as the grass caught around his ankles.

"But it beats school?"

"For sure."

Wade stopped for a second, let Gill go ahead and then fell in behind him on the path he broke through the grass; the ground under their feet lumpy with vegetation left from when the water was higher. Gill slowed, dropped down into the tall grasses and turned to his left. He went crouched up a small incline and Wade imitated his every movement. Then they were out of the tall grass on a knoll with the starry sky wide above.

"We can see the whole thing," Wade said in a whisper.

"This is the spot."

The slough spread out in front of them and beyond under the light coming stronger into the sky. The fields sloped down to the slough from both sides, the treelines of elm running up and out of the hollow, and the slough stretched out to the horizon.

"How far does it go, Dad?"

"Twelve miles."

"Wow," Wade said and strained his eyes to see the slough snaking away. The water out in the middle of the slough shone, reflecting the light of stars. Wade could easily see the water and the shine in the middle and as he looked around, he realized it shone and reflected amidst the reeds as well. The open water was bright and steady but there were glimpses of reflections everywhere in the edges and in the distance; the sound of the geese loud but the sky above still dark.

"Now we wait," said Gill and broke his gun. Wade did the same and fed a shell into the barrel. The air around them hung quiet and still, the only sound the geese calling.

"It's incredible, Dad," Wade whispered.

"Pretty nice, partner. This is why you come."

Wade was about to say something when Gill held up his finger and brought it to his lips. Faintly, he heard the peeping sound of ducks flying close by, like a tiny hinge in need of oil. Then there was the rush of the air cut by wings dropping out of the sky. The ducks skimmed down in full flare, tipping left then right to slow their descent. The sky was still dark and the ducks in the air were invisible. Then Wade heard the swooshes of the water where each duck landed on the surface of the slough while those above kept coming. Wade and Gill stayed crouched on the knoll and listened to the ducks go over. Wade wondered what they would do.

"Do we shoot?" he asked Gill in a whisper.

Gill shrugged. "Do you want to?"

Wade didn't know what to say. "I don't know."

Gill smiled. "Let's wait a bit. We'll see if the geese come in."

Wade bent his neck upwards again and the flight of ducks kept coming in. His foot under him began to fall asleep in his rubber boot and he shifted to ease the pressure. There was a lull in the flight of ducks and then more came right over them, so close Wade could see the wrinkles on their webbed feet, the nostrils in their beaks. The ducks in the slough began quacking as the sun came up onto the mist over the water. Wade was not sure if he heard geese closer or not. He watched his father for a sign to let him know what they would do and he saw the thrill in his father's face.

In the end, they did not shoot. The geese stayed high overhead, out of range. A few more ducks came in to the slough and they let them land. When the sun was hot enough to burn off the mist over the slough they stood up and sent the ducks wheeling into the sky.

They hunted the rest of the morning and ate lunch with Bill Tisdale, who was an old friend of Gill's and fished with him at Lake of the Woods the last weekend every June. After lunch they took their birds out behind Bill's barn and plucked the feathers off the biggest ones and breasted the smaller ones. Some wild cats picked at the carcasses when they went into the farmhouse to get plastic baggies for the meat, and Bill shot one out of a tree where it hissed at him. In the late afternoon as the birds went back out to the fields for the evening feed, Wade and Gill drove back over the fields to the city. Wade woke up when the Land Cruiser stopped. Gill looked over at him, yawned, stretched his arms forward and then smiled. It was dark and they were back on the street in front of the house.

"Some company you are," Gill said in a kidding way.

"I had to chase your birds all day," Wade said and smiled. He opened the door and went around the back and Gill did the same. The night was brisk and the wind cut through Wade's clothes to the skin. He grabbed his duffle bag and Gill carried the rest of his things in. Everything smelled dirty, the sweet scent of the slough.

When they came up the drive, Christine was standing on the front step in her business clothes as if nothing had changed since they'd left. One of the outside lights had burned out and she had been replacing the bulb as they pulled up. She crossed her arms in front of her and smiled at them coming up the driveway.

"The boys are back," she said. "How did you do?"

Wade and Gill looked at each other.

"Good, Mom," Wade said. "My first shot I got a duck."

"He did well," Gill said. "He's a damn good shot."

"That's good to hear."

Wade carried his bag inside while Gill stayed to talk to Christine. The house smelled good, like someone had cooked. He looked back outside to see his mother leaning against the house, her arms still crossed. His father stood a step below her on the driveway, his head visible over her shoulder. Wade knew they were telling each other what had been happening in their separate lives. Christine's hair shone as she nodded. Gill looked serious but not angry and he looked over her shoulder right at Wade and finished what he was saying. Wade smiled at his father through the window and bent over to take off his boots and when he straightened he saw his father kiss his mother and wave to him. He dropped his duffle bag and ran out in his sock feet.

"Dad," Wade called out and Gill stopped and turned back. "Thanks. For this. I had a good time."

"Me too, Wade."

Gill opened his arms and Wade gave him a hug. The slough and the gun oil and his father were all in a smell at once. His father's canvas duck jacket was smoothed by wear and crumpled softly against Wade's cheek.

"Can you stay for dinner, Dad?"

Gill shook his head. "Long road still tonight."

Wade smiled and stepped back.

"Take care, Gill," Christine said.

"You too. You two," Gill said as he walked backwards a few steps down the driveway. "I'll see you soon, Wade."

"When, Dad?"

"When's hockey season start?"

"It already has."

"Then when's your next game?"

"Saturday."

Gill thought for a second. "I'll see what I can do," he said. "I'll call if I can't make it." Then he turned and waited for traffic to pass and crossed the road to the Land Cruiser. The starter motor whirred and Gill pulled into the driveway and clicked on the lights. Then he backed out, stopped, shifted, released the clutch and left a trail of exhaust hanging in the air as he drove away.

Wade and Christine hadn't moved except to wave as Gill had pulled away. They went inside and Christine asked him about the trip. Wade did not say much at first but it was something that came out of him in bits and pieces of stories over the course of the evening. Christine sat and listened and offered what she could, and she told Wade what she knew of his father, and duck hunting, and the way that nothing was the same once you were back in the city and the geese were migrating high overhead and calling.

UP IN ONTARIO
—*June, 1988*—

EVER SINCE WADE HAD STARTED COMING OUT TO LAKE OF THE woods on his own, he and Gill practised a routine. Each morning when they got up they both followed the routine though neither one said a word about it. Gill always woke first and Wade always heard Gill's bare feet slapping across the cold floor and the water run into the coffee pot. The element on the stove ticked as it heated up, the fridge door stuck open and sucked shut, the milk carton patted down on the table. Wade heard Gill get up before him and say to the cabin, "Daylight in the swamp." Gill whistled or hummed an old dance tune as he walked to the front of the cabin and looked out at the weather on the lake. Wade always woke at the first sound Gill made but did not stir until Gill came in to wake him. Wade would lie under the heavy blankets and listen. He liked that Gill always said "daylight in the swamp"; it was one of the things he liked best about being at the lake, and about being with his father, like it was a call to action or to arms. He knew he would like to wake someone he cared about by saying, "Daylight in the swamp," but it would not have been the same; he had tried it once with Christine at Terry's cabin, one of the men she had dated, and it had rung hollow to his ear. It felt good only when Gill said it, only at the lake.

When Gill pulled back the heavy curtain to wake Wade, it often took a few minutes before he said anything. At times Wade wondered about this, when he was not sleeping but not letting on that he was awake, but it did not make him nervous. He liked having his father there with him even if his father did not say anything; he just liked having him in the room. It was the right way to wake from the kind of deep sleep that he only had at the lake, the kind of solid and mysterious sleep he always woke from so easily. When Gill would finally touch Wade on the arm or the forehead Wade would get up to the smell of coffee.

This morning, Wade's first morning at the lake that season when he was fourteen, they were going fishing. Gill had already poured Wade a coffee, and it sat steaming on the rough, pine-knotted table while they both worked around the cabin to warm up and get their things together.

Wade had arrived on the bus the night before from Winnipeg. As the bus pulled in off the highway Wade had seen his father waiting for him across the road from the depot, looking out on the sun setting over the lake. His father had kept looking out on the lake, his hair curling back in the breeze. Wade saw his eyes squinted against the light. His father looked out until the sharp release of pressure from the air brakes caused him to turn, and then he crossed the crowned road in long, slow strides, his hands deep in his pockets, his figure silhouetted by the setting sun over the lake. Wade had climbed down from the bus with his pack slung over one shoulder and joined Gill in a hug. They had walked back across the road to the truck, slammed the old doors, and driven through town; over the concrete bridge with its towering Indian gates that Wade's grandfather had helped build, the log booms lashed together in the water below, and out the far side. At the turnoff to Storm Bay Road, they left the highway and then arrived at the shore of the lake, back together to where they loved to be, with their thoughts full of expectations and the idle chat of hockey games and school marks and fishing rods exhausted.

When the work was done and Wade had warmed up, the coffee was still hot and waiting on the table for them. Wade sat down opposite Gill to drink his coffee and stare out at the water as the light of the day started to reflect off the water. Wade yawned and, in his early-morning clumsiness, spilled some coffee on himself. "Ahh, shoot," he said jerking himself awake.

"What is it?"

"I spilled my coffee."

"Did it burn?"

"Nah."

"Well, it's not the end of the world."

"Yeah, but these are my only pants. I have to wear them all weekend and now they've got a coffee stain on the leg."

"And?"

"Well, they're wet, and stained, I guess that's the worst of it."

"Do you want to wear a pair of mine?"

"Nah, it doesn't really matter."

"Nope, not really. Anyway . . ." Gill's voice trailed off as he stared out at the reflections on the lake. The shadows of the pines fell across the rippled surface breaking the streaks of light.

"Yeah?" Wade said.

"Oh, well, you won't need them soon, it's going to be a hot one."

Wade smiled. He had learned long ago how Gill loved to talk about the weather when they were at the lake. Since Gill had come back to guiding at Lake of the Woods he paid close attention to the weather. Mounted on the wall of the porch, his brass barometer was his guide, and every morning he checked it and set it to see how the pressure changed from day to day. Wade looked out at the sky and saw that Gill would be right, it was going to be hot; one of those high-sky lake days when the water and sky look a hard and painted blue. They finished their coffees looking out at the day and then Gill took the empty cups to the kitchen to rinse and Wade stared out from the porch. Gill came out and they walked down to the dock with their things, ready for the day.

As they loaded the boat with their gear, the calm water spread out in front of them, stretching away from the end of the dock to the thin line of treed shore in the distance. Wade retrieved his fishing rod from the shed and placed it in Gill's new outfit, a sixteen-foot Lund with carpeted floor, swivel chairs, storage compartments, and a thirty-horse Yamaha outboard. Gill threw in his old brown backpack with the filleting knives, Wade's mask, snorkel and fins, the landing net and the ham sandwiches he had made. They stood on the dock looking down at the packed boat, decided they had everything they wanted and stepped in. Gill pull-started the thirty, slipped her into gear and they idled away from the dock. Wade sat in the front of the boat on his pedestal seat and Gill sat in back driving. Wade wondered what he would tell his mother about his coffee-stained pants. He only drank coffee when he was at the lake with Gill, where it came in a coffee pot, with boiled grinds that ended up at the bottom of your mug if you didn't swish them into the last swallow. For the last two years Wade had drunk coffee at the lake with his father. The first year, he had slipped two lumps of sugar into it each morning so he could drink it. Now, he drank it black like Gill. He still drank it from his Coffee Hound mug with its pistol-grip shaped handle and drawing of the Coffee Hound on the side, which he had seen Gill retrieve from the back of the cupboard the night before, getting it ready for him.

Gill drove the boat south across Storm Bay, where there were still no other cottages within a mile of the bay. They passed out of the mouth of the bay and headed farther south into the open water. The wind picked up from the west past the shelter of the point and Wade and Gill both knew the small chop would make for good fishing on the windy shores. Gill steered the boat across the crests and troughs of the waves, listing gently from side to side until they turned east with the waves and towards the opening to Route Bay. They did not slow as they passed a shallow sandbar to the left of the channel into Route Bay and Wade looked down at the water rushing past, the blurred muskie weed and granite-speckled bottom visible only in the shadows thrown by the tallest pine trees, the bright sunlight making the water opaque as Wade tried to see into it. Then the water dropped off and grew dark and Route Bay opened out in front of them with its weed beds and cliff walls along its bottle-shaped length. Gill steered to the south side and slowed as he drew close to the rising cliff faces, the rocks covered in patterns of white and orange and green. He held the map open on his knee with his right hand while he drove the thirty with the tiller in his left, looking alternately down at the map and around at the landscape, making sure he knew where the channel led to the portage to Blindfold Lake.

The first floating Javex-bottle marker appeared and Gill headed the nose of the boat toward it. The channel had been dynamited and dredged in 1952 so a retired senator who owned most of the shoreline of Blindfold Lake could pass his boat through to fish Lake of the Woods. A dam kept the water level of Blindfold Lake three or four feet higher than that of Lake of the Woods and a marine railway with a wheeled cart and hand winch ran beside the dam to portage boats from lake to lake. Gill knew that as long as you steered clear of the markers the channel was at least four feet deep.

"I bet I haven't been through this portage in probably ten, fifteen years."

Wade looked ahead and at the water. "I was down here last year. Me and the MacLeod boys came to dive when you were out guiding. We were catching suckers and that family from Missouri staying at Smith's were giving us two dollars a fish for them. They had this smoker set up that cooked twenty suckers at a time." Wade paused and continued looking at the water, unsure of himself since he had not told Gill about leaving the camp the previous year. He could see the muddled and mossy-khaki bottom and Gill didn't say anything. "I guess the suckers won't be here anymore because there's no water coming through. Usually there's more water than this. They must figure it's going to be a dry year."

Gill nodded and folded the map on his knee. "The water's gone up a good six inches at our place since the first of May. They're letting it in from all these little lakes. Looks like there's none left in them now. As usual, that damn MNR doesn't know when to leave well enough alone. With some of the squalls we've had this year, I don't want my boat and dock too exposed." He snorted while Wade shook his head and felt easier. He started to tell Gill about the storms they'd had in the city, the lightning and the winds and funnel clouds that had forced the Blue Bombers to cancel their home opener, and the rains that had flooded the field. Wade watched the water over the prow of the boat for signs of rocks and the channel widened like a reverse funnel as the boat came within sight of the dam. The trickle of water slipping over the dam made little, rippling currents and Wade could see the pebbled bottom in the smooth-moving water. He cushioned the front of the boat with his leg to keep it off the rocks and stepped onto shore with the rope as Gill cut and tilted the thirty.

"She should stay," Wade said. "I'll go get the cart."

"Do you want a hand?"

"Nah, I've done it before."

The tracks for the cart dipped into the water of both lakes and a red hand winch with a geared flywheel sat anchored in the middle of the dam to pull the cart up the inclines. Wade went to the winch and lifted the piece of shale off the foot brake, then cranked the flywheel until the cart cleared the Blindfold water. He put the shale back, walked to the cart and leaned his shoulder into it to push it the rest of the way to the Lake of the Woods side. The cart started down the slope to Lake of the Woods and Wade went back to the winch and let the cart down into the water with the foot brake. Gill paddled the boat out again and brought it towards the tracks while the cart gurgled and bubbled into the water under him.

"Is the boat in place, Dad?"

"Yeah, go ahead. I'll be there in a second."

Wade removed the shale and started to pull at the flywheel. The cart started to lift the nose of the boat up the track and Wade had to take short, choppy strokes and throw his whole body weight against flywheel. Gill jumped out of the boat when it inched closer to shore and sprinted to join Wade at the winch. There were two handles for the fly-wheel and they both went at it, working at the heavy boat hand-over-hand until it was up the slope on the flat section and they didn't have to fight for each foot. Wade watched Gill like he always did whenever they worked together. Gill knew what had to be done and Wade trusted him to know the best way to do it.

"Wade, why don't you hold the brake and I'll spell you off for a bit. You've been working hard. I'll go push her."

"I'm not tired. I'll go and push her."

"Why don't I put the shale on the brake and we'll both push."

"I can do it."

"I know, you just can't leave me behind."

Gill put the shale on the foot brake and they both pushed the boat until the cord stretched taut back to the winch and the cart started to pick up speed down the slope to Blindfold Lake. Gill went back to the winch and used the foot brake to lower the boat into the water. Wade held the bow rope to make sure the boat wouldn't drift when it floated off the cart. The nose of the boat plowed into the water and Wade pulled the boat off the cart and over to the shore to make it easy to step into. The water of Blindfold Lake tinted the light to rust colour, the minerals in the water staining the pebbled bottom a deep amber. Wade stepped into the boat to get a better look at a painted turtle that had surfaced out in the water beyond the boat. Gill replaced the shale on the foot brake and saw Wade in the back of the boat.

"You want to drive, partner?"

"Sure."

"Okay, be careful."

Wade flipped the latch and lowered the prop into the water like Gill had shown him. He made sure the gear shift was slotted into neutral and twisted the hand throttle to Start. He pulled the starter cord, the engine caught and he slowed the throttle to idle. The gear shift stuck a little as he shifted into reverse and turned the bow out from shore and down the channel, then he shifted into Forward and gave it some gas. Gill looked at the map as the wake behind the transom billowed and churned over on itself and Wade putted down the middle of the channel followed by the small waves of the wake. The channel widened to a fork where two channels angled away and Wade knew to steer down the left one. By now he had lost track of which way was north and understood why they called it Blindfold Lake; once you were on it, you had to know where you were going. Just like Gill had told him, Blindfold was not a big lake, but it was a difficult lake. The shores were either low-lying, swampy bogs, or jagged cliff faces with orange moss growing in patterns resembling continents on a map. The dense growth of spruce, cedar and willow grew down to the water's edge where they could. Gill had told Wade that from the air Blindfold Lake looked like a very wide river with lots of dead ends, false channels and switchbacks. On the water, the lake surrounded you in an envelope of wilderness with plenty of places where the channel widened out from the moss and granite and trees to open water that turned out to be a closed bay.

"Looks like you know where you're going," Gill said, looking up from the map.

"Brian MacLeod and me went exploring up here in the canoe. We brought the map to find our way but still only went a little ways. I've never been past the next corner up here."

Gill nodded and followed Wade's eyes ahead. The granite cliffs fell from high on their left and gnarled jack pine grew angled out of the crags and ridges, hanging onto the small slits and corners of soil collected in the cracks. Wade knew it amazed his father how the trees grew parallel out from the cliff face in the sparse soil. Gill had told him that they reminded him of the trees he saw high up in the mountains when he had worked in the logging camps out in BC; how they lived on nothing but their tiny corner of earth without moisture, and how they lived everywhere. Gill had worked with a guy who called them *wahbashne*, a word that he had said meant "survivors."

"Hey, Dad," Wade said. "*Wahbashne*."

"That's right. *Wahbashne*. Survivors." He smiled at Wade and watched him drive on at half throttle, careful of the rocks and logs in the water. "Up here, partner, it's plenty deep as long as you stay to the right. There's a reef off the far end of that island but you've got lots of water on this side."

"It looks deep on both sides."

"Slow down and we'll take a look. I'm just telling you what the map says."

Wade came off the throttle and the hull backed down to the water. He slowed to an idle when they neared the island and Gill stood up in the front of the boat, both of them searching the water for signs of rocks. A darker shadow appeared ahead and to their left through the grainy water. Wade cut the thirty and released the tilt latch to be ready. He saw the reef only a few inches below the surface as the boat drifted towards it. The waves from the wake of the boat made the water whorl and swirl over the reef and Gill manned the paddle to keep the nose from hitting the rock. The moment the paddle broke the glassy surface a flurry of movement erupted below the surface.

"Holy cripes, Wade. You should see all the crayfish on this rock. Why don't you put on your mask and fins and take a look?"

"How's the water?"

"Warmer than the big lake."

Wade stuck his hand over the gunnel of the boat and the water felt cool to his touch. He knew once he got in it would be all right. He stripped off his pants and sweatshirt and rinsed his mask in the lake. He spit in the mask to keep it from fogging up, rinsed it again, and fitted his snorkel inside the strap. He slid off the leg of the thirty into the water so as not to scare the crayfish and Gill threw him his fins.

"Do you see anything, Wade?"

Wade heard Gill as he dove underwater but did not have time to answer, having already arched his back. The cold jarred him as his head submersed for the first time. He thought about going back to the surface where the water was warmer and where he could get used to the cold, his body told him to go back, but he wanted to do something, something he could do if he forced himself to, and so he kept diving, down to where he had seen the last bit of movement against the dark rock. When he came up he had a crayfish in each hand and blood pounding in his ears.

"Wow, that one's a beauty," Gill said, pointing at the crayfish in Wade's right hand, which was a bluish colour, missing one of its claws and bigger than Wade's hand. Wade had each crayfish grasped on the sides of its abdomen, behind the claws, between his forefinger and thumb. They were confused and caught by something they could not do anything about. They tried to get at what it was but could not. Their hooked claws opened and closed, searching, ready to pinch anything that came near.

Treading water with his finned feet, Wade kept the crayfish

underwater while Gill tied their empty minnow bucket to a cleat. He dropped the minnow bucket into the water beside Wade and Wade pushed open the sprung door to put the crayfish inside. He cleared his snorkel, dove to the bottom, and caught two more crayfish to put in the bucket.

"Now we've got some bait for fishing, right, Dad?"

"You want to fish for bass? Crayfish are great for bass."

"Sure, you know where to go?"

"Yeah. Yeah, I know a spot." Wade climbed into the boat and Gill threw him a white Holiday Inn towel to dry off with while he started the thirty to get them underway. Wade sat in the front with the towel wrapped around him feeling good about the crayfish and watching Gill look at the map while he drove. The channel narrowed and widened and other larger channels branched off but Gill knew the way he wanted to go. They were cruising on plane out in the main body of the lake when he turned in toward shore.

"Wade, this is where Rushing River comes into Blindfold. I think we should go up to the mouth and see what's doing."

"That's where the bass are?"

"I hope so. That's where we used to catch them. I haven't been up here in a long time."

Gill backed off the thirty so it idled in the shallow water. Wade saw that the water coming into Blindfold from Rushing River had changed colour from the brassy colour of the body of the lake to the silver of the flowing water. The bulrushes and cattails grew thicker to the left of the channel and the muskie weed extended out into the body of the lake as if pushed by the current. A swath cut into the bulrushes and cattails on the right side of the channel where the current swept out deep and fast. Gill gave the thirty gas and headed the boat upstream into the swath and toward the source of Blindfold Lake. As they travelled farther up the channel, fewer bulrushes and cattails grew and the water flowed faster, the banks on either side grew steeper.

Wade stared at the bottom of muskie weed waving in the current twelve feet down. He looked up and ahead at a granite cliff on the right side of the channel. On the top of the cliff, flat shards of shale had been stacked on top of each other as a marker shaped like a man in profile against the clear sky, arms out horizontal, feet and legs together. A pile of more loose granite and shale rested in the water at the cliff's base. A thick vein of quartz cut a diagonal crescent moon across the cliff face where nothing grew.

Gill steered wide left of the cliff, around a bend to the right, and then up the swelling channel to where the water slowed. The channel widened to a wooded pool about fifty yards across where the willow and cedar grew tight down to the shore of the pool, and the taller white pines towered above. At the far end of the pool, Rushing River poured over a granite ledge into Blindfold Lake. The current flowed strongly through the centre of the pool and Gill gave the thirty gas while Wade watched the water, trying to see what he could. The clear water gave him the illusion of seeing shapes of fish moving below but the current made it impossible to be sure about anything. He could get only a vague idea of the outline and colour of things in the fast-flowing water, a strand of muskie weed, a school of minnows darting past. He wondered how they were going to fish in the current.

"Wade, look under the front deck and get out the ten-pound anchor."

"This hatch?"

"No, under the floor."

"Okay, I got it."

"Now, I want you to throw it out when I drive us up into the current and we'll drift back as far as we want."

Wade got the red anchor out and tied it to the bow rope. The thirty rumbled as Gill gave it more gas. Wade looked back. "Now?"

"Let her go, but hold on to the rope as it uncoils so I can ease off the throttle gently."

Wade threw the anchor into the rushing current and the boat started to lose ground as Gill slowed the motor. The current caught the nose and the boat swung in the water as Wade tried to play out the tightening rope and heard his father cut the motor. As if on cue, a large smallmouth bass jumped right in front of the boat, so close it almost hit the anchor rope. The bass startled Wade and he lost his grip on the rope. The boat pulled to one side in the current, the slack in the rope peeling out over the side. Then a twang sounded and the nose of the boat jerked back around into the current as the anchor caught and the rope stretched and Wade's granny knot held fast.

Gill laughed out loud. "You should have seen the look on your face."

Wade smiled. "That bass was a monster. I'm just lucky he didn't take me with him."

"Wasn't he a beauty?"

"Yeah, the anchor must have scared him."

"Could be," Gill said, still smiling.

"And now we know there's fish here."

"Yeah, they're here. But them jumping is not a good sign."

Wade hurried and rigged his rod. He nodded as he listened to his father but still felt eager to cast for the bass he had seen. Gill rigged his rod as well and dipped the minnow bucket of crayfish in the water to freshen them. He drained the water, plucked one out, threw it to Wade, plucked out another for himself, and set to putting the crayfish onto his hook.

"Hey Dad, how do you rig these things?"

"Turn them upside down and start your hook at the base of the tail. Thread it through the body and out between the claws so it trails backwards, like they swim."

"Out about here?"

"Yeah, that's it, you're set. It's the best thing I've ever seen for bass."

Wade cast his line into the still water beside the main current, let the bait sink to the bottom, then began to jig it back to the boat. He pulled it and let it sink, pulled it and let it sink; jerking it like he knew crayfish swam. He tried to keep the line taut in the current, knowing that if his line went slack and he had a strike he wouldn't know it until it was too late. He wanted to be sure to set the hook when his strike came. He brought the line in slowly but there were no strikes. Gill had cast and was bringing his in at the same time and Wade saw the quick jerk of Gill's hook set out of the corner of his eye.

"You got one, Dad?"

"Yeah. It's just a little one. Keep bringing yours in and see if we can get a double."

Wade turned back to his line with more attention. He jigged the crayfish up and down closer and closer to the boat. He was jigging the bait so it was nearly vertical now and watched the clear water to see if he could see it coming in. He followed his line with his eyes until he saw his crayfish about twelve feet away. Then he saw the jackfish. The jack made a strong move and the crayfish disappeared. Wade set the hook and felt a steady, live pull on the line. He let out an excited cry, "I got one!" And the rod bent dangerously as he felt the jack shake its powerful head. The drag on his reel whined and Wade let the jack take the line, losing sight of it in the water as it made a run.

From the front of the boat Wade held his rod as tightly as he could while Gill threw back the small bass he had brought in. Then he was beside Wade with the landing net, coaching him.

"That's it, play him ... If he wants to go, let him go ... Don't horse him ... Good ... Good ... Keep your rod tip up ... Good ... I think he's tiring ... Be careful of him on the surface ... Okay, now head him this way ..."

Wade brought the jack to the surface alongside the boat. He started to lead him parallel to the gunnel but as soon as the jack saw the boat, he took off on another run. Wade held on to his rod as tightly as he could, not taking any chances horsing the jack in the current. The jack looked to be a good size and Wade wanted to be sure to land it. It would be his biggest fish ever. He tried to reel and the jack came closer with each crank, not feeling as big as it had before when it had first been on. Wade guided the jack towards Gill holding the landing net beside him. The jack came up alongside the gunnel, gave one last head shake and Gill stabbed the net into the water and scooped and lifted it into the boat in one motion. Water splashed on Wade and Gill as the jack thrashed on the bottom of the boat and wound itself around in the net. The naked hook came out of the jack's mouth and caught in the net but the fish was landed. Wade saw his father sitting on the gunnel holding the net handle. The jack flipped in the net and Wade bent forward to untangle the fish.

"Wade, whoa, look at those teeth. Just let him tire himself out a bit before you get your hands in there."

The jack breathed heavily between flips. Its white belly shone in the sun and the mucus that coated its skin stuck to the net in strands. The green Appaloosa-pattern of its scales glistened in the sun and Wade looked at the jack's toothy grin and understood his father's caution. Wade waited until the jack quieted, then unwrapped the net from the gills and fins and slid his fingers under the gill plate. He lifted the jack out of the net and tried to hold it at arm's length, like he had seen in the pictures at Smith Camps, like he was having his picture taken, but his arm only had enough strength to get it up to his waist. "What do you think, Dad?"

"Pretty darn good, partner."

"These things sure are slimy."

"Yep, they call them water snakes. Look at the shape of him. The slime is for his protection, so don't handle him too much or he'll get infected."

"What're we going to do with him?"

"He's your fish. Do you want to keep him or put him back?"

"I don't know."

"If you want to keep it I can show you how to clean jack so there's no bones."

"I don't know, I still don't like them. I wish I'd caught a bass like yours. They're a pretty fish. But I still wouldn't want to kill it. They're just so nice."

"Yeah, bass are a nice fish."

"Yeah." Wade and Gill stood in the boat and smiled at each other. They had both started to sweat when Wade had hooked the jack and now they had to come down from the excitement. The jack gave a flip in Wade's hand and Gill told him to get the jack on a stringer.

"Or he'll be dead and you won't get to decide what to do with him."

Wade tied the jack over the side of the boat from the oar-lock and then picked up his rod and rigged another crayfish the same way. He cast wide of where he had cast last time and worked the bait back. Gill cast his bait out the other side of the boat. Then, after a while of casting and jigging his bait, he sat in the back of the boat and watched as Wade cast. Wade saw Gill put his feet up on the gunnel and look up at the sky. A few wispy clouds had begun to stretch in. The click of metal from the reel repeated over and over as Wade cast, combing the pool for biting fish.

"Any follow-ups, Wade?"

"No, nothing."

"That big guy probably scared everything else down there."

"Yeah, that's what I was thinking."

"Those fish'll be spooked for a while yet. You ready for lunch?"

"I'm starved."

Gill threw him one of their ham sandwiches out of his bag and picked one out for himself. Wade was thinking about his jack and wondering if he should keep it. He liked that his father would let him decide. He wondered what Gill thought, what he would do if it was his jack.

"These sure are good sandwiches, Dad."

"Tell Nancy Smith next time you see her. The ham's left over from the dinner I had over there on Tuesday. At their fish-fry pow-wow. She made these sandwiches for us when I told her you were coming."

"She sure is a good cook. I remember when we all used to go over there for brunches on Sundays. The three of us. And she'd make those yogurt pancakes with the strawberries on top that Mom loved."

"Those were something."

The waves of current or the push of the wind pivoted the boat on the steady hold of the anchor rope.

"Do they still have those brunches at Smith's, Dad?"

"I think so. But they're mostly for the guests."

Wade nodded and thought about his jack. "Are you sure you can get all the bones out?"

"Am I sure? C'mon, partner. Do you know how many jack I've cleaned for Yankees who can't catch anything but? The only difference between filleting bass and pickerel is the 'Y' bone off their spine. I'll show you how it is when we get back so you'll know."

Wade ran his tongue along his teeth and thought about this a while. "Okay, then I think we should bring him back to Smith's and weigh him and then eat him tonight."

"You got it."

"And if we catch anything else, we should let it go."

"Sure, partner." The wind that had been from the west out on Storm Bay had died down to nothing while the clouds high above scooted across the sky. Gill looked up at the topmost branches of a tall white pine. The long needles did not move in one direction but twitched and couldn't make up their minds.

"Wade, you keep watch on the skies. It's been so hot lately and we're due one of those Storm Bay steamers."

"Will do."

Wade watched Gill as he watched the sky, as he squinted up at the tops of the trees, then as he started to rig his rod again. Wade felt slow and full and drowsy. He dipped his cup into the water over the side of the boat and took a long drink of the clear, sweet water, then picked up his rod.

"I'd better see if I can't catch another fish to feed you tonight." Gill smiled at him. "You want another crayfish?"

"How many are left?"

"One, I had to use another one. This is the last one."

Gill threw him the live crayfish. Wade let it land on the floor of the boat and grabbed it as it tried to crawl away from him, then rigged it onto his hook and cast. He jigged it back to the boat and cast again twice. On the third cast he had a strike and reeled in a small rock bass and lost his crayfish during the fight. Gill laughed at him. "You call that a fish? I wouldn't even bring in something that small."

Wade smiled at his father. Even though he was annoyed he'd lost his crayfish, his father was a good teaser, always kidding around with the guys at Smith Camps after a day out on the water. Wade remembered past years when he had visited his father at the lake, sitting around as Gill had drinks and told stories with the fishermen he guided. Wade had never known his father to get drunk like the fishermen did, but he had never known him to turn down a drink either. Gill joked with Wade as he did with the fishermen, but not exactly in the same way.

Wade liked to be able to kid back at Gill. "You're going to be one hungry man tonight if I don't share my jack. I don't see anything of yours on the stringer."

"Yeah, we'll see about that, big talker. You'll be choking on bones if you keep it up."

Gill cast his bait. He jigged it slowly back to the boat while Wade watched. A few small perch followed the bait but nothing else. Gill cast again and jigged it in, and cast and jigged it in. He cleaned off a weed he had picked up and cast again. The perch followed but there were no strikes. Gill leaned the rod against the gunnel, the hooked crayfish dangling over the smooth, moving water.

"Well, you ready to start heading back?"

"If you want."

Gill looked up at the moving clouds. "We can try some spots on the way back but I think we should get going. I don't like the look of this sky."

"All right, I'll pull in the anchor."

Gill started the thirty while Wade coiled the anchor rope, and hoisted the ten-pound weight. Without the anchor, the current twisted the boat broadside like a leaf. Gill righted its direction with the thirty and they idled down the channel, the jack leashed on the stringer, trailing alongside the boat. The sun slipped behind the clouds and the light became flat and grey, a quick change in the feel of the weather. Wade sat in the front of the boat with his elbows on his knees and looked over the gunnel at the water. He tried to see down and into it but the light made it difficult. As they flowed past the cliff the clouds parted and the sun illuminated the bottom and something caught Wade's eye. "Hold on, Dad. Do we have time for a dive here? With all of the crayfish I can see, there must be some bass around."

"All right. Throw out the anchor again, then. I'll take a couple of casts. We may pick one up."

The boat held on the anchor next to the bulrushes and cattails and across the channel from the cliff and its pile of granite rubble. Wade spit in his mask and rinsed it, fitted his snorkel inside the strap and slipped into the water. Wade could not feel the current but knew it pushed him along. Gill threw him his fins and Wade put them on and swam out into the channel. The water was clear and Wade could easily see the bottom below. He saw the flitting reflections of a school of shiner minnows to his left. A few of them broke the surface as he swam near them and they skitted away. The seaweed grew only on the sides of rocks that were in the lee of the current. Wade took a deep breath, pulled a sharp sweep through the water with his hands and dove. He followed the length of a sunken aspen and counted four perch and a bullhead in the current break. He swam toward the other side of the channel underwater. Three-quarters across he came up for breath and dove again. The rocks became larger and more jagged closer to the rock pile. These were the kinds of rocks that bass liked, he remembered his father telling him, with current breaks and fleeing crayfish all over. Wade swam at the surface and breathed through his snorkel. Two small rock bass darted behind a large triangle piece of granite and Wade came to a hollow in the rocks with three good-sized smallmouth bass suspended in it. The current pushed Wade around the hollow downstream and back towards the channel. Wade told himself there was no need to scare the bass. He would get the landing net and they would stay just where they were. Wade turned in the current and swam back to the boat, keeping his fins under water, careful not to hurry. He poked his head out of the water at the boat and tried to talk calmly.

"Dad, you should see the bass. There's three of them. Over by the cliff. And I'm going to try and net them."

"Why don't you try and catch them with a hook?"

"Dad, I want to catch them in the net. You should see them, they're amazing. They've got these dark zebra stripes all down their sides and gills."

"Really? Maybe I should cast over there and see if I can't get one." Gill kidded Wade and handed him the net. Waves spread out from the boat as Gill rocked it and climbed up on the deck to watch Wade swim back across the channel.

Outlined on the bottom of the channel, Wade saw his own shadow, the net held tight in profile to his body. He swam on the surface and breathed through his snorkel; he wanted to be fresh when he got to the cliff. The sun went behind the clouds again and his shadow blended into the bottom of the channel. Wade felt the surface of the water wrinkle in the breeze as the air passed over his back and head and shoulders. The wind moved across the back of his head and his exposed shoulder blades and he shivered slightly with a chill and with excitement. At the sunken aspen, the four perch and bullhead still held in the lee, watching him kick past.

The rock pile was close now. Wade followed the same course he had taken when he had explored the first time. He had marked where the hollow fell away and could see it as he approached. He stopped to gather himself and get his deepest breath, then he dove. He came into the hollow not from above but from the side, as parallel to the jagged rock bottom as possible. The three bass were still there, their fins waving to keep them in place. They faced Wade and he moved in on them. They turned and moved slowly away, as if one fish. Wade drew closer, bubbles escaping from his snorkel to the surface. He singled out the largest one and started to extend the net from his body. The bass started to swim faster and Wade swam along at an angle to it and extended the net further. He wanted to get his bass cornered in the rocks so he could gather it into the open net. He closed in and the bass swam slowly and Wade kept up. He knew he could not keep up if he spooked the bass. He tried to move smoothly and slowly and be steady and patient as he trailed along. The bass kept moving and watching, wary. Wade followed patiently, biding his time, waiting for the right moment. The bass turned a little, forced out toward Wade by the curvature of the shore, and the time was right. Wade kicked his fins harder and extended the net to arm's length, into the path of the bass. His breath was tight now and his lungs were starting to burn. The bass broke closer to the rocks. Wade jammed the net rim against the rocks in front of the bass and the bass had a burst. The bass and the rim of the net got to the same place at the same time. Wade pinned the bass broadside against the rock for a second, then the bass snapped its tail and was gone, leaving behind the stirred-up water and Wade straining for the surface, trailing the empty net.

"Did you get him?" Gill shouted.

Wade cleared his snorkel and shook his head. He breathed deeply and lay suspended at the surface, floating and replaying the near miss in his mind. If only he had moved more quickly. He kicked to keep himself moving on the surface and heard his own deep breath through his snorkel. The tight feeling in his chest eased and he looked at the bottom, then lifted his head and looked to orient himself with the cliff and the rock pile. The chase had carried Wade downstream past the rubble where he wanted to be. He swam back against the current, and felt the displaced water pushing on his forehead. The rock pile spread out below him, granite rubble lying well beyond the end of the cliff where it had fallen or been pushed, and he realized he had not explored all of it.

From downstream, he could see an old dead spruce tree lying across an edge of the granite rubble. Unfertilized fish eggs and seaweed caught in its branches along with the rotting needles. Small water beetles and snails rested along the trunk in the lee of the current. Wade hovered above the spruce, watching and resting. He arched down into a dive just under the surface to get a closer look. He watched the water beetles scurry away as they heard the bubbles escaping from his snorkel. He watched their movements when another caught his eye. The peak of the spruce overhung its granite support by a few feet and under it Wade saw the largest bass he had ever seen. He was so shocked he almost yelled and breathed underwater. The bass was suspended under the spruce peak and watching Wade as he moved towards it. It watched him with its dark red eyes and toothless mouth opening and closing, while its fins made small twitches to hold it in place. Wade noticed on its gill plate the notch of a white scar from a previous battle. He drifted down to be on a level with the bass, watching it as it watched him. He moved the net from his chest outwards, slow and easy. He did not look at the net but kept looking at the suspended bass. He moved the net further out, like he felt the water move, slow and easy. The rim of the net surrounded the bass and still it did not move. The green netting floated all around the bass, encasing it, and it kept watching Wade. The bass was inside the net but it had not been touched. Wade started to turn the net, to twist closed the opening and tighten the filaments that would hopefully hold this huge bass. The green netting cinched in and when it touched the bass, the bass exploded.

The sound of the struggle frightened and thrilled Wade, the explosion of jerks and lunges reported through the handle of the net to Wade's hands. The bass snapped its strong tail over and over, trying to push through the constricting net. The snapping, snapping, snapping was all Wade heard, feeling the bass pulling him back down to the bottom, knowing that if the bass found the opening or broke through the net it would be gone for good. He strained to the surface, pulled against the force of the bass, pushed the thrashing net up ahead of him. He kicked as hard as he could, up to the blurred shapes and colours of clouds and trees and rock. It seemed to take forever for the net to pierce the surface. He thought it would never happen. He kicked and spit out the mouthpiece of his snorkel and then the rim of the net broke the surface and there was the sky and clouds above. Wade gasped in a breath of air and looked over at the boat where his father almost fell in, he was leaning so far forward over the gunnel to see.

"What have you got?"

"E mahs." Wade spit out the water he had swallowed and took a breath to answer. "A bass." The bass struggled against the binding net but the only sound now was the splashing of the water. Wade could barely keep his head above water as he swam towards the boat, trying to keep the net as high out of the water as he could.

"Oh, wow, what a beauty! What a brute!"

Wade swam closer and Gill kneeled down against the gunnel and his face was flushed. He reached out to take the net handle Wade pushed at him.

"What a beauty. Ho-ly cripes! Is he ever a brute."

Gill hoisted the net and the fish into the boat and as soon as he let go of the net Wade tucked his hands under his arms, hugging himself and shaking too badly to get into the boat yet. He let the current sweep him slowly along the hull and to the motor as he waited to calm down. Gill went on talking about the fish and Wade smiled bigger as his teeth chattered. He suddenly felt very cold. He squeezed his legs together and felt like curling into a ball. He tried to call out to his father but only a whisper came out. He shivered harder and tried to call again but couldn't. He banged on the boat transom and felt it cut the heel of his hand. The boat jumped on the water and then Gill's face appeared over the side, smiling down at Wade and reaching out to pull him over, next to the thirty, to climb back into the boat.

"Are you okay, son?" Gill said and Wade shook his head. Gill reached over the transom and lifted Wade until he could get his knee onto the edge and climb in. He wrapped him in the Holiday Inn towel and talked to him. Wade's lips and eyelids and fingertips were blue and the heel of his hand stung. Gill stood him up and rubbed him dry with the towel. "Keep moving Wade, you'll warm up. Guess you shouldn't have been in that long this early in the year. Keep moving, that's it. Come and see your fish."

Wade sucked the blood from his cut hand. His skin was pulpy and shredded from the water and the sharp metal but he wanted to see his fish. The bass flopped on the bottom of the boat where Gill had untangled it from the net. It had been out of the water for over a minute and its rich striping had not yet begun to fade. Its toothless mouth opened and closed as its gills worked to breathe. Wade ran his fingers along the grain of the rough scales.

"Do you want to put him on the stringer, Wade?"

Wade thought about it and looked at the bass. It was a huge bass, certainly a trophy. Wade wanted to see how much it weighed and that would mean getting the bass back to the scale at Smith's.

"I want to weigh him, but I don't want to kill him."

"There's a pail up front we could keep him in while we're running."

"Will he be okay?"

"He might be, he might not. You never know."

Wade did not think about it. "Let's weigh him and then let him go under our dock. We can keep him as our own."

"It's your fish. You're the boss."

Gill got the bucket and filled it from the lake while Wade put on his pants and sweatshirt. Gill handed the bucket to Wade and pulled in the jack on the stringer. They put the bass into the bucket head first, its tail in the air, swimming side to side, some water in the base to breathe. Wade held the bucket between his shins as Gill drove the boat down the swath, out of the channel and onto the main body of the lake, the clouds ahead gathering darker.

By the time they got back to the dam, Wade had warmed up but fits of shivers still seized him every few minutes. He and Gill hurried to portage the boat under the threatening thunderheads in the distance. They put the bass on the stringer with the jack while they worked with the boat, the two fish opposites side by side: the jack long and sleek, the bass short and stocky. Wade and Gill both made guesses for how much each fish weighed. The colour of the jack had faded, its Appaloosa pattern now smooth and milky from being out of the water on the floor of the boat. The colour of the bass had also paled but its skin still held more colour. Side by side, both fish swam as deeply as the length of stringer allowed in the rusty Blindfold water.

The air grew thick with moisture as Gill drove the boat out into Route Bay. Sheet lightning lit the sky in the distance where the clouds loomed in the low sky. Gill had the thirty wide open. No wind blew and the boat cleaved across the mirrored surface at full speed. They passed the sandbar, turned northwest to Smith Camps and, just as they left Route Bay, as if a light switch had been thrown, the skies opened up. One moment there was no rain, within five seconds it was pouring. The huge rain drops fell and splashed on the water where they landed so that the lake surrounding Wade and Gill appeared divoted. The thunder crashed in the distance and rolled across the sky as their boat cut across the pocked water and Wade turned to face the back for shelter. He could see the rain drops beating against Gill's face. Now that they were caught in the rain and wet, they backed off to half-throttle. The rain fell hard on the jack lying in the boat; it splashed against the tail of the bass where it stuck out from the bucket. Gill drove on through the rain and Wade shivered in the front of the boat. The rain kept up so that by the time they had the boat tied to the dock at Smith Camps they were both drenched to the bone on the side they had faced to the storm. As Wade carried the bass up the length of the dock in the bucket, the rain drops felt like they were getting smaller. Gill followed behind him, carrying the jack on the stringer and his brown bag over his shoulder.

They took shelter in the fish house at Smith's where they stood and watched the rain through the insect screens, heard the rain on the corrugated steel roof. The hard, rhythmic rain pelting the roof made Wade feel like they were inside a ceremonial drum, a drummer somewhere above keeping a beat, changing intensities, returning to the same beat. The fish scale hung on the wall of the fish house above the stainless steel countertops where the fish were cleaned. Ken Smith had rescued the scale from an auction at the Safeway in town where it had been a produce scale in a previous life. Wade and Gill laid the two fish beside each other on the counter top and stepped back to look at them. The jack did not move while the bass's gills rose and fell slightly.

"Which one do you want to weigh first, Wade?"

"Bass."

Gill slid the bass into the basket and released it slowly. The basket drooped under the weight, the red needle rebounding, wavering and then resting on five and a quarter pounds. Gill exhaled in a whistle. "I think that's the biggest bass I've ever seen."

"He's a big one, all right."

"It must have been hard to swim with him back to the boat."

"Yeah, he's a strong fish. He fought hard."

"Yep, bass are a strong fighter. They've always been my favourite fish because of that. And they're such a pretty fish, too."

Wade listened and nodded but all he could think about was how the bass had remained still as he had fit the net around him; how the bass had not been afraid, how he had seemed to be waiting for Wade, how he had looked at him the whole time, the whole time until the net had touched him. Gill lifted his hat by the bill and perched it onto the back of his head. He leaned against the countertop as the bass creaked and swung in the basket, rubbed his hairline lightly, and stared at the bass.

"Dad, don't you think we should get him back into the water?"

"Yeah ... I ... Yeah, sure."

Wade grabbed and held the bass tight by the tail as he lifted it out of the basket and back into the bucket. The bass slid in gently, making a half-moon of its body against the plastic walls, facing and leaving the same direction. Wade lifted the bucket by the handle and hurried back down the dock. The end of the bass's tail fins slid down into the water of the bucket and came out again at every step. Gill did not follow Wade down the dock to the deeper water. He held the fish house door for him and watched from the shore where the dock began. Wade stopped where the water would be deep enough for the bass to swim away. He put the bucket down on the edge of the dock and crouched down on his hands beside it. He dropped down onto his chest like he was going to do a push-up and lowered the bucket to rest on the water's surface. The half-empty bucket sunk into the water but stayed upright and bobbing. Wade held it upright with one hand while he reached in with the other. He grasped the bass like you were supposed to, his thumb in its mouth, its lower lip between his thumb and fingers. The bucket tilted towards him and the water came out and went in and the bass slid out with it. Wade held the bass in the cool water and moved it back and forth, talking to it the whole time. "C'mon, buddy. C'mon. You can make it. Almost there. Just get you back here. This looks good. Okay. Just turn you a little. Now, stay still. There's your lip. Okay. Here we go. How's that? Better? Yeah, c'mon now. You can do it."

Wade worked the bass forwards and backwards in the water. He worked water into its gills by moving it like it would have swum. He worked at it and talked to it as he worked. The bass was still alive and Wade tried pushing it through the water and letting go of it. He tried working it forwards and backwards while holding its tail, tried stroking it gently on the nose. He kept waiting for the bass's strength to come back, for it to pull away from his hand when he worked it forward, for its body to bend on its own, alive and ready to flex the opposite way. He kept waiting and trying but every time he stopped working the bass, it came back to the surface broadside up, still trying to swim down into the cool water, but unable to.

Wade moved back from the water onto his hands and knees. He had let the bass go and was waiting. Maybe it just needed more time to revive and maybe the pressure and stress of his hands was not helping. The bass floated broadside on the calm surface, moved its gills in a small out-in, out-in motion. Wade watched for a long time and knew it was not going to make it.

The rain had slowed to a mist when Wade reached down into the water to lift the bass back into the empty bucket. The wind ruffled Wade's wet hair as it picked up and swirled around, creasing the water in the calm bay. Wade got up from his knees with the bucket and began to carry it back towards Gill, who stood on the dock watching him. Wade looked at the bass in the bucket as he walked as if still hoping it was going to make it.

"He's not going to make it?"

Wade shook his head. "I don't think he wanted to go, Dad. He was still alive but didn't go. I tried to make him but he wouldn't go. He just wouldn't go."

"Why don't you bring him inside? I don't want you to catch cold standing out here."

The rain began to fall again in a broken rhythm on the corrugated steel roof. Wade followed Gill into the fish house. They put the bass onto the stainless steel counter and for a good while looked out at the rain, falling on the lake, finishing or starting the water cycle. Later, they took the bass out of the bucket and weighed the jack. Then they cleaned both fish and Gill showed Wade how to get the "Y" bone out of the jack; the length of the knife-stroke, the depth of the slit, the angle that had to be cut. They wrapped the boneless fillets in brown freezer paper and marked them in black felt-pen: Gill + Wade DuB—1 jackfish, 1 smallmouth; 5 1/4 lbs both. Then Gill hiked up to the Smith Camps lodge to see if they could stay for dinner. He offered the fillets as a contribution.

Wade and Gill stayed after the potluck until the storm cleared and the sun touched the horizon, under the clouds and above the lake, before they set out home to the cabin. As they pulled out from Smith Camps, the sun's last rays left the water ablaze, waves licking around the hull of the boat. Gill shielded his eyes with his hand and smiled at Wade, asleep in the crook of the bow in his borrowed outfit: Ken Smith's old overalls and work shirt. Gill drove at a good clip across the bay and docked gently in front of the cabin. Wade woke only to walk up to his bed and get out of his wet socks; he was asleep by the time Gill came in to see him after putting the boat and gear away. Wade did not feel Gill cover him with an extra blanket and smooth his hair from his forehead. He did not see Gill go to the front window and look out at the sun setting beyond the tallest pines; the light going out of the day across Storm Bay, the loons starting their laughing calls. The last thing Wade remembered of the day was the sound of his father's boots as they echoed up the wooded stairs to the porch, stopped by the doorway, and were replaced by his sock feet padding softly across the floor to get the coffee pot ready for tomorrow.

KENORA

WHEN THE HUDSON'S BAY COMPANY ESTABLISHED A TRADING POST on the north shore of Lake of the Woods, they translated the name the Ojibway had given the place and called it Rat Portage. In 1905 the Maple Leaf Flour Company felt concerned about building a mill in Rat Portage; they didn't want the word "rat" on their bags of flour. Prominent members of Rat Portage understood the concerns of Maple Leaf and initiated a plan to change the name of their town, which had dissatisfied townsfolk in the past, but which had always seemed like too much trouble to change. As the name-change discussion began, prominent members of neighbouring communities, interested in economic opportunity, met with the Rat Portage naming committee and decided that by combining the first syllables of Keewatin, Norman and Rat Portage they would create Keenora, and move forward into the new century united. The final spelling remained flexible. In 1907 the Kenora Thistles won the Stanley Cup, and in 1917 a syndicate of lawyers purchased the SS *Keenora*, a renowned steam ship on the waters of Lake of the Woods, Lake Winnipeg and the Red River that accommodated 65 passengers at a speed of 15 knots, for use as a floating dance hall. The parties they held became legendary, as police boats topped out at 12 knots and sergeants routinely watched the steamer pull away into the night.

The Maple Leaf Flour Mill burned to the ground in 1962. At a distance of over two miles, people stood on the Keewatin Bridge and felt the heat of the flames. Murmurs of insurance fraud began to circulate, since the mill had fallen on hard times, but calls for an investigation were never taken seriously because one of the mill's investors was related to former Prime Minister Arthur Meighan.

In more recent years, a new version of the SS *Keenora* takes Smith Camps' guests out fishing and on eco-tours to photograph bald eagles. Parties can be booked with one-week advance notice.

AT THE LOCKS
—*January, 1991*—

ON THE FINAL DAY OF HIS TRIP, ONCE HE HAD SHOT HIS MOOSE
and it was field-dressed in the garage back at Smith Camps, a
man Gill had guided for too many years to remember named
Dick Cleary asked Gill about why he lived on his own in his
cabin on Storm Bay. Gill had taken a long sip of his beer and
thought about the differences between Americans and
Canadians.

"I've heard you never belong to a place until you bury your
dead there or have a birth there," Gill said. "My family has lived
here for generations. I like it here. Either you belong to some-
place or you don't. If you don't, you can go anywhere. If you do,
then the place belongs to you too."

Later that evening, Gill thought more about why he stayed at
Lake of the Woods, as he had thought about it many evenings,
and the first thing that came to his mind was the solitude,

though it was not something he thought he could find only at Lake of the Woods. What was it that held him to this place with the tenacity of a wolf? He had tried to live in other places, out west in BC, an apartment in Winnipeg, but he had always felt out of place until he returned; claustrophobic even. In the end, Gill had trouble imagining himself living anywhere but Lake of the Woods, and so alternatives became unreal compared to the life he had, and he stayed and bore the cost.

And at times, the cost felt very high. Winter was the season Gill liked best at Lake of the Woods, when it was quiet and he could spend a whole day without seeing an RV trailing a boat or a fisherman tossing his cigarette into the water; but winter also remained the saddest time for Gill, a time when the loneliness and absoluteness of his choices were not dulled or displaced by chores and clients calling, demanding his attention. In the winter, Lake of the Woods existed in a different world from the place most people knew. The day before Dick Cleary asked Gill what kept him at Lake of the Woods, they had been tracking a moose through the bush and Dick had wondered aloud if any animals were awake, or if they all hibernated until the spring. Dick knew Lake of the Woods only in the summer, and the quiet and still-ness of the season stood in stark contrast to the place he knew. Gill showed him how the sound of two men on snowshoes stuck out; how if you stopped and stood in the middle of the bush, the sounds returned as animals moved under the surface of the snow and in the branches of the pines. Later that same day Dick asked Gill if the wind ever stopped blowing, since now he heard the particles of snow ticking across the drifts and the bare branches creaking as they rubbed against each other. Snow covered the rocks and roads, and weighed on the boughs of the spruce and pine trees; it froze to the thin branches of the poplar, maple and aspen. Ice formed over the water, making a black and cracked sheet that heaved in ridges under the pressure of the winds and current, and rolled in little waves from the pressure of the heavy trucks carrying lumber down the lake to building sites. In the sky to the south the sun shone for eight hours a day and made the long shadows look blue on the snowy shores.

A few days after Dick returned home to Denver, Gill drove in to Kenora to meet his friend Andrew Allen for lunch at the Husky Diner. He and Andrew had met on their snow machines out on the ice road between Hay Island and Heenan Point, each on their way back from checking their traplines, and had agreed to have lunch. Gill settled in across the table from Andrew and felt the familiar slow and deliberate rhythm of their lunch renewed for another year. Outside, the snow continued to fall over the sleepy town. Gill and Andrew ended up together over lunch or dinner or drinks a couple of times a year. From their early teens they remained good friends, and since it felt to Gill too early to go anywhere for a drink, and in winter he was not much of a drinker, lunch would have to do.

Living in Kenora, Gill ran into his neighbours at regular intervals; the people he shared an interest with he crossed paths with often; others he saw on fewer occasions. Gill and Andrew ended up almost always seeing each other a few times each winter, with the trapping season in full swing, and the ice roads crossing the lakes and islands all the way from the Manitoba border to Sioux Narrows provided the only means of travel over the frozen lakes. At lunch Gill and Andrew talked about women and trapping and life in Kenora, and enjoyed not having pressing business to attend to. The waitress who served them was named Justine and she was the sister of a woman they had known in high school who had married young and moved to Thunder Bay, and who Andrew had seen dancing as a stripper at a motel bar in Dryden.

The conversation Gill and Andrew enjoyed at their lunches always played out in a similar vein. They discussed guys they had both known when younger and impressionable and feeling as if they could be who they chose to be. Gill wondered how closely the guys he kept in touch with resembled the guys he had known in the past, and how much of a chance any of them really had to create themselves in the image they wanted. How much did anyone really change? How much of their life did anyone choose?

Gill remembered the stories Andrew's grandfather Elmer, who used to get called Clipper because he loved sailboats, used to tell them about the sturgeon rolling in the shallows of the Winnipeg River, when there were so many of them they looked like logs you could walk across from bank to bank; back in the 1920s, when Lake of the Woods supplied most of the caviar of North America. A friend of Elmer's, who he always called Sloopy, used to buy the caviar from the Indians to sell in Europe as beluga caviar for four dollars a pound. Sloopy was part of a prominent town family so Elmer would never tell Gill his real name, but he did eventually cut Elmer in on the deal, and then a few months later Sloopy died. Elmer took over the business and amassed a quiet fortune that ended up buying the Allens' parcel of land at the end of the narrows leading in to Kenora, which people started calling Allen's Narrows.

When Andrew was eleven, a boating accident killed his parents and brother, and he went to live with his aunt and uncle who lived next door to Gill's parents. So growing up, Andrew and Gill had always played together, and as long as Gill had known him, Andrew had been impressionable; trying the latest styles of hair, getting his ear pierced, talking about finding himself and travelling around Europe with Australians in a minibus. In Gill's mind, Andrew remained in many ways the same person he had been as the left winger of their midget hockey team, the selfish star looking to receive the pass, loyal and friendly and nice as long as it did not take too much effort, but not ready to lead himself or anyone else.

When their lunch finished, neither Gill or Andrew had any pressing business to attend to, and so they decided to drive down to the Winnipeg River locks to see if the suckers were running in the open water flowing from Lake of the Woods into the

Winnipeg River. They drove down off the Trans-Canada Highway on a gravel road, the land around them rising and falling over rock and scrub bush, down to the winding shoreline. What people called the mouth of the Winnipeg River was not so much a mouth as a dropping away of water from the expanse of Lake of the Woods; through passages and islands the water collected again behind a high point of land to create a channel where the water rushed and swirled under the weight of its own momentum, and then spread out again through a jagged pattern of islands and reefs. The land where the locks were finally built was called Johnson's Portage and it divided crown land from the Anicinabe Reserve. Log booms chained together in rafts floated below a bridge that Andrew and Gill crossed, where the current of the Winnipeg River curved up and pulled anything on the surface of the water under it as it rushed past. Gill had once heard the story of a moose swimming from the mainland out to an island, a moose whose antlers had caught on the log booms so that for the week before the logs were brought in to the mill you could see the antlers sticking up between them.

Gill drove the Land Cruiser down through the residential neighbourhoods where snow machine tracks ran along the shoulder of the road, fresher than the tracks from the cars. When they came to the opening in the bush below the hydro dam, two pickups were parked on the side of the road and they saw four men out on the bank of the river, one with a spear in his hands and a length of rope to retrieve the spear coiled around his shoulder. Gill recognized two of the men, Carl and Benjamin Desmarais, two Métis brothers he knew from high school, and the other two he had seen around town before: one was named Flett and the other was Henry Campbell. He waved at them when they looked up at him and Andrew driving past, looking for the head of the trail to the Diving Pool. Andrew started to talk about the good times he remembered at the Diving Pool, and he asked Gill if he remembered.

Gill said, "That's when Christine first met you and Joan. We came down here with a lunch on a weekday I had off from work and swam and ate all afternoon. Then you and Joan came down when she finished work and the four of us took the inner tubes you used to keep behind the shed up to the dam and floated down here." Gill did not mention to Andrew how he and Christine had been sunning themselves naked on the rocks and had scrambled to dress when they heard the noises in the bushes just before Andrew and Joan had appeared, or how the photos Christine had taken of him balancing on the diving rock that day remained some of the only things he kept from the times they had together. Andrew talked about his daughter Carrie, and Gill remembered when she was first born with her head pointed and the red marks on her forehead that persisted until she was three months old. Andrew had asked Gill and Christine if they would be Carrie's godparents. Gill remembered how at the christening, Wade had squirmed in his arms, anxious to see what was happening, and it amazed him how fast the events of life passed by.

They arrived at the trail to the Diving Pool and followed it down through the bush until the trees ended and water flowed past looking black and sleek against the snow on the rocks. From upstream came shouts and splashing that echoed off the cliff walls. Someone yelled, "Pull it. Go Carl, pull it in."

Gill packed a snowball and threw it out into the water where it splashed and broke up to join the river. He thought about asking Andrew how he and Joan were, since the last time he and Andrew had spoken there had been trouble and talk of separating. He thought of ways to phrase the question that had been on his mind since they had met at the diner and finally just came out and said, "So how are you and Joan?"

"We're working on things," Andrew said while the yelling continued from upstream. Gill wondered whether he should call bullshit on Andrew and tell him just to come out with it, since he already knew better; or, whether he should let him off the hook, to keep private things private. It bothered him not to talk about it.

"Listen," he said as gently as he could. "I saw you with Claire Kozak at the gas station a week ago and it didn't look like you were just helping her pick out a motor oil."

"What are you talking about?"

"Come on, Andrew. I'm not blind. I was in Fort Frances picking up a gas stove for Smiths."

"Fuck, Gill." Andrew looked at him as if he had slapped his face. "I've been trying to get through this thing with Joan and we've been working at it and seeing a counsellor." He picked up a handful of snow, packed it into a ball and threw it into the river. "But it just doesn't feel like it's going anywhere. I think that Joan's made up her mind and is just putting in the time to see if we can patch things up because she doesn't want to be divorced. Not because she wants to be together."

"So what happened?" Gill asked and Andrew started in on how things were going well; life around the house had been better for him and Joan and Carrie. He did not know if they were going to pull through, but things were better. Then he started a job in Fort Frances on the pipeline and ran into Claire, who had been transferred from Toronto a couple of years ago. She had a son but was not seeing anyone. Andrew said he went out for dinner and a drink with her, talked about old times, and Gill could feel the bullshit being dished to him. "You know, she and I never really did break up, she just went away to work," Andrew said and the next thing he knew she was crying on his shoulder, she didn't think her life was going anywhere, she was alone. They were back at her place on the couch and "things started happening."

"So you slept with her?"

"Yeah."

"Just once?" Gill looked at him and he could see Andrew thinking about how much he should tell him, the polished version he sounded like he had worked out for himself or the real version that involved an ugly side of himself.

"A couple of times on that trip. And one time after. I didn't mean for it to be that way. She talked for a while and cried and then listened to me tell my story and we talked about how things are never the same in your life once you've got kids. We both were scared that the best we had to hope for in life was behind us. Then things happened. You must have seen us on the second trip. We were pretty stupid going out there together, weren't we?"

"You should tell Joan," Gill said, not knowing why he had said it, or if it would make things better. Andrew looked at him and Gill felt like he could almost smell the fear in him. Tears started to fill Andrew's eyes and he looked away and wiped his face with the back of his hand. He told Gill he did not know what to do. He had broken things off with Claire but he kept thinking about her. Joan knew nothing about what had happened, or at least he assumed she knew nothing, and he did not think he could tell her.

As Andrew rattled on about the situation he was in, and how he could see no way out of it, the shouting from the men at the dam got louder and sharper and Gill heard one of them cry out what sounded like "*Help!*" He looked upstream and saw nothing moving except a group of about twenty bluebills diving for minnows in the steaming water. The ducks popped up in a small group in the shallows, then Gill saw someone scrambling over the rocks along the bank, slipping and falling and getting back up, looking out into the river.

Gill scanned the water and saw something being carried along: a head. "Oh shit," he said. One of them had fallen in.

The bluebills took off in a flurry of movement while Gill jumped upstream from rock to rock. If he reached the outcropping of reef at the head of the Diving Pool there was a chance to save the man in the water, but if Gill missed him the man would be swept under the ice and dead for sure. Andrew fell behind Gill and yelled out in pain as Gill carried on. He landed on the big flat rock they used to dive off into the current and slipped down on his hip into the water. He pushed himself up and crawled out off the rock.

"Grab my belt!" he yelled at Andrew, who arrived right behind him.

Gill lifted his jacket at the back so Andrew could grab him, never taking his eyes off the head in the water as it came over a rapid and turned and Gill recognized Carl Desmarais. Carl lifted one arm out of the water and tried to swim over to the rocks, but the cold had sapped his strength and the stroke was feeble. Gill started to wade out in the numbing water, careful about where he put each foot, trying to judge how far he had to go to reach the place where Carl would pass. He took another step forward and found nothing under his foot; he was as far as he could go. He would have pitched forward and been lost if Andrew had not held him fast from behind.

"Swim to me!" he yelled. The strokes Carl Desmarais took in the current looked like they were in slow motion, his body so cold it could hardly move. "Come on, swim to me!" Gill yelled again.

"Swim, Carl!" Benjamin Desmarais yelled as he arrived from the shore, and splashed into the water to grab on to Andrew. Gill heard Andrew tell Benjamin to grab his belt, then he felt pushed out further into the water. His chest went under as he stretched out into the current and he felt his breath catch in his chest. He could not inhale but he held on. Carl's strokes slowed and only one of his arms lifted out of the water. Gill could not feel his feet as they bounced off a rock and he reached further into the current. Carl was almost there and Gill did not know if he could reach.

"I've got you, Gill," he heard Andrew say and he kicked forward another few inches in the water. Something slipped in the chain behind him just as he stretched to grab Carl by the collar and one of his braids. Gill locked his hand and felt himself moving in the current. He reached back with his other hand and felt for Andrew. Someone caught their footing and they jerked to a stop.

"Puuullll!" someone yelled and they were moving back, toward the rocks and the shore and home. Freezing water flowed down the back of Gill's collar as someone pulled him back towards shore. All he could think about was holding on to Carl and being part of the chain and not letting go. He felt rocks grind against his back and Andrew pulled him out of the water. Benjamin hit him on the hand and he realized they were up on the rocks and he could let go of Carl. They had made it. Gill tasted blood and found he had bitten his lip. He bent over and felt like he would be sick but all that fell on the white snow were bright, round drops of blood from his mouth; tick, tick, tick they dropped and stained the snow.

Someone Gill did not know arrived and started shouting at Carl and Benjamin. He leaned on someone and felt heavy as they started walking up the path to the road. Then he heard the sirens and everything afterwards happened fast. Andrew carried Carl up the path to the road where a fire truck and paramedics waited. Gill helped load Carl into the ambulance and it took off to the hospital. A fireman wrapped Gill in a blanket just as his clothes started to stiffen and freeze. Andrew came with the Land Cruiser and picked him up and took him to his house where Joan ran a hot bath and Gill borrowed some dry clothes. They ordered in a pizza to eat and watched the local news coverage of the event, which consisted of a reporter standing on the side of the road in front of the dam and getting the names wrong. The bath and food and warmth revived Gill. After the sports report, he felt well enough to start the Land Cruiser and head back out to the cabin. Andrew fussed over him and offered to have him stay in their extra bedroom but Gill told him he just wanted to get back to his own bed. What he did not tell him was he did not trust himself not to keep the truth from Joan, a great girl who deserved better than to have her husband cheating on her, and that he could not stand being in the same room with the two of them and remaining silent about what he knew.

The amber lights at the outskirts of Kenora faded in the rearview mirror and Gill clicked the Land Cruiser's lights up to high beam. Seeing Andrew and Joan together, he felt like he did not understand what it was that they could not get over to keep themselves happy and together. They had a terrific little girl who was sharp as a whip; they had their health and a great life together. How hard could it be for Andrew to think well enough of himself and just be good to the other people in his life? Gill had surely made his share of mistakes and misjudgements but he had never lied to Christine. He had fucked up and done things he wished he could have back to do differently, and he had tried, the same as she had, to make a relationship work that they both should have known would never work, but he had never cheated. He had given it his best shot and learned the things he could and could not reconcile.

So it continued to amaze Gill as he got older and expected people to behave more reasonably, with more thought given to their actions and the consequences, that they kept doing stupid things, unstable things that wrecked their lives; things that if they saw someone else doing they would tell them to give their head a shake, but that they were not willing to stop themselves from doing. Gill turned onto the Storm Bay Road and watched a red fox slink along the edge of the road and jump over a drift into the bush. Did people just have a fixed amount of happiness they allowed in their lives? He pulled into the driveway to his cabin, in over the fresh snow that flew up into the beams of light from the Land Cruiser and the quiet of the place.

The embers in the stove had turned grey during the day and Gill lit a new fire to heat the cabin. He brought in the groceries he had bought and stowed them in the cupboards, put the supplies where they went, then retrieved Gramp's old mechanical typewriter from his days at the *Kenora Miner and News* and set it up on his table beside the bills, account statements, invoice books and records from the taxidermist. Something had come to him. As he thought about what he would write, the keys started to warm up and the action of the hammers and ribbon became smoother. False starts and ideas on scraps of paper littered the desk beside the typewriter before he felt ready, and then once he started it all flowed out at once. His fingers, which had seemed so skilled and nimble as they worked the skin from the beaver carcass that morning, could not keep up with his mind. The sound from the keys shot through the empty cabin in rapid fire. Gramp had been a powerful two-finger typist who had worn the action of the keys, so that the touch typing Gill had learned in high school brushed the paper with smudge marks when what was needed were strong strokes to make bold letters. Gill reared back and pounded at the keys with his index fingers and the words started to reach across the page. After a few lines, he pulled the typewriter back to him and went at it again, just as he remembered Gramp doing on those early mornings, as if he had to jam the words onto the paper as the machine tried to get away. A wreath of smoke would curl around Gramp's head from the cigarette he clenched in his teeth, the smell of scotch mints lingering in the room. Gill went at his letter with great concentration until he was through it and both his hands and his mind were spent. Then he pulled the sheet of paper from the roll and set it on the desk to flatten. Tomorrow, he would decide whether or not he would fold it and slip it into an envelope at the post office. The typewriter went back into its case, the case went back on the top shelf of the closet and Gill busied himself around the cabin getting the coffee pot ready for the morning. A few more logs needed to be brought in from the wood pile to dry out for the fire tomorrow, then it was time for bed.

As Gill lay in his bed and let his eyes adjust to the darkness, he felt empty and exhausted. All the things that had happened since he left the cabin that morning came rushing back to him: the paralyzing constriction of the cold water as he had watched Carl Desmarais pushed towards him, the taste of blood in his mouth, the scared look on the face of Andrew when he realized that Gill knew about his cheating, someone saying, "Fucking Indians, fishing out of season" when they had brought Carl up to the fire truck. As his mind calmed he almost forgot the letter lying on the table just outside his bedroom. Whatever happened with Andrew and Joan, or the Desmarais brothers, or the Land Cruiser, or whatever, Gill felt that the letter he had written would be something he could hold on to, and something he had done to be good to someone he cared about. And as he lay in his bed alone, with the cold retreating from the blankets as his body and the fire heated them, he felt like part of the solitude he found at Lake of the Woods became more negotiable. The good and the bad of what had happened in the past remained in the past. He had to live in the present.

Christine,

I almost saw a man die today. He had fallen into the water below the dam of the Winnipeg River where we used to go and eat our picnics—at the Diving Pond. Do you remember? I remember. It made me think of you today. I think of you lots of days. Over the years I think we have done a great job of being good to each other. We have not been selfish or weak. There were times when we did not agree (camping comes to mind), but we never let that get in the way of the respect we had for each other.

We have a great son. I wake up some mornings here in the cabin and wonder how this happened. We had some great years together and I wish we could have worked things so we had more years together. We never did or said too many things to each other that we would take back (at least me, I assume we're OK on this since we're still friends). Do you know there is almost nothing in the world I would not do for you?

In the years since we divorced I have blamed myself for not being a better husband and father and for not being around as much as I should have. Lately, I've started to believe that we're actually better off in our separate worlds than we would have been living together. Strange, isn't it? It has taken me a long time to realize this. I remember telling Wade years ago that sometimes people are just better off not being together. Now I think I know what I meant.

Like I always said, you were the first girl I ever loved and you will always be special to me.

Gill

ONE NIGHT
—*June 1992*—

WADE DUBOIS GRADUATED WITH A HUNDRED AND SEVENTEEN other boys from St. Paul's High School on June 19, 1992. Of the days surrounding his graduation from St. Paul's, two things stood out in his memory. The first was the way those blurred few weeks of May and June and July felt magical, as if he lived with the circus and any consequences of his actions would never catch up with him or his friends as they stayed awake late into the night around steaming swimming pools and talked about the future. The second thing Wade remembered was things starting with Murryn Carlyle. A great anxiety took root in him as he watched her take ten dollars from Darren Reed, a tall boy with a gawky appearance and a wounded demeanour, in a double-or-nothing rematch of a game of pool, right after she had lost the first game without sinking a ball. Wade felt struck by how Murryn could handle herself; in a group, at a party, at a game of pool, or on her own. She seemed to possess another kind of maturity than that of other girls trying to be women. Wade felt a tremendous tightness in his chest when he spoke to Murryn, and from this feeling a connection existed before he knew her; a connection different from his relationship with any of the other girls who moved in the same circles of friends, even though he knew they said yes when he asked them to the movies. When Wade and Murryn spoke for the first time at a barbecue on the May long weekend they shared jokes and references with an ease and naturalness that made Wade conscious of how well it was going. He found himself telling Murryn exactly what he was thinking before he could stop himself. He stood next to the smoking grill, sipping a can of beer and telling Murryn that she had a beautiful smile and that her looks would endure, which he could see made her pause before taking it as a compliment. Only years later, when they reminisced over a plate of oysters and lemon wedges about the first time they had met, did they finally figure out the date and decide they had met once before but did not remember each other. Whether this was charitable to Wade, since he had been drunk at their actual first meeting, or whether it was the truth was something Murryn would never tell him.

St. Paul's High School described itself as a Catholic school in the Jesuit tradition. Winnipeg's leaders and prominent families, whether Catholic, Jewish, Protestant or Sikh, sent their sons to St. Paul's to form the social connections that would see them through their professional lives. Wade had mentioned attending St. Paul's to Christine one day as they drove home from hockey practice. Some of his teammates on the hockey team had started to talk about going to St. Paul's, and Wade wanted to know more about going too. Older brothers of Wade's teammates went to St. Paul's and their parents made donations to the school and wore pins on the lapels of their jackets with the school motto: *Sigut Miles Christi:* Soldier of Christ. Wade had been twelve at the time, big for his age and strong in sports, and looking at his teammates' siblings, Jason Rosen's older brother Reeve, and Trevor Clarke's older brothers Jeff and Mike, Wade could see himself going to St. Paul's and playing on the Crusader football and hockey teams just as they did.

And so it turned out. After collecting a letter of reference from the minister of Westworth United Church, and sitting through an interview with his parents and the Principal of the Administration, a bald, French-Canadian man with playful eyes and an outdated suit, Wade found that St. Paul's had determined it had a spot for him.

Time then blazed past, marked by birthdays and holidays, successes and failures, so that when Wade remembered his four years at St. Paul's he thought of changes more than specific events, and his life around graduation stretched out about as ideally as he could imagine. The rush of time from the end of the hockey season in late winter, through the rugby season in spring, to exams for all his classes, SATs for American college entrance scores, applications and letters of acceptance contingent on his upcoming marks, made life flow past in a surge of events and preparations. Wade took to getting up late in the morning and lolling around the house where Christine would have left him a note with the details of her plan for the day. Errands he had to run for her came with some money to buy himself something nice. Together with his friends he would go to the gym to lift weights. They might swim in a backyard pool or drive an hour north to the shore of Lake Winnipeg where Grand Beach stretched out in white dunes further than you could walk, and where the bouncer at the door of the beach club let them in without ID or a hassle. Exams and parties and sports and barbecues kept his 1984 Honda in motion, and gym bags and athletic shoes and sports-drink bottles began to pile up in the back seat.

In all of this the one thing Wade never missed was the daily arrival of the mail between noon and one. He would search through it for letters from coaches and university entrance committees. He picked out these letters and read them in the bright sunshine of the front porch and knew that he should be paying attention to how things were happening, that this time of motion and privilege would have to end at some point with talk of buckling down and getting serious about the future, topics already alluded to in conversation over dinners with Christine and her boyfriend Gary Shewchuk, a tall man who had given up smoking when he joined the provincial Progressive Conservatives. Gary always paid for their meals and this seemed to entitle him to some opinion over the events of Wade's life. But exceptions continued being made to the rules that had been enforced up until then. Phrases such as "You're only young once" were spoken in sentimental tones by Christine and by the parents of Wade's friends like Marion Pringle, who stated that nothing was going to ruin the time she had left with her Charles before he went off to Columbia to become a lawyer. At the dance party following the St. Paul's graduation dinner seventeen- and eighteen-year-olds ended up drinking beer from the bottles their parents handed to them, and kissing in dark corners of rooms and outside the hall with girls from the sister school, St. Mary's Academy.

The weeks of parties and fun eventually led to one party, one night which rumour and promotion promised to be the pinnacle of the grad experience. When Matt Kowalski's parents left for Palm Springs they were aware their son planned to throw a party, and that the party would likely be big and wild, not unlike previous parties he had thrown, but they did not need to know, and did not want to know, anything more.

The night of the party came. Wade sat in the front room of the Kowalskis' sprawling Tudor home with his friend Sully, a tall and lanky kid who had starred at wide receiver on the football team and underachieved to a C average for the past three years, and watched the guests arrive through the rain-spotted picture window. Around them, the party gained momentum as people arrived. Drink orders started in the kitchen and Sully, who acted as bartender whenever there was a party, left to keep the people happy. Wade heard the glasses clink together on the wet counter, ice rang in them, bottles cracked open, and more orders were yelled. A minivan pulled into the Kowalskis' driveway and a girl in a yellow slicker crawled out of the side door. The slicker's hood was up and the girl kept her head bowed, making it impossible to see her face. Wade half expected her to jump in a puddle on her way up the walkway. And then, just as he caught himself thinking he recognized the girl, he knew he recognized her: it was Murryn Carlyle, the one girl he hoped would show up for the party.

Wade knew from past parties that Matt Kowalski likely would remain in his basement bedroom with his girlfriend Sari for most of the evening, and he felt obliged to make sure the house was not torn apart. People stood with drinks, talking about school and universities and test scores, what they were doing for the summer, how much time they thought they would be able to spend at their family cottages at Whiteshell Provincial Park or Victoria Beach or Lake of the Woods, and what kinds of parties they would have there. They tried to act cool while checking new arrivals or what the popular girls were wearing, tried to fight off the little shiver they felt from the stiff drinks Sully poured. Bottles clinked against each other as a case of beer passed overhand between boys; a few girls waited in the hallway to use the bathroom. At the dining room table a card game called Asshole started up until all the chairs filled and girls sat on boys' knees or shared chairs to participate. A girl Wade had never met before dropped her gin and tonic on the living room carpet and he handed her a roll of paper towel to clean it up. Many more drinks would fall before the end of the party, and some glasses would break, a chair collapsed, a towel rack was pulled from the wall when someone grabbed it to steady themselves; the basics of what made for a party had established themselves.

Wade circulated and laughed with his friends. Every now and then he caught sight of Murryn and his attention strayed from the conversation he was having as he tried to follow her movements and catch her attention without letting on his intentions. Out in the back yard he stood beside the pool and talked to Sully's cousin Sarah from Brandon, who would be moving to Winnipeg in the fall to live in residence at the University of Manitoba, and she flirted with Wade and told him she wanted him to go and change into his bathing suit so he could join her in the pool. Chad Moritz, a short boy with dark features who'd studied in France for a term and whose father ran a chain of Ford dealerships, yelled from the pool, "You coming in, Wade? We cranked the heat this afternoon. The temperature's over ninety-five. It's a hot tub, man."

"I don't have my trunks."

"'S okay. Neither do I." The swimmers laughed as Chad pushed off from the side of the pool and dove deep, showing his beluga-white bum. The shimmering underwater lights made the scene seem foreign, Californian. Wade stayed and talked to Sarah. Sully came out in his white uniform with a towel over one shoulder and a cocktail shaker in his hand to pour drinks for the swimmers who held up their plastic martini glasses and toasted, "To the Queen."

The party carried on and even when the police knocked on the front door to tell them to keep the noise down, no one left. An air of purpose remained attached to the evening. People vomited in the bathroom and outside the back door in the yard and a couple emerged from Mr. and Mrs. Kowalski's bedroom, but basically everyone behaved. Sully gave the bar over to anyone who wanted to make the drinks after midnight. Cigar butts littered the dining room table and the smoky smell hung over the room, though they had seemed like a good idea at the time. A poker game which had erupted under the low ceiling of the basement almost broke into a fight when two guys accused a third of cheating and stashing cards. A bout of pushing ensued, with a lot of big talk about ass kickings and ass whippings, which amounted to nothing in the end except for a crack in the drywall and a swollen finger on the guy accused of cheating. Wade thought that over the course of the evening almost two hundred guests had passed through the Kowalski house, and that all things considered, things looked pretty good; Jenny Feldman, who had graduated from St. Mary's, had even flashed him her tits as she went into the bathroom to change out of her wet bikini, and they were fine tits that she was well known for. Only a tumble down the stairs by Trevor Acheson, a barrel-chested boy with a ready smile who loved to wrestle, that resulted in a pressure cut on his forehead and a debate over whether he should go the hospital to get stitched up or not, kept the evening from being an unqualified success.

As the evening wound down and the usual time when people would have started to go home for curfews passed, it became apparent that no one wanted to go home. Some partyers who had left to go to Scandals Niteclub returned to the party at two a.m. with more people to inject the party with new life. Pizzas were ordered and the Kowalskis' liquor cabinet raided while people skinny dipped in the backyard; the guys coaxed the adventuresome girls to go without their bras and panties, and the girls called for someone to bring them towels after they had swum around a while.

Around three a.m. Wade and Sully perched themselves on the kitchen countertop, both feeling no pain, and a high-level conversation ensued, instigated by the shirt Sully wore under his white apron. His older brother, a master's student in philosophy at McGill who grew marijuana in his closet for personal consumption, had given Sully the shirt and advised him to wear it to pick up older chicks. The shirt had printed across the chest "Those who do not remember the past are destined to repeat it";

and across the back, "Chaos is perhaps at the bottom of everything." The party had by then mostly burnt itself out. A few nighthawks watched Hitchcock's *Rear Window* on the television in the living room and lights were on all over the house showing the remains of the party: ripped beer cases, sopping towels hiding bathing suits in puddles on the linoleum, beer bottles filled with flat beer and cigarette butts, McDonald's bags and McChicken wrappers on the table, torn plastic packaging lingering beside ripple chip crumbs and dip cups. Beer caps had been pushed under chesterfields and bookshelves. Wade walked through the house surveying the debris and found Murryn in the front hall putting on her coat. He felt like he should stay and help his friends clean up but there she was, standing in front of him, leaving, and he fought with the tight feeling in his voice and chest. The feeling of responsibility and the intention to stay to help his friends clean up disappeared the second Murryn smiled at him, and instead of pouring out the bottoms of beer bottles he found himself offering to walk her home.

Then, Wade was outside in the fresh air waiting for her as she went to the bathroom. A half moon shone from behind the broken clouds that raced across the sky. The lawn under Wade's feet released wet fallow smells that reminded him of the smell the marsh let out when he and his father went duck hunting. Streetlights reflected across the wet roads and Murryn clicked the door open.

"Ready for the long walk?" Wade said and Murryn nodded and walked ahead of him down the driveway and jumped with both feet landing at once in the puddle at the curb, and they laughed, each for different reasons. They cut across the boulevard, the toes of their shoes collecting moisture, and fell into an easy pace talking about their plans for the summer; she planned to continue working at the Safeway, the money was good because she had been there for two years and she could get flexible shifts and weekends off. Wade told her he planned to work out in Kenora and stay with his father for the summer. He didn't have a job lined up yet but he could always fill in as a dock boy again, as he'd done the summer before at Smith Camps, where he ran boats and cleaned fish for the American families.

Past the end of the Kowalskis' street, Wade and Murryn cut through some yards to Grant Avenue, the main street running from downtown out to the suburbs, where passing cars sucked up a mist behind them on the wet street. Murryn asked Wade if his parents were split up and then told him hers were too; she and her sister lived with her mom, her brother lived with her dad in Ottawa, and she didn't see them except for twice a year when she travelled out to ski at Mont Tremblant, Quebec.

"You're the youngest?" Wade said.

"By five years. I've considered I could have been unplanned."

"I'm an only child," Wade said. "And I think it was planned that way. But I don't know. Maybe I was unplanned too."

A van passed, kicking up a mist Wade could feel on his face. The road straightened ahead of them through the Assiniboine Forest Park, a few kilometres of hardwood trees and sloughs with paths for dog walkers and cross-country skiers.

"But my mom and dad split up when I was pretty young. My dad lives out past Kenora."

"How come he lives out there?"

"He's always lived out there. Ever since I was born at least. He's a fishing guide. Lots of Americans come up and go out fishing with him." Wade didn't know what else to tell Murryn about his father, he didn't know himself if his father was happy as a fishing guide and what kept him there. It had always just been that way. "In the winter he's a trapper and a handyman. He even works at the pulp and paper mill sometimes."

"Lake of the Woods?"

"Yeah. Have you ever been there?"

Murryn nodded and told Wade about the camping trips she used to take with her family in the summers when her parents were still together. They would all go on an annual camping trip to an island whose name she couldn't remember on Lake of the Woods.

"The water was really cold and we had to bathe in it. Brrr. Makes me cold just thinking about it."

Wade looked over at her and thought about putting his arm around her to cuddle her against the cold like she was his girl. Buds on the trees they passed had sprouted and filled the air with the smell of sap. Wade and Murryn walked on and talked about school. Murryn planned on going through a year or two of sciences, then transferring to medicine or veterinarians' school while Wade planned on going straight into commerce, majoring in finance of marketing and one day starting his own business. "Maybe with my dad doing tours for Americans at fishing camps." Both of them agreed they thought they knew what they wanted to do but weren't sure that in a few years they would end up feeling the same once they had some experience.

The sidewalk skirted the division between the Assiniboine Forest and Grant Avenue, its crooked slabs cracked by roots, stubborn trees growing between the sidewalk and the boulevard. Murryn told Wade that sometimes she wished she could leave and go see the world, like her mother had done when she was Murryn's age, and like she encouraged Murryn's older sister to do all the time since she had graduated from arts and not found a job. Going and seeing the world was popular; Sully had an around-the-world ticket booked to depart in September, starting off in Ireland. Wade listened and laughed at Murryn's story.

"What are you laughing at?" she said and hit him on the arm.

"Nothing. We're just a lot alike. We'd both love to do things at the drop of a hat but most of the time are too responsible to."

"Well, if I were going to go I would need the right person to go with. Someone who I wouldn't end up hating two weeks into the trip and then having to travel on my own."

Wade laughed and Murryn hit him again.

"What?" she said. "What are you grinning about?"

"Nothing. Nothing. You're cute when you're trying not to say something."

"I'm not trying to be. You know when you just have a thought spring into your head and you don't know where it came from but you know it's a crazy thing."

"Yeah, I know. It happens to me all the time."

"Really," Murryn said. "Like what?"

"Oh no. Don't try and distract me. What were you thinking that was so crazy?"

"It's stupid."

"No it's not," Wade said. "How do you know it's stupid unless you say it?"

"It is. Forget it."

"I'm sure it's not. I promise I won't laugh or make fun of you."

"Yeah?"

"Yeah," Wade said. "Except if it's stupid."

Murryn butted him with her shoulder, her hand in the slicker pocket, knocking him a step off the sidewalk.

"No. Hey," Wade said. "I'm just kidding. Tell me. I won't laugh. Promise." Murryn fixed a look on him, her steps carrying her along as he kept up. "Promise."

"Okay. I was thinking that because you want to travel but are going to school first for your degree, and at the same time I want to travel, that we could maybe travel together. Because our plans are pretty much the same. And we both thought of doing it and we're both here right now. And we're talking about it." She stopped walking and talking. "I told you it was stupid. Since we know each other so well. Just, don't listen to me."

Wade stopped and smiled at her with a rising feeling inside of him. "Hey," he said reaching his foot towards her, one step, two; now in front of her, her head tilted up to his face and her cheeks full of colour. "It's not stupid. I thought the same thing."

"You didn't."

Wade nodded. "I did. But I'd have to meet your parents first."

The details of Murryn's face smoothed out; Wade smelled vanilla from around her neck, saw the silver chain and cross she wore and just as he moved to kiss her a pair of high beams flashed up at them and hoots and yelling rang out. Leering faces appeared in the window of a car that passed on Grant Avenue. "Do her!" someone yelled as the car slid away on the wet street and the moment passed, and Wade felt caught too close to Murryn but neither of them shied away, they kept smiling at each other and the moment stretched out until finally Wade reached over and touched Murryn's warm hand under the cuff of the slicker. He could see her eyes sparkle and they started off along the sidewalk hand in hand. Wade remembered how his mother had told him to always pay attention to a woman's hands, that touching them as if they were precious was the key to impressing anyone worth impressing.

Ahead of Wade and Murryn, a deer stepped out of the tree line and looked around with its black eyes, then flicked its tail, and bounded out onto the road, across two lanes of pavement, the boulevard and two more lanes, into the Assiniboine Forest on the other side. They watched the deer disappear soundlessly into the bush and Wade hoped aloud that it was alone. They walked a few more steps and another deer raised its head. They could see its eyes glowing green, its ears cupped forward to listen.

"Ohh," Murryn said, seeing why they'd stopped. "She's beautiful."

"Yeah, a big doe."

The doe lifted her front hoof and stretched forward onto it, moving toward the road. A car approached and sped past. Wade looked back along the road to see if any more cars were coming and when he looked again toward the doe she was gone. Then she was back, her head bolting up, chewing the grass between her teeth, swivelling her head twice to look around, then dropping her head again for another mouthful. No wind carried the scent of Wade and Murryn and the doe kept eating, her head coming up every few seconds, then taking a few steps to find the tender shoots of grass.

Wade and Murryn became so absorbed watching the doe they didn't hear the car approaching behind them. They noticed the doe's head bolt up and she was closer to the road. Headlights made a light silhouette over her; made her black eyes glow green; froze her there, staring. Then in one motion the doe dropped her body, twisted her head and bounded away, each jump carrying her through the air. The car rushed past Wade and Murryn and their hand-hold tightened. The doe bounded alongside the road in the soft turf. The brake lights of the car flashed on, its nose diving as its tires locked in skid and its headlights twisting to the side. The doe changed direction in one jump, out onto the road, her hooves scratching the pavement for grip. A loud, sudden whack shot out into the night. The doe's whole body bent over the angle of fender and hood. The windshield shattered. The doe rolled up over the car, the dull sound of metal thudded when her tail hit the roof and hooves cut in, her body cartwheeling in a limp drop to the pavement. The car hit the curb and came to a stop facing the wrong way, one headlight cracked, the other still on. Wade could hear the radio playing. The doe started straining, her front legs pushing her body up, trying to get away from the road. The back legs dragged. Wade and Murryn ran to the accident.

The doe's coat had pulled away from the purple muscles underneath, her pink tongue hung out between her teeth and bubbles of blood ran out of her mouth. Wade knew the doe was hurt deep inside her lungs. Her front hooves clattered on the pavement and Wade could see her wild eyes watching them as he and Murryn came to the scene. Everything had happened so fast there had been no chance to say or do anything. Wade smelled burned brake pads. They arrived at the curb as the amber hazard lights blinked on around three corners of the car and the driver's door opened. A woman's leg in a white tennis shoe and white tights dropped to the pavement. Wade pulled the door open and there was a nurse inside looking up at him with big eyes. He made sure she was okay and then helped her stand. "Take it easy," he said. She told him her name was Carol Baker and she lived on Laxdal Street, only four blocks from where they were. She was on her way home from her shift at the Victoria Hospital and she didn't see anything, then there was this deer running out in front of her and she tried to avoid it but she couldn't.

Wade left her with Murryn, as he could see another vehicle coming along the road. He went around the car and heard the wheezing breathing as the doe strained on the pavement with one black hoof on the end of one brown leg. Her leg collapsed and did not push her up again. All she had left in her was the strength to lift her head, her blood pooling around her on the pavement like oil. Wade stood in front of the accident and flagged an approaching pickup to a stop. He stepped to the driver's window and looked in.

"What happened?" The man inside the pickup asked and pulled on his hazard lights.

"A lady hit a deer."

"Oh shit, oh yeah," the man said as the doe lifted then dropped her head. "Is she hurt?"

"No, she'll be fine. Just shaken up."

"She's lucky it didn't come through the windshield. Have you called the police?"

"No. It just happened."

The man looked at the scene again with Wade. The doe's head swung up in the lone headlight of the smashed car, dropped and lifted again, trying to lead the body back into the trees.

"Jesus," the man said and stepped out of the pickup to walk over to the doe. "I've got an ax in the back," he said to Wade. "We should do something. Put her out of her misery."

"Yeah. We should."

"It's awful to see her struggling there."

"Poor thing. She was eating on the side of the road. Then just decided to run out in front of the car. You could see it happening."

"You don't understand it."

"Yeah, no, it just doesn't make sense." The doe lifted her head again and then sagged. "It's a shame they don't do something about this."

A warm smell coated the scene as Wade and the man from the pickup watched the doe twitch and take her last breath. A red sports car idled by in the free lane with the driver gawking at the scene then stopping, rolling down his window and saying he was going to call for the police.

The man from the pickup left when the police arrived. Wade and Murryn gave their statements, then were free to go, and they walked away from the accident and held hands again; the three blocks from the end of the forest to Murryn's house were quiet, Wade saying a few words, Murryn answering, saying a few of her own. It was the first dead animal she had seen except for baby birds in the back yard or meat from the grocery store.

"It's strange," Wade said. "We've only known each other a little time."

"And you feel like it's been so much longer?"

"Yeah. It's like we've known each other for years. At least I feel like I know you like I've known people for years. Better even. Even though it's early." Wade and Murryn turned up her driveway and headed toward to the door and the light above it. "Does your mom wait up?"

"She doesn't wait up but I tell her I'm home."

Wade nodded and they were at the top of the driveway, as far as he would be going. Every step was a little slower until Murryn asked Wade if he would stay so they could sit together on the porch and talk. She disappeared into the house and the lights went out and then she reappeared with a blanket.

"I thought we could sit on this," she said looking at the blanket. "It's nicer than the stairs."

Of the three steps up to the house Murryn stood on the middle one and Wade stood on the bottom one, she taller than he. His hand touched hers and then they kissed, not waiting for the right moment, not waffling and stalling through a conversation occupying neither of their minds. They kissed awkwardly and fumbling, at first, then gentler, finer, with their heads tilted to the proper angle. Later, they opened the blanket on the step, and then kissed again, and by the time Wade left to walk home his lips were rubbed smooth and he didn't know what time it was, though it didn't matter. The piece of paper he held in his pocket had Murryn's phone number scrawled on it. As he came within sight of the porch light at the top of his own driveway, thoughts and feelings churned through Wade's mind. He had crossed Grant Avenue in time to see the Animal Services van driving away from where it must have picked up the dead deer. It was sad to see the doe die and it was incredible to kiss Murryn, and Wade swung one leg then the other home to bed wondering how so much could happen in one night, so much that seemed so important. The sky above started to lighten and a few cars passed him with the headlights on in the dawn. He had kissed Murryn Carlyle! In his imagination, Wade could not understand how so much could happen in one night, and how the most important thing of all could not have happened in a more perfect way. As he replayed the events of the night so he could save them in his memory, he remembered that she had even kissed him first.

CONTINENTAL DIVIDE
—April, 1994—

WADE RELEASED THE CLUTCH AS MURRYN FASTENED HER SEATBELT and waved one last goodbye through the window to her mother. After so much talk around the kitchen table following dinners that started with the Lord's Prayer, they were finally leaving. The silver Honda accelerated as Wade shifted gears and they joined with the traffic flowing out of the city, past intersections and service stations, around an overpass, to the west-bound lanes of the Trans-Canada, where cars jockeyed for position and the trucks swayed in the crosswinds. Murryn watched as the puddles of melted snow in the fallow fields wrinkled with waves. She put her pillow in the back seat and sat and read the words on the cabs and trailers of the trucks: Reimers Transport, Gershman Trucking, Sunshower Sprinklers, Paul's Hauling. Did Paul really work there? The land stretched out around them in perfect flatness and they burst through the city limits to a flat horizon that surrounded them.

At eleven, they stopped to eat in Brandon. The wind tingled on their skin with the cool of winter. Murryn went in to the McDonald's to pee while Wade parked the Honda. She told him the only times she had eaten breakfast at McDonald's were after her brother's Saturday morning hockey games when she ordered hot chocolate and wrapped her hands around the cup for warmth. One thing she knew she could count on while on the road was that the bathrooms at McDonald's would be clean. She felt good to be on the road and with Wade. They had talked about going on a trip together, to get away from the city and to have an adventure with each other. "We're taking a big step here," Wade had said to her the night before as they took the car through the automatic wash, and she had wondered if the step was not in fact bigger for him, and, even though he kept trying to pay more attention to making sure her mother was happy with what they were doing, it seemed to Murryn that it was Christine who needed the reassurance that everything would be all right.

Murryn returned to the car, handed Wade a Sausage McMuffin from the bag, and they passed out of Brandon, rejoining the traffic streaming along the Trans-Canada past the RV parks and car dealerships and fast-food outlets and motels. A half-hour later, the flat prairie fell away and they dropped down and across a wide valley to a bridge above the muddy water of the Assiniboine River that made her think of hot chocolate again. Just before they crossed into Saskatchewan they passed Virden and Murryn grabbed Wade's arm and told him to pull over to the side of the highway so she could snap a photo of a huge statue of an oil derrick. She remembered driving to Expo '86 in Vancouver with her family and seeing the huge statues that seemed to be in every small town along the way: a moose in Moose Jaw, a dinosaur in Drumheller, a Smokey the Bear in Revelstoke. She wanted to photograph each one they passed to create a scrapbook of their adventure.

They crossed into Saskatchewan and she noticed a new image

of a deer on the yellow deer crossing signs. The Qu'Appelle Valley rolled along to the north, providing glimpses of bright blue water every few kilometres between the patchwork colours of the prairie fields. They passed through Regina, gassed up and rolled westward at a pace easy enough to put Murryn to sleep. When they slowed at Swift Current and she realized they had passed Moose Jaw and the statue of the moose, half of her wanted to ask Wade to turn back, but she felt it was for a silly reason, and he would make fun of her, he made fun of his mother for being sentimental about photos of fishing trips with his father, so she said nothing.

Wade stopped in front of a motel in Swift Current that advertised good rates. The motel looked like a low bunker, built of cement blocks, its twelve units each had the same pattern: door, number, window. As they had discussed, Wade went to the office for a key and brought it to Murryn so she could look in at the unit. After she had inspected the shower and sheets, she handed Wade forty dollars to pay for the room. Murryn could not believe Wade had been set to put down their cash without checking the room. Of course it was more important for her to have things clean—she could not have had a shower if it had not been clean—but it also made her wonder about the things men really needed to live, what they thought of when they looked for somewhere to sleep. Her father's apartment had always been dirty. Things had always been picked up, but it had been dirty and she had hated to shower there. She thought she knew one of the reasons why her parents had divorced. It was the fresh smell of Javex that she liked, a sure sign things had been cleaned by someone who cared.

Once they had brought their things into the room, Wade stood and washed his face, and it reminded Murryn of a night they had danced together at a wedding, and he had drawn a sheer scarf from her shoulders and held it up and watched her over the top of it just as he did with the towel he was using to dry himself.

That had been the night they had danced together, the first time they had danced the ballroom steps they had learned taking classes together with the seniors at the local community centre. All she remembered of that night was him, and the dancing, and the music never stopping. Towards the end of the night, whenever they had left from the dark hall, she had told him she loved him.

Murryn sat on the corner of the bed dialling the phone and Wade put the towel down and started brushing his teeth. The ringing of the phone cut through Murryn's daydream and when her mother picked up, Murryn almost told her about dancing the waltz with Wade and telling him she loved him. She almost told her mother where they were and what they would be doing on the bed in the motel in Swift Current, but she knew that her mother, with her Catholic beliefs, wanted to know none of it. Instead, she said they were fine, the drive had been long, but easy, the roads safe, the other drivers not worrying. Her mother told her she was cooking a roast for dinner, and she would save the leftovers for when she returned. Once Murryn signed off with her mother she untied her shoelaces and when they were loosened on her feet she lay back on the bed and sighed and stared at the cracks in the ceiling.

"I think I'll take a shower," Wade said.

"Come here for a second first. We have to decide a few things."

"Like?"

"Which side do you usually sleep on?" Murryn said and patted the spot beside her as Wade came over without his shirt on. She turned her eyes to look at him without turning her head. He lay down beside her and she curled towards him, his warmth, that mix of smells. "You should have let me drive too, little boy. Now you're all tired out and can't play with me." He smiled and his regular breath moved against her. She watched the rise and fall of his chest and heard the little noises he made as he breathed.

"Just give me a minute to rest. Then we can play."

Murryn put her head down on his chest and felt it move under her, heard the slow thump of his heart. The next thing she knew she woke and wiped her mouth where she had drooled in her sleep. Her stomach growled. Outside the window, the sky looked purple in the dusk. She brought her hand up onto Wade's stomach and undid the button on his jeans. The zipper unzipped tooth by tooth and she slid herself down his body, having always imagined waking him up this way, by fondling and then sucking him. She felt him lift his hips to help her push his jeans down and then she took him in her mouth, the soft skin hot against her lips, tasting salty on her tongue. When he came, she felt surprised by the violence of it as he clenched all over, and she kept playing with his softening penis, looking up at him to see his reaction. Whatever she wanted now she could have. She could strip off her clothes and make him beg to have sex with her, she could make him get down between her thighs and follow her directions. But right then she felt hungry, and she had to pee, and the blowjob had been mostly about performance after all. She stood and walked to the bathroom. When she opened the door again she told Wade that she was hungry, that they needed to have some food soon or she would become crabby. They walked to the Boston Pizza and ate all but two pieces of a large half-vegetarian and half-Hawaiian pizza, then carried the left-overs home in a box and fell asleep watching videos on the motel-room TV.

The next day they passed Climax, Saskatchewan, and Wade asked Murryn if she thought they had a Miss Climax pageant. Somewhere after the Alberta border where the signs warned them to watch for antelope, and the tumbleweeds snagged in the barbed-wire fences, she leaned over and touched him on the inside of his arm. Then she touched the back of his neck and slid her fingers into his hair, and he cranked his window down halfway. She touched his neck with only her fingernails and smiled and kissed at the inside of his elbow and then sat back up as he cranked the window down all the way.

They switched drivers at a gas station in Medicine Hat and he read a magazine and she told him to talk to her, to tell her a story about a princess and a ranch. The speed limit was 110 and she set the cruise at 130 and still cars passed them. Oil derricks dotted the fields while Wade slept and Murryn wondered how each little town got its name, if the towns were like children to the people who had named them all those years ago. These people stayed with them or returned later and talked about the town's changes, talked about how the town had grown up, how it had changed. She thought mostly they would wonder how they themselves figured in, would try to figure out the what-ifs: What if I had done this then, what if I had done that there? What then would have happened?

In Calgary, they stayed with Murryn's uncle in his house on a cliff that looked out over a canyon where Canadian geese swam in the river and flew in and out in small, noisy groups. She felt disappointed in what the city offered to see, a dun expanse except around the river where some pale greens existed and wound along to the high-rises downtown. They sipped their drinks on the back porch and her uncle told them about the growth of Calgary and how hard it was to find a good house or good help for his carpet-cleaning business. The three of them went out for dinner to a steakhouse and then when they got home Wade stayed up with her uncle to hear stories about when Murryn was younger. The next day she told him she did not think she had slept at all; she had dreamed about rivers and not sleeping, and had rolled over in the night to say something to him and he wasn't there. "Oh, yeah," was all Wade said as he concentrated on driving and reading the traffic signals that were turned on their sides, red lights on the left and green lights on the right. Murryn decided not to tell him how she missed him even though she had just seen him, and how she felt cold without his body there beside hers where she could rub her toes against his shins.

They pulled out of Calgary against the press of rush-hour commuters, onto the highway that started to roll as it approached the snowy mountains in the distance. In Canmore, they stopped for gas with the mountains towering around them, sheer cliffs rising up above the treeline from the steep slopes of thick evergreens. Murryn went around the back to the bathroom and Wade went in to pay. When she got back in the car he was flipping through a local real estate guide and started to tell her about the cover story, how real estate prices had boomed in the area with property values tripling in the past five years, how local residents had been pushed out by commuters from the city and retirees looking for summer cottages.

"This is what my dad's afraid will happen with Lake of the Woods," Wade said. "If there was more money in Winnipeg it would have happened already. I keep telling him he's the one who owns the land, it would be good for him. But he doesn't see it that way."

Murryn noticed Wade talked more about real estate values, investments and the stock market in the last little while, and she wondered why these ideas interested him so much when to her they seemed like the boring domain of old men in suits and luxury cars.

"It would be the trade-off," she said. "What would you do if your dad sold his place?"

"He would never sell it."

"How can you be sure?"

"I just am. I don't think he could live anywhere else. He's told me so."

Twenty minutes later they passed through the Banff National Park gates and Murryn read Wade the visitor information from the pamphlet they had been given. High fences bordered the highway on both side and when she pointed them out Wade told her they kept the elk off the highway. The sun shone off water that seemed to be everywhere: standing in the ditches and rushing in the creeks and pouring out of cliffs. Signs indicated the turnoffs to Banff, to Sunshine Village ski resort, to Lake Louise. The traffic thinned as they passed higher into the mountains, and then, as the highway parted from the river it had followed, they saw the signs for Kicking Horse Pass. Wade slowed the car and parked in the "Point of Interest" lot and they stretched and got out into the bright day. More signs at the edge of the parking lot listed facts about Kicking Horse Pass, its elevation at 1,647 m (5,320 ft) above sea level, its history beginning with the Canadian Pacific Railway, its place as a boundary between British Columbia's Yoho National Park and Alberta's Banff National Park. But for Murryn and Wade, only one fact mattered about Kicking Horse Pass: it was the continental divide.

They packed their backpacks and locked the car. A worn path led them up to a picnic site overlooking a clear river rushing over rounded stones and they were suddenly alone in the wild. Murryn imagined trout and salmon living in the river. She crouched down on the banks and placed her flat hand into the water and it felt so cold she could not feel it was wet. From his pack, Wade passed her their blanket and she spread it out where the ground felt level and the roots of the trees burrowed underground. She fished out their lunch and they ate sandwiches as the water rushed past. The size of the place felt so foreign to her, the mountains right there in front of them looked so close; she could see the trees on its flank and the bare rock face up higher, but in her mind she knew it would take days to walk to it. The scale of the landscape fooled her eyes: eyes used to the prairies where if you could see something you could get to it in a day. They ate alone on the bank of the river and she felt the expectations rise in her chest and said, "This can't be the continental divide."

Wade swallowed his mouthful. "What do you mean?"

"The sign at the highway said this was the continental divide but this river is still flowing west to east." She held her hand out toward the river. "We haven't reached the divide yet. The real divide must be around here but this isn't it."

"So lead on, intrepid, let's find it."

Back into the backpack went the blanket and the sandwiches, and they hiked upstream on a path that ran along the bank of the river. Murryn smelled the trees heated by the sun and the rotting leaves underfoot. The brush began to get closer and the hiking tougher as the path started to zigzag back onto itself up a steep incline. She heard the sound of the river grow louder in the distance. The brush crowded the path as it climbed in switchbacks away from the river, and they stopped and then decided to press on. At its peak, the path flattened out to a clearer spot where the brush thinned out. Murryn led Wade to the edge of the clearing where the land fell away. Beyond them, the river boiled down in a wide swath. The noise of the water swelled as they climbed up onto the rocky bluff and took the last few steps to face the river. The cool air pushed by the flowing water blew in their faces. This was it. The water and air rushed down toward them with such power that Murryn felt pulled into the current, as if the outcrop where they stood moved upstream and split the river in a perpetual fork, sending it east and west, tumbling from the glaciers high above to the creeks of the foothills and the rivers of the prairies where it fed cattle and watered gardens.

They retreated to the clearing and Murryn set their picnic on a section of tree stump she found while Wade spread their blanket under a pine tree. The carpet of pine needles and dried leaves wavered in the sunlight as the wind moved the branches of the pine and she felt chilled even in the bright day. They finished their lunch and relaxed. In time, she pulled out and read a biology textbook to prepare for her exam and Wade slept beside her with his head on his bunched up jacket. At some point she must have put her head down and fallen asleep as well. When she awoke it was later in the afternoon and the sun had slipped behind the mountains. She pressed closer to his side and wondered if they were reaching for something they were not ready for; something she might look back on in months or years and feel foolish about in a private way. It almost made her sad to feel so good, with Wade there beside her, with the ground all around them still warm from the heat of the day. They stayed pressed together until the shadows covered more ground than the sunlight and then they descended back to the car, the highway and a chalet on the main street of Banff that they had reserved. The white sheets on her bed felt too clean as she slid between them. She remembered the pine needles crushed under their blanket, the sap coating the stem ends, sticking to the blanket where her and Wade's bodies had pressed down on them. She imagined the rich smell of the sap and decided that she wanted to keep it, for the smell of the sap to be what she remembered from the trip; it made her aware of her clean skin, her movement.

By this force of will, the smell of sap became the clearest thing in her mind when they left for home the next day in the wind and rain and dangerous roads, cars and trucks resting at the end of dark tire streaks on the shoulder and in the ditches. Murryn drove east of Calgary when a television news van raced by and sped into the distance. Wade offered to drive until they passed to calmer weather and Murryn slowed her speed and leaned forward to see the road as the wipers swept across the windshield at high speed. They overtook the television news van just as a camera crew were filming a report at a crash site where a red pickup had gone into the ditch sideways and rolled several times. One of its doors had twisted open and flapped in the wind like a broken limb, the flashing lights of emergency vehicles reflecting on the scene.

Around the middle of the day, the skies cleared and she passed Climax with the cruise control set. Wade slept in the reclined passenger seat. In glances stolen from the road, she watched him breathe. She reached over and stroked the back of her finger across his cheek and swept his hair from his forehead and could hear his breath entering and leaving his body, saw the little hairs that curled and covered the top of his ear when he needed a haircut. Murryn kissed two fingers and brushed them to his lips and then drove on all the way to the border with Manitoba where they switched drivers and pressed on past midnight to get home.

Two months and three days later, they celebrated her birthday and Wade gave her a wooden box he had made lined with a linen napkin wrapped around a pine cone. It was a warm summer evening when she opened it and the sap inside the pine cone had softened and run out of its casing. She lifted the box and pulled out the pine cone and smelled the sap, which was soon on her fingers and on his hands and on his neck. They went out for dinner and their utensils stuck to their hands through the appetizer and main course. At the end of the night, Murryn took the pine cone, wrapped it again in linen, placed it on a shelf beside her bed so she could dream of rivers and adventures. When she and Wade had tougher times through that summer, with him working at Lake of the Woods and with her trying to keep up her grades while in a work-placement for her program, she forgot about the pine cone and she went out to concerts and festivals with her girlfriends, and danced with the boys who asked her. Once Wade returned in the fall they went for a drive out to the west, to the open prairies where the blue sky extended down to the flat horizon in a huge arc of distance, and he told her he had missed her, and had needed some space to see just how important she was to him. Part of her believed him and part of her did not want to be taken in, and in the end she kissed him and told him they were both older and wiser and better for their experiences; though in her heart she did not feel so sure they were better for it, and wished in a way that everything could have stayed perfect forever.

THERE AND BACK AGAIN
—October, 1998—

IT WAS JUST AFTER WADE AND GILL TURNED ONTO THE HIGHWAY leading to Mariapolis that the light began to seep into the day. The flat farmland spread out around them as Wade took a sip of his coffee and felt the warmth spread through his chest. Smells of leather and gun powder and hunting hung in the Land Cruiser as the tires hummed along the highway. Wade yawned and opened up his layers of clothing, unbuttoned his green sweater from the collar and laid his toque on the dashboard where silver frost rimmed the window. As he looked out at the southern horizon, he saw stars on one side and a milky sky on the other. This early drive had become a ritual for him and Gill, and every year since Wade was twelve they had set out from Winnipeg, hunted the sloughs and potholes for ducks and geese, and stayed over in Mariapolis to do the same the next day. Every year a few things changed, new gear bought, the timing of the trip, the number of birds in the sky, but looking back at the photos of previous trips, not much marked the changes, and years blurred together so ages became hard to recognize. Wade and Gill talked about the city, how Winnipeg always seemed locked in a struggle between decay and rebirth, each chance at renewal never quite living up to expectations as the weight of history hampered the present and the city's people ran out of energy. The tall shapes of the grain elevators and silos began appearing against the eastern sky. The telephone poles and wires, roads and train tracks stretched across the landscape they passed, the right angles shaping and cutting the land, every mile marked by a new road at a new section. The only other vehicles passing them on the road were the big transport trucks pushing walls of air. Silhouettes and shapes showed in the dim distance, a herd of Holstein cattle in front of a tree line, a bluff containing a farmhouse and silver grain bins pushed back in perspective against bluffs on the horizon.

"It's funny," said Gill after a few section miles. "When they needed navy boys for the war, they chose them from the prairies. Not much to see but a whole hell of a lot of it. "

Wade nodded and sipped his coffee again and did not give away to Gill the tickle he always felt when Gill surprised him with the things he knew. Instead, Wade told Gill about the Natives who lived on the prairies, which he had learned about in a third-year humanities elective. "When the buffalo herds used to spread to the horizon," he said. "They had directions, north, east, south, west, before white men came."

"Those were the Assiniboine or Cree?"

"Assiniboine. The Cree were more north and east of here. In the forests where you are."

"And the Ojibwa," Gill said, knowing the people at Lake of the Woods.

In the brightening dawn they slipped through a motionless small town. A few farmers' trucks sat at the coffee shop with the big-rig operators and Wade kept a sharp eye on the skies for birds. As the years had passed, and Wade had changed, these hunting trips had changed as well. He still felt the excitement. He still woke as soon as the alarm went, his things sitting by the door packed from the night before, his sandwiches in the fridge waiting, his thermos cleaned and sitting on the counter. The headlights of the Land Cruiser swept up into the driveway and he had the front door opened before Gill stepped out. But as he had grown older, the apprehension of being with Gill fell away, and Wade began to feel at ease with his father.

Gill swung the Land Cruiser off the highway and along a gravel road heading south between fields of sunflowers with their heads bowed. For the last half-hour the ducks had been flying over the fields on both sides of the roads and, as Wade and Gill watched the patterns of ducks, they talked about where they would hunt first. A big slough would be tough to hunt without good cover. They could set up in a big slough and wait for the flights of ducks to return from the fields or sneak into a smaller slough. The small slough on George MacKinnon's land, west of where they saw the ducks stubbling in a harvested wheat field, seemed to present the best opportunity. Wade and Gill knew George from past years they had hunted with him. In those years, George had always given them permission to hunt on his land, and, in the past few years, he had said not even to bother asking him, just to go ahead and shoot, as long as they brought him a few of the ducks they shot.

Wade and Gill drove past the road into George's empty yard and only a black mongrel dog trotted across the lot. The slough lay beyond the yard after the rise in the land. Gill retold Wade the story about how George had polio in the forties, the same way he always told the story when they arrived at George's farm. Wade watched as small flights of birds banked and angled around the sky over the slough. Wade and Gill came to the top of the rise and before them, looking promising, as a few birds wheeled down to land, the MacKinnon slough spread out between the fields to the horizon. Gill inched the Land Cruiser by the slough on the cattle path to get a good look at where the ducks were holding and where the cover grew well. Wade rolled down his window and the loud quacking of mallards drifted to his ears. Gill pulled the Land Cruiser off the road opposite the slough and he and Wade got out to get ready. They pressed their doors closed so they clicked shut with the least amount of sound. Wade popped off his boots heel on toe, heel on toe, and wriggled into the hip waders. Gill cinched the suspenders tight over Wade's shoulders and tied the drawstring tight around the top. Wade held his arms out at his sides.

"How do I look?" he asked, setting his hands on his hips.

"Like a hunter," Gill answered, shaking his head. "I won't say what kind."

Wade smiled and reached into the back of the Land Cruiser for his gun case. He unzipped it and pulled out his shotgun, a semi-automatic twelve gauge. Gill pulled out his own shotgun, a newer version of the classic twelve-gauge, 101, over-and-under. They each grabbed half a box of number four shells for their pockets and whistles on lanyards for around their necks. Dressed and ready, Wade and Gill crossed the crowned road and kneeled in the ditch on the other side. Wade dropped a shell into the action of his gun and slid it shut, holding the lever to keep the metal mechanisms quiet. He slid two more shells into the chamber of the gun and made sure the safety stuck out to the right of the trigger guard, clacked on. Gill was ready too and they whispered together.

Wade asked, "Did you see the birds on the south side?"

"Yep. And the west too. Two groups," Gill said and gave his whistle a toot to make sure it was clear and worked. "Which way's the wind from?"

"North. Northwest maybe."

"Good. We'll come in from this side and then spread out."

Wade pointed at a point of higher ground to the southwest

where the cattails stood taller than anywhere else. "Okay, you head there. I'll go around further to the west, then into the wind. Give me ten minutes. If they get up, they should head away from us. But the wind's pretty strong, they'll struggle."

"Yep. And they'll stay low. The birds who peel off should be in range."

"Okay. Ready?" Wade looked at Gill crouched beside him and their eyes locked, both pairs blue and clear and bright. A pair of mallards went over, the sun glinting off their feathers as they swept around and down into the slough.

"Good luck," Gill said.

Tall grass around the slough bowed low as the wind pressed over it in waves. A chill remained in the air and some of the grass still held drops of dew frozen on the underside. Wade pulled his camouflage hat down to his brows and set out through the grass down to the reeds and into the edge of the water where the soft ground sucked at his waders and he sank to his ankles. After about ten minutes of waiting for Gill to get around to a point of land, Wade set off again, careful where he placed each step, aiming his feet at solid points he could be sure of, letting the grass sweep over his body and close behind him. "Always look back when you go in so you'll know what to look for on your way out," Gill had told him when they first hunted together, and Wade followed the instruction without thinking of it.

They shot the MacKinnon slough, then others along the chain of roads around George's farm, and got some birds and missed some birds that they shot at late or at the ends of range. Some sloughs held wary birds that had been shot more than a few times already and they got up as soon as the Land Cruiser stopped. Other birds in other sloughs had to be startled to take to the wing, and Wade snuck so close to a group of four mallards he had to yell at them when he popped up out of the reeds to get them to fly.

Wade and Gill stopped for lunch when the heat from the sun

made the many layers of their clothing too warm to continue. Wade started plucking the birds they had shot and was into the down by the time Gill brought the orange cooler from the Land Cruiser. Wade and Gill had shot four mallards, a teal and two canvasbacks, and planned to take the mallards to MacKinnon's. They talked about how they would hide the meat from the dog so that George could still find it. At the same time, Gill put together his sandwiches and Wade kidded him about his skill in the kitchen. Since he had turned twenty, Wade had made his own sandwiches, always the night before in an assembly line on the counter. Gill never made his sandwiches the night before, preferring instead to bring everything with him in his cooler and assemble them on the spot. He liked to be flexible, to make them on an as-needed basis, one more if he felt hungry, half if he was close to full. It never failed that Gill ended up complaining about a sprig of grass or the grit of dirt in one of his sandwiches and Wade gave him the speech they both knew: "If you'd only do it my way."

The plucked mallards lined up on the flattened grass, their wings drawn tightly in, their orange feet cramped, the webbing folded together. The only feathers left on the birds were on the heads and ends of the wings; everything in between looked the same as a skinny chicken, ready for the freezer or, with a little cleaning, the oven. Wade nipped and tossed the fine grey down to the wind and it floated away like cattails gone to seed. Gill finished making a sandwich and walked over from the Land Cruiser, two hands on the sandwich to keep it together.

"You're doing a fine job," he said to Wade in between bites. "Maybe you should do them all this year."

"That's okay. I wouldn't want you to get out of practice."

"I've done plenty," Gill said. "That's not a worry."

He supervised beside Wade, eating and watching him work. The white and pimpled skin of the ducks was dotted with small spots of blood where the shotgun pellets had hit. Wade wiped the sticky blood off his hands on the grass and asked Gill what time they had to leave the next day, since they had to be back in the city at three for Christine's wedding. They agreed to get in the morning shoot, clean the birds and be on the road by eleven, since she wanted them there at two-thirty.

Wade unlatched the cooler and fished out his ham sandwich while a few clouds appeared in the sky and skated across in front of the sun. He saw Gill watching the clouds and asked him if he had ever met Gary, the man Christine was marrying. Gill said he had met Gary back when Christine had been in law school, and that he had actually introduced them to each other at a party for an old-timers hockey team both he and Gary played on. The guys on the old-timers hockey team called Gary "Slick" and he had a reputation with the ladies.

"You think he's slick?" Wade said.

"I haven't talked to him in almost twenty years. I understand he's a good businessman though."

"Yep. He's always on some deal."

"Is he still in real estate?"

Wade nodded with his mouth full of sandwich and grabbed the canteen of water from the Land Cruiser. He drank some and rubbed his hands together to clean the blood and mustard, then wiped them on the waders, leaving four long dark streaks on either thigh to wash off next time he went in to get a duck. "He's got his own company."

"Does he still have that partner? Arlen or Aiken?"

"Aikens," Wade said and took an apple from the cooler.

"So what do you think of Gary?"

"He's okay. Mom seems happy when she's with him." Wade felt like he did not have much to say to his father about Gary. Wade did not know Gary well and had no interest in knowing him well. The one day they had spent together golfing with Gary's buddies at St. Charles had been fun for Wade, since they treated him like one of the guys and bought beers from the drinks cart and told the same tasteless jokes that Wade thought they would have told if he had not been there. "But I don't see them much. And he doesn't have to make me happy. I went for dinner with them last week at Le Beaujolais." Wade saw Gill raise his eyebrows and he explained to him Le Beaujolais was a fancy French restaurant in St. Boniface. The clouds had grown thicker and darker and heaved across the sky in layers of whites and greys. Gill asked Wade about the house he had just bought, and what it felt like to own his own place. They talked about the renovations Wade planned to make, and having Murryn move in with him, and the way the planning for Christine's wedding had occurred. Wade noticed for the first time how Gill's hair around the temple had begun to grey, and he told Gill that he thought that Christine's marriage could turn out to be a good thing. He thought she had waited for him to get set up on his own before she had decided to marry, and then he asked Gill how he felt about the wedding.

"Sounds like it'll be a good meal," Gill said as he looked at the sky and leaned back on his elbows on the tall grass. The wind flapped open the collar of his green hunting sweater under his down vest. "Do you think it's strange I'm going?"

"I think an ex-husband going to his ex-wife's wedding is strange. But I don't think you going to Mom's wedding is strange. What would be really strange is if you were giving the bride away."

Gill snorted and laughed. "That is so," he said. "That is so." A few ducks flew under the moving clouds while most rested in sloughs for the middle of the day. "What do you think about all this marriage talk?"

"For Mom?"

"Yep," Gill said. "And for yourself. You think you and Murryn will get married?"

"Mom and Gary have been dating awhile. But she's dated guys before. So I never really thought about her getting married. When she told me I was surprised. I didn't know what to think."

Wade broke a blade of grass and told Gill he had been pretty suspicious of Gary at first, but then he saw Christine happy with him and what else could he want? He knew it was not really his business but he would be lying if he said he did not think about it. In the end, he wanted his mother to be happy, and she seemed happy, and so he guessed he felt happy for her. Gill told him he thought it mattered to Christine what Wade thought, since it would matter to him if he ever thought about getting remarried. They talked more about getting married and Gill told Wade he had been seeing a woman from Kenora named Cheryl who ran the local radio station, though he did not think they would get married since they both had tried it before. Wade said that he remembered how all his friends thought it was strange how Gill and Christine remained close even though they were divorced, how lots of other parents had awful divorces involving lawyers and custody battles that lasted years.

"With you and Mom it's like you were the right people but under the wrong circumstances, or the wrong institution." Wade looked at his hands and the blood in the folds of the skin, under the nails. "Maybe that's just me hoping. But you guys were honest about things. You respected each other enough not to be petty. You liked each other enough as people to do good things."

"And we liked each other enough to know we couldn't be together."

"Yeah."

"And you, Wade," Gill said. "You were a big part of it."

Wade nodded and wanted to say something else but as he started the wind snatched his words and carried them away into the rustling grass, and he did not know what to say. He pried one fingernail under another to scrape the blood out and knew there had been a lot of things his parents had done for him in their lives, and how different their lives would have been without him.

"How old were you when you got married, Dad?"

"It was 'seventy, so I was twenty-two. Your mother was twenty."

"You were twenty-two?"

"Yep. Two years younger than you are," Gill said and with a little grin passing to his lips. "That's why I was asking about it. Don't think you can duck things so easily. A little heart-to-heart and I'll forget what I asked you?"

Wade smiled and flicked dried blood into the long grass.

"Me and Murryn," Wade said to himself as much as to Gill. "Well, we won't be married for awhile. Her parents are divorced and my parents are divorced and that doesn't invite us to rush to the altar." Wade told Gill that he had thought about getting married to Murryn, and they had talked about it in a joking way, as if the whole thing were hard to imagine. Right then, Wade and Murryn were moving in with each other, and if anything changed, Wade told Gill he would let him know.

Distant goose calls sounded out from the sky and drew the attention of Wade and Gill to the high, migrating flock passing overhead, a long, trailing, unbalanced V of specks in the sky. As the calls passed Wade wondered how women saw his father. They must think good things of him, he was attractive in his own way, fun and honest and interesting, good to spend time with. Wade had met a few of the women Gill had dated over the years but none of them had lasted very long, though Wade had liked them all. He watched as Gill stood and stretched his back from sitting on the ground in the grass, brought the plucked birds over to the Land Cruiser by their feet, the wingtips fluttering in the wind. More dirty clouds rolled in from the west. Once the cooler and birds were stowed away, Wade and Gill got into the Land Cruiser, spun up through the ditch and sped back along the road to MacKinnon's; the tires threw mud cakes into the air.

The rain finally started falling as Wade and Gill drove out of George MacKinnon's yard and turned south onto the road. They had almost slipped away from MacKinnon's with George being out. They had left the ducks inside the front door and been back in the Land Cruiser turning out of the yard when George's red International clogged the ruts of the drive. He had offered them coffee inside and, because George lived alone since the passing of his wife Clarice, both Wade and Gill saw that going inside meant no hunting done for hours. Instead, they had pulled off the track and yakked through the windows while the clouds ploughed across the sky, and after ten minutes, they had made their escape.

"We just made it," Gill said, heading south out on the road and clicking the wipers on.

"You were lucky to get a word in edgewise."

Gill told Wade he did not feel great about leaving George, but that he had trouble understanding what he said. Only half the conversation ended up out loud, and Gill could understand how this could happen since he lived alone as well, and some days he ended up not seeing another soul and his own voice sounded strange. The wipers squeaked across the windshield and Gill clicked them off. There was no intermittent setting and so a regular on-off click every ten seconds kept the windshield clear.

"Cheryl stays with me sometimes."

Wade looked at Gill steering the big black wheel of the Land Cruiser. His eyes wandered the fields along the road as he thought about his father and Cheryl, dating and kissing and washing each other in the shower of the cabin after having sex. Gill looked back at him and they smiled at each other.

"That's real good," Wade said. "She stays with you sometimes."

The Land Cruiser came over another rise in the road and a large slough that they knew well from past trips spread out in the hollow. The road passed through the edge of the slough; reeds and water rippled in the wind on both sides, ducks traded back and forth over the road, circling and landing in wakes. Wade wanted to say something to Gill about Cheryl; he had a notion to kid him about her, to flip roles and ask him the same questions Gill had asked him about Murryn. But he could see things for Gill felt new and exciting and undecided. And so he said nothing. The wipers continued to click on and squeak across the windshield and click off, and Wade held his eyes on the slough for flying ducks.

The Land Cruiser crept by and Wade glimpsed open water through the reeds. Out from the road, where a smaller section of the slough was flanked by harvested wheat fields, and it looked good for a sneak, the birds concentrated in the corners. Wade suggested they walk up on the ducks to see if they could get some shots with the wind coming in at them. Near the top of the next rise, Gill swung the Land Cruiser off the road and through the ditch. Wade and Gill got out and touched their doors shut, pressing them to latch. They retrieved their shotguns from the back, a few more shells for their pockets to replace the ones discharged, and set off in the ditch opposite the slough. Wade walked below Gill, in the water of the ditch, the hip waders creaking as they folded into the wrinkles at the knee and ankle. When they descended closer, Gill duck-walked up over the crowned road and angled himself into the reeds a few steps. Wade creaked on in the ditch and then duck-walked over the crowned road to the cover of the other corner by the road. Wade knew that he had to be quiet as he moved; if one duck grew too wary and jumped up into the air, the rest would follow, and unless a foolish young bird wheeled over in range, the hunt would be over.

Wade took a few steps into the reeds and waited for Gill to find cover before he descended into the slough, the reeds thick and crackling, the ground soft and sucking. He strained his eyes ahead to see as he heard swishing splashes of moving water: not a good sign. The ducks might not know what he was, but they could hear something big moving and would not wait around. He stopped and tried to see ahead but the reeds made it impossible to pick anything out. He took another step and the ducks were up, the splash of their leap, the whirring of their wings, followed by the peeping sound they made when they flew. Wade could only hope the ducks would fly over Gill or wheel around in the wind so he could get a shot. A few minutes passed and nothing came over. Then he heard Gill's whistle and knew the hunt was over. He slogged back out to the road along the crease he had left in the reeds, and Gill walked towards him on the road.

"Nothing?" he called out and Gill shook his head and pointed off to the other side of the road where the ducks had gone.

"They knew what was happening," Gill said when he came closer. "As soon as I came close they were up."

"Yep. They got up right away but didn't go far. I watched them land. They must be about a hundred yards in on this side," Wade said and pointed to a larger slough across the road from the one they had hunted.

"You want to give it a run?"

"Yeah. One of us should be on point and the other go in and flush the birds. The same as we did here last year."

"Okay, you give me the waders."

"I'll flush," Wade said, knowing it would be tough walking and he had the young legs.

But Gill shook his head. "I'll put the waders on and go. You know how to get in on the point."

Wade nodded and he and Gill laid their guns down on the grass, the two wooden stocks spooned. They swapped the waders for the rubber boots and Wade uncoiled and cinched the suspenders tight on Gill's shoulders, bunched the drawstring around the top to keep water from splashing in. Wade turned to the slough and crossed the road into the edge of the reeds. The falling mist blurred his sight for a second as he looked back and gave Gill a wave before starting in, headed for an isthmus of land that stretched out into the north end of the slough. Wade had discovered it the previous year, the willow and cattail growth covering him to the shoulders as he waited for the birds. With the right wind, anyone could sneak out and wait on the isthmus without being seen or heard. The southwest wind had picked up to a perfect pitch for sneaking in. The fine mist spit straight into Wade's eyes as the sound of his approach was carried away behind him, up beyond the rise of harvested field, away from the ducks. Wade stopped for a second and put the butt of his shotgun on the ground, let it lean away from him, suspended by the rigid, corded strength of the reeds. He unwound the tangles of grass hooked around the crook of each ankle, retrieved his shotgun and slung it over his shoulder. Thinking better, he unslung his gun and held it ready in his hands, diagonal in front of his chest, a quick snap to bring the butt to his shoulder, ready for the chance at a shot. The safety clicked off and then back on, back and forth through the trigger guard, between his finger and thumb. He settled onto one knee and waited.

Sometimes, when he waited in a slough with his gun in his hands, when he knew the safety was on, he pressed the trigger and felt it rest against the catch, locked into place. Wade tapped it with his finger as he waited on the isthmus, keeping the muzzle pointed at the sky or the ground. With the fine mist on his face, Wade wondered what would happen if once, the safety was not on. He imagined the feeling of the impact of the shot right before the sound of the explosion, the texture of ground beef and thick, rich blood. The thought of what could happen remained a cold reminder that it was a loaded gun he held in his hands.

Some ducks took off, swung into the wind and landed in a different part of the slough. Wade pulled his gloves from his pockets and smelled the dry, tanned leather. He put them on and rested his gun on his bent knee in front of him. The quiet tension of getting in to the isthmus faded, replaced by the calm of waiting. Where Wade crouched he was hidden in the wavering reeds. He looked around and blinked away the accumulated mist on his eyelashes. It was funny, he thought, the way you could squat down amongst the tall reeds and the wind would disappear, and you could feel like the world was small and consisted of just you and the reeds surrounding you and the patch of sky above. Wade thought of the men in the trenches in World War I; soldiers who spent so much time staring up at the sky, they could map the stars by memory, day or night. He felt sure he never would be in a trench in a war.

A rotting smell came from the reeds that fell year after year and now lay matted underneath his feet. New reeds grew up through the old and stretched straight and tall, up through the brown bodies of past years. If Wade stood up the fields of wheat would roll out in rows in every direction and he would be tiny and the sky all around him huge, so huge it was dizzying to look up at. And it was even funny too, that sometimes, when you were waiting for the ducks, after you had busted your ass to get out on point, it would be just as easy to fall asleep in the soft marsh grass as to wait and be alert and squint into the sky.

Dressed in their best, guests milled around the family, chatting and laughing and waiting to be summoned for the start of the wedding. Circles of friends and acquaintances mingled and mixed with other circles, and people called to each other while introductions were made. A few folks mentioned how nice it seemed to have a wedding in your own house; how it seemed like a really nice way to symbolize new beginnings in the place they would occur. Candles glowed on shelves and tables and ivy curled around the banister. The furniture had been moved out of the living room and folding chairs set up for the guests during the ceremony. The dining room table stood at the front of the room acting as the altar, flowers lay arranged on it around more glowing candles.

By the time Wade and Gill arrived almost everyone else had a drink in them. Wade's mother had told them to be at her house by two thirty and now it was five to three. The ceremony was set to begin at three. Wade and Gill went around to the back door instead of going through all the people at the front. Just as they entered the kitchen, a woman's voice started herding people into the living room where the ceremony was ready to begin. Wade wondered if Christine had been watching at the window and waiting for him and Gill before giving the cue.

The traffic of people bottlenecked into the living room full of humming and talking and motion. The post-ceremony spread of food lay plattered-out in the kitchen. Wade and Gill looked at each other and at the food, feeling the same hunger. Their rush to get back in time for the ceremony had precluded their usual stop at Nick's Inn, where the burgers came with chili and onions and the french fries were served hot and crisp and almost burnt.

"It looks good," Wade said.

"Yep, your mother can still cook."

"She and the corner shop. But we shouldn't touch it."

"She'll know," Gill said and scratched his head.

"But it looks good."

"We better go."

"But it looks good," Wade said, grinning to Gill as they headed through the rooms for the living room. "We could volunteer to help with the serving."

"That's always a good plan."

Wade and Gill clicked over the tile to the gaping front foyer of the house. Cleaned up and shaved, they looked sharp in their suits. The peach and grey and navy backs of the last few guests filed into the living room from the foyer and Wade and Gill prepared to fall into line.

At the same time, the front door sucked opened and presented Gary and his best man in their tuxedos. Wade and Gill halted in mid-foyer and Gary and his best man halted on the grey mat. For a second, Gary's face showed surprise, then searching, questions, and a toothsome smile. Wade did not know what to do or say; a moment of chances hung in the air. A fight scene flashed into Wade's mind, the actions ruthless. If Gary or his best man ever made a move for him or Gill he knew what he would do. Then, as quickly as the thought came, it changed and he worried about getting blood on his white shirt.

"Gary," Gill said, taking a step forward and holding out his hand. "You look nice."

"Gill, you too," Gary said, shaking his hand. "You don't look any different than the last time I saw you. Less hair that's all."

Gill rubbed his stubbled scalp and smiled in a friendly way.

"Wade," Gary said and Wade stepped forward, shook his hand.

"Gary," Wade said.

"This is my best man, Mike Tinkham," Gary said, making the appropriate gestures. "Mike, this is Gill Dubois. And this is Wade, Christine's son." Wade and Gill shook hands with Mike and it was like a meeting of the board. Wade's hand closed around Mike Tinkham's and he knew he could squeeze it if he wanted. It was a stupid thing to know. But his hands were bigger and he was stronger and that was his first thought. If he had to he could handle Mike Tinkham and his cold smooth hands.

"Well, we should get in there," Gill said, raising an arm and side-stepping towards the living room. "Don't want to miss the ceremony. Good luck, guys."

"Thanks," Gary said.

Christine had name tags on the seats and in the second row, Wade Dubois and Gill Dubois found their spots. They pocketed their tags and sat down and smoothed their jackets. A violinist in a black suit stood at the front corner of the room, set his bow to his instrument and introduced a gentle melody. People chatted with their neighbours as everyone waited for the ceremony to begin. Wade recognized the minister from the church off to the side at the front, swaying along with the violinist. The minister's grey robe was harnessed at his waist by a golden rope and the folds below it softened his girth.

"It's baroque," Gill whispered to Wade.

"What?"

"It's baroque. What the violinist is playing." Gill linked the fingers of his hands on his lap. "Your mother and I used to listen to it. She loves this music so we used to listen to it. In the car." Wade saw his father's lips move slightly, dahing and deeing to the music. "I can just imagine her trying to explain to this fellow what she meant." He nodded at the bent soloist. "She has an awful ear for music and I'm sure she would have hummed it."

"You miss her sometimes?" Wade asked.

Gill listened and looked at Wade. "Right now, yes."

"What's the song called?"

"I don't know. I can't remember. The ink on the tape I have rubbed off years ago. Some of the tape's stretched too. In places it plays like molasses and there's a lot of sound in the background, like bacon frying."

The violinist let the song trail off in a long swooping note. The chatterers sitting in the room had all stopped and the intensity of the song, as it had risen and captured more and more of the attention of the gathered, lingered over the crowd though the song had ended. Slowly, someone clapped their hands and then everyone clapped, as if the intimacy acknowledged itself. The violinist bowed without looking out and then reconfigured himself for another song. The applause calmed and Wade felt a fullness in his chest and a tightness in his throat. He had known for a long time that this event was coming; Christine and Gary had been engaged for two years, they had lived together for six. Wade looked at Gill seated beside him, still dahing and deeing to the music of the violinist, and then he had to look away. It was just his father sitting there beside him, right? Wade felt like something escaped him. Since he had been seven and Gill had explained to him that he and Christine would not be getting back together, Wade had not held any illusions about his parents. His mother was a city girl and his father belonged at the lake.

Somewhere along the line, they had both recognized they could not be happy and together at the same time. Wade wondered, was it not just as simple as that? The same collar he wore five of every seven days to work suddenly grabbed at his throat and he turned his eyes upwards to keep his tears from falling.

The violinist ended the song and looked to the back of the room for instructions. The ceremony was set to begin. Gary stood ready at the door. Mike Tinkham and the bridesmaid Judy linked hands on their way down the aisle. Wade concentrated on these things, the details of the ceremony. The cuff links on Mike Tinkham's wrists could not be rented. Rented ones were never as nice. What kind of flowers were in Judy's bouquet?

Wade stood and smiled as he heard the familiar notes of the wedding procession played. Christine entered and cameras clicked as people leaned around each other for better sightlines at the bride. A murmur went through the room as the wedding march continued to play: here comes the bride. Wade lost sight of Christine behind a throng of wide-brimmed hats. He turned to the front where Mike and Judy had split to either side of the altar and Gary stood tapping the shining toe of his left shoe. Gary shifted his weight on his feet and smiled at Wade, the same smile he used when he closed a deal, all teeth, twin rows of incisors and canines, even and uniform like rows of corn. Wade smiled back at him and for a second he wanted to stop the wedding. How was his mother marrying this fucker? Didn't she know what a prick he was? And at that same moment, as Wade felt seized by the feeling that he had to do something, he realized that he could not. The relationship between Christine and Gary worked for them for their reasons. They had been friends before they dated, they shared common interests and played tennis and golf together, went out for dinner and on cruises in the Caribbean. It worked for them and Wade had no right to question it, because it worked for him as well. He was the one who joined them at the club and played the back nine with Gary when Christine wanted to quit. He benefited when Gary made the call to a friend in Human Resources at Great-West Life to get Wade's resumé flagged and brought to the top of the stack.

Wade saw Gary continue to smile, then take a step forward. Christine looped her arm under Gary's arm and they strode forward together to stand before the minister. The guests sat and some fanned themselves. Over the next twenty minutes they stood and sat again as they were instructed by the minister. Readings came from Corinthians and Blake and Shakespeare. Wade counted five instances of God mentioned, but only in passing; three from the minister and two from the readings, though Blake was never clear in his meaning. Before Wade knew it, Gary and Christine had kissed and signed the register and the ceremony had ended. A 1930s roadster pulled into the driveway and its vintage horn groaned. Gary and Christine stepped into the back seat and waved, then departed to have their photos taken and to meet the guests at the reception at the old Fort Garry Hotel. Gill and Wade walked out to Wade's Honda and drove to the reception making small talk about the ceremony and the decorations and the way everything had come together. They had drinks and mingled, ate dinner when it was served to them and gradually, Wade started to enjoy the evening. He talked with Gill about the wedding and listened to Gill talk to the rest of their table. It was a new experience to see his father at a fancy social occasion and Gill impressed Wade with his ability to make small talk with people about Okanagan wines, World Cup soccer and travel in Greece.

By the time Murryn entered the Fort Garry ballroom, dinner had finished and the dancing had begun. Her conference had run late and since she was still new to the position she did not feel comfortable leaving before the end. Wade saw her come in from the marble foyer because he had watched for her, and he walked over to greet her with a smile.

"Hi," he said and kissed her on the lips. "You look good. Great, really."

"You too. You hunters clean up pretty well."

"Did my best," he said and kissed her again. "I'm glad you're here."

Wade held her hand and walked with her into the ballroom. He told her about the wedding and the 1930s roadster and his impression of the minister. Murryn had questions about everything and the details Wade provided did not satisfy her curiosity. When Murryn asked how the ceremony had gone and how Christine had looked, Wade told her what he thought, that the ceremony had gone smoothly and his mother had looked pretty, but Murryn wanted to hear more; more about the colours of the décor and the nature of the vows, what the bridesmaid's dress looked like and how Christine had done her hair. She also wanted to see the wedding ring, which Wade had not noticed. By the time they arrived at the table where Wade had sat with Gill, he recognized he was frustrating Murryn, and told her to get the full story for herself from Christine, who was out of the hall but would be returning soon.

They sat together on one side of the table and Murryn told him about the conference, a disguised trade show, companies trying to gain the attentions of clients for the coming season. Wade listened as he always did, enjoying the stories and rumours from a company other than Great-West Life. Murryn's position as a product representative for Dynomex Pharmaceuticals netted her a good income at a medium-sized company as well as a good benefits program and growth potential. Wade remembered his shift volunteering behind the bar and decided it could wait a few minutes. Murryn told him she hated the conferences she had to attend. "Most of the other reps are middle-aged men. Nice family, kids, minivans, suburbs. They don't blatantly hit on me. But I feel sick after I talk to them. Like they're thinking about me in ways I don't want to imagine. I'm the pretty girl to them."

"They don't say anything though?"

"They're in town for two, three days at most and it gives them a kind of courage," Murryn said and put her hand on Wade's leg. "But I can't do the pretty girl routine much longer." Wade listened as she told him how she just felt gross, that it was no mystery how attractive women helped the sales process, that her boss did not help and had made it clear that nothing would trouble him but falling sales numbers. At a break in the conversation Wade told her he had to tend bar for an hour.

"Okay," Murryn said. "I'll go and see your mother. Congratulate her." They both stood up and kissed, Wade still holding her hand. "I'll come and see you in a bit."

"Okay. See you."

"In a bit," Murryn said and they separated.

As Wade and Murryn had spoken, Gill had watched them acting their life right beside him without them noticing. Wade was so close and casual with this girl who Gill knew mostly through his son's words and actions. Gill watched as they fractured off in differing directions. The crowd closed around Wade in a second but Murryn remained visible and Gill continued to watch her. She waited for another woman to finish talking to Christine, then Murryn walked up and hugged her. The hug was not as Gill had hugged Christine with his arms wrapped around her, but a girl's hug, their arms bent up over the other's back instead of circling around embracing. Murryn then talked to Christine for a while and they laughed and gestured like friends. Soon, Christine was pulled away by another friend, her attention never able to rest in one place too long, and Murryn circulated around the hall, stopping to talk, waving, smiling her public face until she was back at Gill's table.

"Anyone sitting here, Gill?" Murryn asked as she stood over him.

"All yours."

Murryn slid down beside Gill at the round table and crossed her legs. He offered her a drink from the water pitcher full of clicking ice.

"I'd love one," she said and flipped over a glass. "Thanks."

"You're welcome," Gill said, refilling his own glass as well. "Now, what should we drink to?"

"Health and happiness for the bride and groom, of course."

"To health and happiness for the bride and groom, of course," Gill said. They clinked glasses and drank their water. "Powerful stuff," Gill said and wiped his mouth.

"I'll have another," Murryn said and pushed her glass over.

Gill filled her glass and watched her drink it and understood his son's attraction to this girl.

"So why're you sitting over here by yourself?"

Gill leaned his elbows on the table. "I don't know too many people. I've seen the one I wanted to see."

"Christine?" Murryn said and Gill nodded once. "She looks great." Gill nodded once again and looked at the bride dancing rings around the dance floor in the arms of her father.

"What do you think she sees in him?" he asked Murryn.

"Gary?" Murryn said. "He's good looking for an older guy. He's a good talker, outgoing, gets along well with people. I don't know, I haven't thought about it. He seems to know a lot, worldly, if that's the right word."

Gill craned over the edge of the table leaning on his elbows. "He's got money, he's stable."

"Yeah, I guess as much as we'd like to think those things don't matter, they do in a way. Not so much to me, but maybe more when you get older. When you've left your ideals."

Gill weighed this assessment in his mind. "Maybe that's true."

"It's hard to find something that's always true," Murryn said. "I think that's why lots of people get married. To have something that's supposed to be permanent and stable. To have something to be sure of."

"That's pretty wise of you."

Murryn stopped to look at her hands, clipping her growing idea. "I didn't mean to get up on my soapbox."

"No, that's fine. It's good to talk like this. I like it." Gill had an impulse to reach across the table and touch her hands but he did not. Instead, the dance floor caught his attention and he watched Christine finish dancing with her nephew.

"How was hunting?" Murryn asked, trying to return to easy talk.

"Good. It was good. We got a limit of mallards the first day. But no geese. Saw some, but none within range."

"You boys had a good time together?"

"We did. Wade's a good lead shot and he knows the wind well, which is important." Gill dug into bird talk and hunting talk like a teacher. Murryn's conference and the wedding ceremony slipped into words between them and it started to feel easier. As the people at the wedding walked by, Gill and Murryn laughed and shared stories. Wade played in some of the stories but not all. Often in the Wade stories, they each only knew one part of the story and this was their chance to hear another record of the events. As Murryn finished telling Gill about the time Wade taught her to fish, Gary stopped at the table and held out his hand.

"Murryn, do you want to dance?" he said.

Murryn looked at the hand with the big blue and gold Grey Cup ring Gary had won as a board member of the Winnipeg Blue Bombers. "Thanks, Gary, but my feet are sore and I might lend a hand at the bar in a few minutes."

"Wade's doing it right now," he said and looked at Gill. "He's fine. I just saw him."

"Well, I'm going to go see him too. There's something I wanted to ask him." Murryn stood, straightened and patted her hand onto Gary's palm. "I'll go and do it now," she said and slid past him.

"Sure," Gary said and flicked his eyes over at Gill. "How about you, Gill, do you want to dance?"

"Not for me, Gary. I lead."

"Then no dancing," Gary said and sat in the chair Murryn had left, pushing her glass into the wrinkled tablecloth. "What do you say, old Gill?"

Gill leaned back in his chair and raised his eyebrows. Gary looked around at his guests and the tables. "Not much, old Gary."

"Gill, do you know what a newly married guy needs?"

Gill shook his head.

"A couple of hours alone with the bride between the ceremony and the reception."

"That's an idea," he said to Gary. "Did you run it by Christine?"

"I'm just kidding, buddy. There's no way she'd go for that. No negotiations." Gary spun the big blue and gold ring on his finger. "Listen, Gill, there's something I've wanted to ask you. You know the land around Lake of the Woods as well as anyone, right?"

"I suppose."

"Well, I've been looking at it for a long time. Maybe not that long, but since Christine and I've been together, I don't know, three or four years. She told me stories about how she loved to go there. At the same time, I've heard stories from friends about developments out there. They're looking for investors on the front end, to start things up. Have you heard anything about that?"

"I have," Gill said nodding a short, up-down motion. "They've been talking about developing the east arm of Hay Island and the Route Bay area."

"That's right. Those names sound familiar. What do you know about it?"

"A motion to zone and sell the land went through council a week ago. The surveyors will be out to the island in two weeks." Gill said.

"And when's it up for sale?" Gary asked.

"You'll have to find that out."

"But it's good land? Not swampland?"

Gill laughed in a short exhale of breath. "If it's Hay Island and Route Bay it's good. It's really good." Gill stopped for a second. "You know, they've been talking about subdividing and selling that land off for years. People who live around it have been against it.

"Are you against it?"

"Yep."

"That's too bad. It could be a good deal."

"Good deal? You have to understand, to me this is not cottage land. It's the land I work with to make a living. That's a good deal to me. Why should I want someone who doesn't understand that to move in next door and play for twelve weekends a year?"

"Why should it bother you? If they're only there twelve weekends a year?"

"How would you like someone living in your office twelve weekends a year?"

"Ahh, that's not the same. No one would want to live in my office," Gary said and smiled, showing his teeth. Gill smiled and sat back in his chair. Gary rubbed the end of his nose between his thumb and fingers. "You know Gill, we could make this work. I've got some dividends coming up. End of year stuff. I thought that after Christine and me were back from the honeymoon we might swing out past your place and you could show us around. Some of the good spots. I'll get Christine to call you. She has your number right?"

Gill nodded. "Yep, she's got it."

"Good. I better get going but we'll call you. Probably in late November or early December. Who knows? It may be Christmas. Whenever it is, we'll make it worth your while."

Gill held himself rigid, his head still as Gary turned and walked away. Gill followed him with his eyes, aiming at the point of the spine between the shoulder blades, where if you shot any animal it would drop and never move again. It was not an option to shoot a man for no reason, but it was something you could think about. Gary flapped over to his new bride who was in a conversation with someone Gill couldn't see. The coloured lights glistened on the bald spot topping Gary's head like a guillotine had missed its job. Gary waited for her to finish her sentence then he turned her to him and kissed her. Gill's eyes jerked away, to his hands resting together on the table. They glistened in the lights as well, the blued veins, white scars, wrinkles at the knuckles, the shapes of flesh and bone and tendon he used every day. He squeezed them until the four knuckles pressed up white through the skin and his nails gouged his own palms. Like that he held them and looked at them: their ends like blunt objects, their white scars random slashes of history. When he felt his pulse thumping inside each fist, he released them, got up, and went outside for fresh air.

After Wade dropped Murryn at her apartment, he returned to the Fort Garry to pick up Gill. The two of them were the last to leave the reception as they walked out to Wade's Honda. Their ties were loosened, the top buttons on their shirts undone. Wade's joints had an easy, loose feel like their fluids had just been changed. The air brushed over the streets in cool, refreshing strokes, into lungs used to the stuffy heat of the hotel. The sky looked clear, stars shining all across the blackness, the moon a slice of light resting in the west.

Wade had his hands in his pant pockets, against his thighs, around the car keys. His steps unrolled along beside his father and his legs felt tired from standing. He peered up at the twinkling sky and felt good to have gotten through the day. It always felt good to work with his father and Wade was finding out it also felt good just to be with him. An easy silence traded back and forth between them like wind.

"Well, partner," Gill said. "It went off without a hitch."

"Yeah. And we had that good meal."

"Wasn't it great?"

"It was good," Wade said, twisting the key to unlock Gill's car door. Gill got in and reached across to unlock the driver's door. Wade got in and fired the ignition.

"You're a good date," he said to Gill.

"I am, why?"

"You unlocked my door. Apparently that's the way to tell if the girl you're with is a good date."

"Does it work?"

"I don't know, I've never paid attention."

"I'll give it a shot on Cheryl. See what she does. What does Murryn do?"

"Sometimes she unlocks my door, sometimes she doesn't."

Wade clicked on the lights and shifted into first. He released the clutch and the Honda eased around the parking lot and out onto Broadway. A navy ghost-car cruised by and Wade released the clutch and the Honda pulled into the curb lane. He changed lanes and pulled a U-turn around the meridian to head west, over the Assiniboine River and out towards the suburbs along the winding path of the river. Only a few cars skimmed along the road, cars filled with teenagers or couples returning from dates, or solitary people on their way to or from parties or odd-hour shifts. Gill unrolled his window and cool air buffeted through the car. Wide oak, pale elm and black and white poplar trees guarded both sides of the road. The lanes of the road cut through the forest. Heeding a yellow sign, Wade watched for deer cross-ing and ran his hand through his hair with the circulating air.

"It's been a long day, hey, partner?" Gill said.

"Yeah. Seems like a week ago we were in Mariapolis."

Gill nodded and watched out the side window as the trees blurred past into greys. "Are you tired?" he asked Wade.

"A little. You?"

"Not really."

Wade tapped the brake pedal as a shadow approached the side of the road. The Honda slowed and rolled past a young doe, her head up and alert, the headlights shining on her side. Her large ears pricked forwards and her white tail flickered. Her eyes reflected the headlights as the Honda crept past and Wade tapped the brakes again as a warning for cars following them.

"Her winter coat is coming in," Gill said, looking at the thick fur on the doe.

"Pretty. It's a shame there's so many deer around. You see them hit on the side of the road almost every week."

Gill nodded, pushed his hands out the window and clapped. The doe dropped its body at an angle and sprang back from the road toward the bush, its white tail up and waving side to side. In a few seconds she was gone from sight. Wade accelerated along the road, shifted to second, rolled down his own window to feel the air, shifted to third, and drove on. The air was wet and cool and fresh and a mist edged out from the trees bordering the road.

"Do you want to go somewhere and get a drink?" Gill asked.

"What do you want? I've got some good beer in the fridge at home."

"That sounds good."

Wade turned on the third street after the end of the trees, went south four blocks and turned west again.

"It went pretty well, don't you think?" Wade said to Gill.

"Pretty well. Yep. The ceremony was nice. The violinist especially. And the food after was excellent. Then the reception. Pretty damn good."

"Mom looked nice."

"Yep. Your mother looked great. She always looks great."

Wade nodded and the air spread out over his face. Questions still rattled in his mind about the wedding and his father. "You didn't feel awkward?"

"Not especially. I think other people felt awkward for me. Everyone feels awkward at weddings. Don Silas: he didn't know what to say or do with me at all. And his wife Brenda, she talked about lakes and water and camping like that's all I can talk about. She told me she bought a fur coat last year and couldn't understand what all the fake-fur fuss was about. That's what she said, 'fake-fur fuss,' like she'd just read an article in *Chatelaine*. She patted me on the wrist and told me real fur was fine with her."

"What did you say to that?"

"I told her that made me feel better. Because sometimes it isn't easy being a trapper. I told her about shooting a marten that was jumping around in a leg-hold trap and my shot missing and the marten running away on three legs because I had shot the trapped leg off."

"Is that a true story?"

Gill smiled and his eyes reflected the streetlights. "She thought so," he said and laughed. "It was the last thing I said to her before she excused herself."

Wade slowed the Honda and made a left off the main road and made a right into his driveway. The house he had bought sat at the edge of the city, on the far side of the last road before the open farm fields and at the end of municipal water and sewer service. The lot covered four acres and the white cottage at the head of the driveway was eleven hundred square feet. It pleased Wade to own the house. The green Land Cruiser rested alongside the garage with strands of grass hanging from the bumper and frame.

"The old Cruiser," Wade said and pulled the Honda into the garage.

"Yep. I have a hunch it may retire soon."

"You're getting rid of it?" Wade asked and got out of the car.

"Nah, there's not much money in it. Just seeing about something newer," Gill said as they walked over to the Land Cruiser

"Good. You can't get rid of it. I'd buy it off you if I had to. She's still a beauty."

"She runs well," Gill said and stepped along beside the Land Cruiser. "She runs well. I've kept her for many years."

"And she's still in great shape."

"Yep, she is that. A lot of care went into her?" Gill said and wandered around to the hood. "And what would you do with her if you bought her?"

"Run it in the winter," Wade said. "Keep it for a few years from now."

"What would you do with it then?"

"I don't know."

"Then why would you want it?"

Wade didn't know what to say to Gill, the challenge in the conversation surprised him. He didn't tell Gill the simple thought that he didn't want the Land Cruiser sold to someone else. "I have some ideas," Wade said and stood still with his hands in his pockets. He wanted to wait for the right time to tell Gill what he had on his mind, an idea about them working together on a business that offered his father a new way of looking at guiding. "Come on inside, Dad. We'll have a beer and go out on the porch and I'll tell you about my idea."

"Okay," Gill said but kept walking around the Land Cruiser. "Go on ahead, I want to clean up out here a bit."

Wade looked at him in his suit, the tie twisted around so the white strap holding the short end showed.

"Go on," Gill said. "I'll be there soon enough."

Wade nodded and turned and went through the garage into the house. The storm door thumped closed. Wade pulled a set of sheets from the closet and made up the bed in the guest room where Gill would sleep. He smiled to himself as he thought of all the times he had seen his father make up beds for him when he arrived at the cabin. Now the roles were reversed and he was playing host. Around the house he busied himself, checking for phone messages, cleaning up in the kitchen from his quick departure. The events of the day, the dressing up, the re-acquaintances, the noise and ceremony, tears and stares, laughs and stumbles, played through Wade's mind. By the time he heard Gill come in, he felt like he was approaching the end of the longest day of his life.

Wade lit a fire in the fireplace and Gill washed his hands in the kitchen sink. Wade took two beers from the fridge and handed one to Gill and toasted the wedding. They went out through the patio doors onto the deck and into the strong smell of cedar. The edge of the deck dropped off to a lawn speckled with fallen leaves that stretched away into the darkness. Deer often fed at the back edge of the property where a tilled garden appeared as a dark patch cut from the lawn.

Gill asked, "What are you going to do with a garden like that?"

"I don't know yet. I may plant it myself. Or Murryn and I. I met a neighbour through the back there," Wade said pointing past the back end of his property. "Mrs. Dunn. She's got a garden. She might want to plant it. Or I might let it go wild. Reclaimed by nature."

"Really?" Gill said.

"No, probably not. But it sounds good."

Wade and Gill sat for a while not saying much. Gill burped a carbonated breath and sighed. "You think you'll be staying here for a while?"

"At this house?"

Gill nodded. "At this house, in Winnipeg, all that."

Wade pulled his face, "Yeah I'll be here for little while. Things are good but there could be more."

"More what?"

"Better," Wade corrected himself. "Better work. It's nice finally having a regular salary, being done school. But I can't see myself staying an employee benefits consultant for Great-West all my life. Who knows? I may be. But I try and think ahead and there's nothing too promising I can see." Wade sipped his beer.

"I've been thinking about doing other things. Some days at work are good and some days are lousy. Like anything." An owl flew just over the bare tips of the back trees, hunting, flying without sound. "On the lousy ones I can't wait to get out of the office. I end up dreaming about things I'd rather be doing."

Wade sipped his beer again. Gill listened and followed the silent shape of the owl out over the yard. He looked strange to Wade, like he'd joined the world at his office for a day, like a new, entry-level employee. Gill wore his suit, his tie loosened, his top button undone, and Wade couldn't remember if he'd ever seen his father in a suit before. He must have, at graduation or convocation. But he could not remember any clear images of those times with Gill in them.

Gill looked at him and said, "So, what were you saying about an idea you have?"

"Right. I have this idea that I've been thinking about for a long time. Since before I started at Great-West Life. Since I used to work the summers with you, out at the lake. You're the one to talk to about it. I thought of it when my friend Sully's dad went on a fly-in fishing trip. He tried to find out about operators and lodges; where to go, who to go with. He had a tough time. So I thought we could start up a company that did travel brokerage for fishing and hunting trips. Like a matching service. What do you think?"

Gill's eyes flickered over at Wade and then back out to the darkness. "Tell me more. How does it work?"

"We set up an office for bookings, then get linked to the provincial and regional and federal tourism networks. We make all the connections so clients know where to find us. We go to trade shows, advertise. Then we approach the lodges in a similar way; find out the details about them, talk to people about what they want. We make up two profiles databases. One is for customers, the other is for the lodges. We match the customer to the lodge."

Gill sat and sipped his beer. A car sped past on a gravel road and stones pinged off its underbelly. "How do you make any money? It seems like you're doing your clients favours more than selling anything."

"Yeah, in a way. But you charge for the favours. It's a value-added service," Wade said and felt excited as he explained his idea, finally sharing it with Gill. He had thought about the idea for so long that now it all started coming out. "The purpose of the broker is to match clients to the right trip. The more volume we do, the more money we make. We advertise in the US and Europe for all the hunters and fishermen to come to Canada and see what they've been missing. We make Lake of the Woods into a world-class travel destination."

"What about people who don't want to go to lodges? People who can't afford fly-in fishing?"

"They don't matter. You would target the people who wanted to go to the lodges. Work deals out with American companies for their tourists," Wade said, pressing on. "It's the same thing you do, Dad. It's guiding but in a different environment." The owl swept over the tips of the trees again, its shape solid and dark against the starry night sky. "I have a rough business plan of the way I would run it. It would be lean in the first few years but as your clients grew, and your reputation, it could be a good venture."

Wade watched Gill as he spoke. He felt that, apart from being a good business model, his idea offered Gill a way to keep his lifestyle at Lake of the Woods while also getting a chance to compete and make money. He had to make Gill see that a bigger world was right there waiting to be seized. He went on into further details about his idea and he saw Gill begin to understand the process of servicing the customer. He explained further how he saw it happening: questions determined what lodge and what package at the lodge was right for a particular tourist on a particular trip. What was their budget? Their time frame? The purpose of the trip? Their desired comfort level? The questions and ideas rushed out of Wade. Some details he passed over quickly and came back to again and other details he said would work themselves out.

Wade went on forecasting until there was nothing more he could think of. He nodded along at the ideas as they came out and took shape in his words.

"And you, Dad," Wade said looking at Gill. "I want you to do it with me."

After a long pause and a sip of beer, Gill said, "Well. I'm not sure, partner. What do you mean?"

"I mean I want you to be a part of it. I mean I think you could be perfect for it."

"An accommodations guide? An adventure-travel agent?"

"You'd be perfect. You know the types of places, the types of people. They would trust you." Wade rolled out the reasons to Gill. "You can't trap and guide forever. You can see that. It's a wonderful life. But not forever."

"What about that life then? You used to tell me you wanted it to be yours too."

"Yeah," Wade said. "Yes I did."

"And I can see you don't now."

"But that's what this would be like."

"You think so?" Gill said and looked over at his son in his suit. "I know you're not going to join me at the lake. You have your life here, where you belong."

Wade looked at his hands around the bottle of beer. It was good beer, imported beer from Europe. "I wanted to before. To be like you."

"But it's not for you," Gill said, finishing the thought.

Wade shook his head.

"You ever wonder why?"

"Because it's not real. It's from the last century."

"It's unsure."

"Damn right it's unsure. All the growth in our economy is elsewhere. It's unreasonable to be a smart guy like you are and to not see the future."

"Maybe you should just leave me behind then," Gill said and stared at his hands between his knees. "In the last century." He looked down to the cedar deck boards, sanded smooth under his feet, the good craftsmanship of even spacing between each board. He wondered if Wade had built the deck himself or if he had hired someone to do it. He wondered if he and Wade could not have done a better job given the chance. "Wade, my life, the life I've led and still lead. It may not be for you. It's not for you, that's pretty easy to see. You rightly have your own life and ideas about how you should live. But this is my life and I chose it."

"Dad—"

"No, listen," Gill said. "You don't have to like it. Just because my life isn't your idea of forever, no pension and benefits package and regular cheques, you can't take it apart. You can't take it and do what you want with it and make it into what you want it to be. I'm not a tour director. Sure, things are going to change. But I can still choose to live how I want."

Wade took a breath to tell Gill that of course he could do what he wanted, but Gill held up his hand to stop him.

"Did you think I could just be the company mascot? Like Gretzky is for hockey?"

Wade shook his head and said, "I'm just trying to offer you something you can keep doing and make some money with."

"Okay, I appreciate that. But what I do, what lots of people in this country do, trappers and loggers and miners, that's what makes this country exist. Not having people visit us so they can take their photos home and show off how they love nature. The smell of a place and the stories we know, what it's all about, it's what makes a place special. And none of it is to get a pension or have security. Companies and offices and Americans and businesses, they're

215

important too. But they're the same everywhere. They always want to take more and they never want to give more. But you can't change the history and nature of the lake."

Wade looked at Gill and Gill said, "I'm not done. I listened to your ideas, now listen to mine. There's more things to say. What happened tonight, with Gary following me around at the reception, when you saw us shouting out in the hall. That was what I'm talking about. He asked me about the cabin, how much I'd paid for it and when, how much I thought the land around was worth, how much I thought I could get for my land. He asked these things like there wasn't anything more important than that in the world. How much can you get for it? Like everything could be for sale. He asked me how the water quality was in Storm Bay, if it was good enough to drink and swim in. He had heard about a venture to bottle it and sell it and wondered if he should get in on the ground floor. He thought he would invest in a development there, like in Florida. It would be a good holding for him."

Gill stopped and let himself breathe. He brought his hand to his neck and pulled his tie away from his collar. "And this thing," he said. "I wish I could tie it around his neck." He stopped and dropped the tie and shook his head. "Ahh, that's not it," he said. "It's just a fucking hell of a life we live here." He shook his head and tipped his beer back and wiped his mouth. "Excuse my language."

"No problem," Wade said and sat on his chair with his hands wrapped around his beer. He noticed Gill's back rising and falling and the angled line of skin where his face stretched over his jawbone. A blood vessel pulsed under the skin of Gill's neck.

Wade watched the man wearing the suit on his deck, the man he thought he knew as he thought he knew himself, the man who was somehow strange to him in the most familiar way, the man he had thought of as an entry-level employee.

Wade asked, "Isn't there anything that'll make you consider my idea?"

"Wade, I tried going to university and working and living in the city for your mother and it's not for me. Being out at the lake and doing what I do works pretty well for me. I like it there, I have something that I think is worthwhile to do. I show people a good time and share with them some of the things that I think make it such a special place. Some days are better than others and lots of days I wish for all the good things that you're talking about: a pension and health plan and security. But I do what I want, and even on the worst days, that's worthwhile. I think I learned a while ago that you're best off being satisfied, not happy or rich or famous."

Gill pulled the loop of his tie over his head and the blood vessel in his neck continued pulsing. "After I'm long gone," he said. "The lake'll still be there. And part of me wants to make sure it's still the place it is. Tourists are fine so long as they understand the place and make an effort to know what it's about. But people don't want to be treated like they don't matter, like they're interchangeable; neither do places. And they're not."

Wade met Gill's eyes and saw the same eyes he had wanted to please his whole life. He felt his idea slipping away. None of it made sense anymore. He still understood the economics of the business and the market opportunity and how it would all work but none of that mattered there on the deck in a conversation with his father. Things Wade did not understand had always existed between him and Gill; things that he could never control, like those that had compelled him to bite through Gill's skin when he was five. The things they had wrestled fiercely about when he was eight. The things that caused Wade to wonder what it would be like to shoot Gill when they were duck hunting and he was thirteen. The things that made him correct Gill on a point of grammar with rigid, regimented precision just yesterday. And now here he was, sitting on his cedar deck as the fall chill snapped into the ground, not able to understand how his father could not see that he could be so much more. A part of him wanted to stand up and shake hands with Gill and go in to bed for the night, having tried to appeal to his father's reason and having gone nowhere. To cut the losses, restructure the dynamics and get the most sleep he could.

"But," Wade said, "people like to travel and go to lots of different places."

"Yeah, you're right. You sound like you know the business side of things."

"I think it could really work if we did it."

"It probably could, but it's not right for me."

"Are you sure?"

Gill nodded. "When you travel you always go home. Just like everyone. We all have a home. We all have a family. Right, partner?"

And at that moment, when Gill looked right through him, the feeling shocked Wade like the kick of a gun: how lucky he was to have his father. He had been frustrated and determined to make Gill see what he was missing out on, to help him understand the opportunities he had. And then his desire and his belief and his idea and his argument that he knew anything about the importance of things in life was gone. It disappeared.

Wade rocked on his elbows and saw a gleam of light on Gill's cheek and then he knew his father was crying. Wade put his beer to the side on the deck and reached into his pocket for a tissue. He leaned forward and let himself fall onto his knees toward his father, stretched his arm and touched Gill on the shoulder. He held his hand there against his father's shoulder, holding the tissue in his hand and then Wade let go of his idea and it left him. At the moment when he knew a difference of values could have driven a rift between him and his father, when he could have staked himself to his business plan and carried on alone, he let go and felt it all melt away.

"It's okay, Wade," Gill said and wiped the tears from his cheeks with the palms of his hands. "I knew this a while ago. I should have let you know."

"About what?"

"About me. About myself." Gill spread the last wetness of tears out of his eyes.

Wade brought his arm back and pressed the tissue to his own cheek where a tear had slipped down and dropped to the deck. He looked up at Gill and a part of him wanted to lay his head on his father's knee, for Gill to cup it with his hand and stroke his hair like he used to lying in bed at the lake, and to let the feelings inside him flow out. Then Wade looked up at his father and put his hand on his knee. Gill looked down at him and pressed his hand with its warm, rough skin over Wade's hand. Wade pushed himself back up into his chair and they sat on the deck for a few more minutes, until both had finished their beers, then went in to bed.

And after he had finished brushing his teeth, Wade went to the door of the guest room and looked in and said goodnight to Gill. He thanked his father for listening to him and for being honest with him. He stood at the door and watched Gill prop himself up on an elbow in bed and he wanted to say more, to tell Gill how proud he was of him and of being his son, but none of that came out.

"Goodnight, partner." Gill said after a moment. "Have a good sleep."

"'Night, Dad." Wade said and started to turn to his bedroom, then stopped. "Dad? I'm sorry, for what I said before. I thought it was a chance for us."

"Don't be sorry," Gill said "I know you did."

Wade stood at the door for another few seconds and said goodnight again and then turned and walked to his bedroom. As he lay in his bed waiting for the sheets to warm from his body, he started to think of all the things that had happened that day and what he valued and where he belonged in the world. But he did not get far before he fell asleep.

The next morning, sunlight crackled over a landscape covered in the bright white of hoar frost. Straight across the sky, the light shone and the world outside the windows of Wade's house glistened in the frosty dust. Gill rose and finished his shower before Wade heard him. He had dried and cleaned himself and was headed back to the guest room to dress when Wade poked his head out of his bedroom.

"Daylight in the swamp," Gill said.

"Daylight in the snow," Wade said, looking out the window.

"Isn't it pretty?" Gill called back, opening the drapes in the guest room.

"It's bright," Wade said, squinting his eyes. He smelled coffee brewing and saw Gill folding and arranging his clothes into a duffle bag.

Wade asked, "You're not leaving yet, are you?"

"I thought I would get out of the way."

"You're not in the way," Wade said. "Murryn's coming over at eight-thirty and we thought we'd do a brunch. She brought the food over last night."

Gill stopped packing and stood at the door of the guest room. "How'd she get in?"

"She has keys."

Gill smiled and shook his head and it looked to Wade like his father was enjoying himself. "We'll sit," Gill said. "And have coffee. That'll be good enough." He pushed his hand down into the pocket of his pants to smooth out the leg. "After that I ought to get going."

By the time Wade had dressed and brushed his teeth, the coffee was gurgling and Gill was waiting for him. Wade poured out two cups and saved the remainder of the pot for Gill to take in his thermos. He put water in the coffee maker for another pot. Gill opened the patio door and stepped out onto the deck. Wade retrieved his hunting boots and jacket and followed Gill, careful not to slip on the slick boards. They sat in the same chairs as the night before, each in the same spot. The frost glistened in the bright sun and their breath jetted out in clouds. A few songbirds flitted amongst the hardwoods at the back of the property, waiting for the sun to burn off the frost.

"It's beautiful," Gill said.

Wade nodded and watched the steam rise off the cup between his hands. "Murryn'll be disappointed," he said.

"Nah, she won't."

"Yeah, she will. She's the one who wanted to have breakfast. She's got it planned: omelettes and panfries and bacon and toast and fruit."

"There'll be more for you guys then."

"Too much for us," Wade said and blew rings around his coffee. A fine breeze nipped around the yard brushing hoarfrost from the tree branches. Wade slurped some of his hot coffee off the rim of the cup and felt it scald down his throat. "Why're you really going, Dad?"

Gill leaned forward with his elbows rested on his knees and his cup of coffee between his hands. He looked down into the black hole of his coffee, inhaling the steam.

"There's things I have to do today."

"They can't wait?"

Gill shook his head. "I'd like to stay. But I have some important things that I have to do." He took a sip of his coffee the same way as Wade, slurped off the rim of the cup.

"Like what?"

Gill turned his head to Wade and smiled; there was no putting him off the scent.

"They're trying to move me out," Gill said. "I told you a motion to subdivide Storm Bay has gone through town council?

Well, the developer wants the whole parcel of land, right through Route Bay, past the Blindfold dam. If that happens, this may be my last year there."

"You're going to sell?"

"Yep, I guess so," Gill said.

"What about Smiths? I thought they owned all the land around Storm Bay."

"They did until about six years ago. Then the government started buying it all back. For crown land they said. Crown land my ass. This deal has been in the works for twenty years, the government knew exactly what they were doing."

"Isn't there anything you can do? Sue them?"

"Not likely. That's what I'm going to see about, but I'm not holding my breath."

"They can't just tell you to sell," Wade said.

Gill shook his head and blew at the steam from his coffee. "We'll see," he said and squinted to the treeline at the edge of the property. "I don't intend to go quietly, but we'll see."

Songbirds skipped from branch to branch, tree to tree, chirping and leaving tiny nicks of footprints in the hoarfrost. The air slid around Wade and Gill and they heard the distant calls of geese. Right away they swung upright, swivelling their heads to the sky, searching for the dark specks swept back in long, uneven Vs. The calls grew louder and carried over the land as the geese came closer. In a wide sweep, the geese descended out of the sky, circling lower and lower, aiming to land in the field behind Wade's house.

Wade and Gill watched the geese and spoke no words. They looked at each other once as they both recognized what the geese were doing, where they planned to land. The calls swelled until no quiet existed between them; the calls vibrated across the land as thousands of the brown and black bodies landed on the white fields just beyond the back yard. Wade and Gill watched the geese descend in waves as they drank their coffees.

When it was time for Gill to go, Wade walked with him out to the Land Cruiser and hugged him. The engine cranked and Gill let it warm up for a minute. Wade opened the passenger door and leaned in.

"You're sure you've got everything?" he said.

"Yep. If not I'll be back in a month."

"Okay. So drive safe. Make sure this old beast gets you home."

"I'll be fine. Say 'hi' to Murryn for me. Tell her I missed dancing with her last night."

"Will do."

"And keep in touch. Even for no reason. The ice'll be in soon enough and we'll make it out ice fishing."

"That sounds good. I'd like to catch some trout."

Gill nodded once. "We'll get you a couple."

Gill's hand reached out and opened and Wade took it, holding it.

"Take care, Dad," Wade said. "Come in and stay any time you like, there's always a bed."

"And there's always a place for you at the lake too, partner. As long as I'm there."

Wade and Gill laughed and shook hands, strong and rigid, then Wade brought himself back outside again, holding the rim of the door.

"Thanks for the hunt, Dad. It was great."

"Thank you."

"Okay. Drive safe."

"I will."

"And I'll see you soon."

Gill nodded and strained to smile as the tears pushed into his eyes. Then he blurred as tears welled up in Wade's eyes.

"Are you getting sentimental in your old age, Dad?"

"It happens. Or you let it happen more. But it happens. See you, partner."

Wade sniffed a deep breath, wiped the tears from his face and nodded quickly to his father. Gill pushed in the clutch, shifted the black gear stick to reverse and scuffed his shirt sleeve over his face. Wade closed the door, put his hand on the window and felt the Land Cruiser start to roll back. He lifted his hand, tapped the green window rim twice and stepped back. He saw Gill turn his head over his right shoulder, swing his arm over the headrest of the passenger seat and twist to look back along the driveway. With a high whir of gears, the Land Cruiser backed up, crossed the ditch and swung out onto the road. As he stopped, Gill hoisted his right hand and touched it against the window. He clicked the lights on and tooted the horn twice. The gear linkages slotted in and the Land Cruiser rolled forward, straightening out and speeding up. Wade stood where he had last touched the Land Cruiser and watched Gill roll along the road and out of sight. He shivered and turned to go back into the house to refill his coffee cup.

When he came back out the calls of the geese seemed to echo and surround the house. Wade sat on the front steps and waited for Murryn to arrive. The sun climbed in the sky and warmed him as he started to plan how to get out to the lake to ice fish. Wade thought about ice fishing, and laughed to himself, since it was not the ice fishing that made him want to go to the lake. It was the chance to be with his father; that man who had been with him all yesterday and all his life; his father, the man he watched and thought of and loved. No matter what, they were both Dubois. Wade thought about how he had aspired to make Gill into an entrepreneur, a success; how he had rehearsed the idea in his head, and he knew it was shit. It was unreal shit and he had tried to sell it and he felt sorry. He had said he was sorry and he believed Gill understood that he meant no harm.

And so Wade sat on his front steps and only one thought came to him, over and over: that's my dad. That's him, that's my dad; over and over, that's my dad. He was the one who loved my mother and his own life at the same time. He chose, with his wife, to be divorced and live in his cabin at the lake. He watched me play hockey and showed me how to fish and breast a duck and whistle show tunes and talk to people and care about them. That's my dad, Gill Dubois, driving back to his cabin at the lake. And when Murryn tells me I'm talking like him or laughing like him or looking like him, then I am, because I am. Because I am.

And as Wade waited for Murryn he could not know that Gill would be killed two hours, forty-two minutes later; on the far side of Kenora where the highway narrows to two lanes, no shoulders, and the sheer granite cliffs rise up on either side of the road. He could not know that a transport truck with a blown tire sent Gill spinning the Land Cruiser's black steering wheel. Gill spun the wheel too tight trying to save himself; the Land Cruiser rolled twice, side over side, side over side, an explosion of sound and dirt, Gill suspended by his seat belt when the Land Cruiser slammed into the cliff. Wade would be told that the impact killed Gill instantly, the vertical dynamite drill-lines in the cliff face forming ridges in the Land Cruiser roof as it collapsed and ended his father's life.

Wade sat on the front steps of his house and waited for the woman he loved and there was nothing he could do. Life was to end for his father that day, the same as it was to end for Wade one day, the same as it did for everyone, no exceptions. The cabin that Wade dreamed about all those nights as he returned on the bus from Kenora was never fully finished and never saw another Dubois generation. Two days after all the legal challenges from residents were defeated, bulldozers would move in and start clearing the shoreline of trees and buildings in preparation for construction. But as Murryn's blue VW pulled into the driveway and Wade stood and saw her smile through the windshield, he felt like the luckiest man on earth and wiped his tears and went to kiss her.

A FOOTHOLD

WADE PULLED THE LAND CRUISER INTO THE CLEARING AT THE end of logging road 341 and engaged the emergency brake. The rough gravel crunched under his feet as he stepped out, closed the door and listened to the echo fade over the quiet country of rock and moss and trees. The burned-out land where the forest fire passed nine years ago fell away before him down to the shore of Lake of the Woods where his boat was beached. As he did every weekend, he planned to hike down to the boat and mount the old Mercury on the transom, then travel out to the island he had purchased with the money from Gill's life insurance policy, and set up his tent in the clearing for the cabin. From there he had watched the sun set over the water and breathed the air blown in off the prairies that made the sky light up in oranges and reds while the thunderheads piled up in the distance.

Wade snugged his pack around his hips, set his Tilley hat on his head and stashed an extra set of keys in the wheel well of the truck before locking up. He hiked down past the sifting needles of the pines just getting their foothold in the acidic soil, over ridges and past saplings he had marked with orange tape, down to the wetter land ringing the shore where pine and spruce and alder stood untouched by the fire. A turkey vulture circled above the treetops and Wade watched it soar around on a wheel of air as he hiked along. When he reached the underbrush that bordered the clearing where he kept the boat, another turkey vulture croaked and took off. The smell of rot hung in the air. This was not what Wade had expected. Getting to the boat on the shore always rewarded him, the end of his hike and the start of the last leg of his journey out over the water of Andrew Bay to the island. Now something had died. As he broke through the brush to the shore, he saw a long bone picked clean sticking out from under his overturned boat. A gust of wind pushed in from the lake and a cloud of tiny flies picked up and milled around in the air like sand. He stood and closed his mouth and eyes and felt the flies hitting him on the face, on the hands, on the neck. The image of the bone sticking out from the boat burned in his mind. It had to be the leg of a bear.

Wade felt a fly enter his nose and he swung out, cleaving the air around him in wild swings. He yelled and swung his hat through the air and dropped his pack. By the time he crouched down beside the boat, sucked in his breath and leaned in closer so that his eyes were in the shadow and he could see the bear's skin caved in around its bones, he knew it was a mess. He needed a plan. His lungs burned and his eyes watered. He watched the shiny beetles thick on the carcass, the black fur up on the leg under the shadow of the boat where the turkey vultures had not been able to get at it. He rolled away from the boat and drew in a deep breath, choking on the smell. Clouds had started to spread across the sky like ash. The forecast called for a seventy percent chance of rain in the afternoon. If he wanted to get out to his island, and set up his tent, he needed to flip over the boat. Wade gathered himself at the side of the boat, squatted down and set his grip. The boat rose with a groan of aluminum, the stench of the bear almost visible in the air that swept out from under the shifting hull, the gunnel pressing down onto the leg bone. It cracked. Wade gave the boat a final push as he always did to finish the roll, when the boat always picked up momentum and rolled down onto its hull. But the boat stopped, hung up on the carcass. He shoved the boat with his shoulder and his legs, with a two-step run at it. It rocked but did not roll over.

Wade walked to the other side of the boat to try and pull it. He reached up and steadied his feet and his grip and pulled. Aluminum pressed into his flesh and the boat rocked toward him as he adjusted his grip to catch the weight. The bone cracked again and the boat shifted in a groan and started moving. Wade stepped back and let it come down towards him, onto the rollers he made sure he placed every time he left the lake. The boat picked up speed as it came towards him until it was dropping the last twelve inches and he had to snap his hands out of the way. The curved base of the gunnel where the red paint of the side panel met the silver paint of the base fell and crashed against the leather ankle of his boot. Wade yelled out and jerked at his pinned foot. He jerked again and it moved. He lunged with his whole body away from the boat, pulling the long reeds at the end of his fingers from the boggy soil. His boot popped loose from its trap and Wade sprawled onto the ground where it felt soft and marshy against his shoulder and cheek, smelled as if it hadn't been disturbed in decades. He stood and tested his weight on his ankle and winced as he walked to the boat. Not broken, just tender, he decided. He dragged the boat to the edge of the water and prepped it to go, mounted the Merc on the transom and chaining it on, made sure the plug was in the drain.

Now he needed the gas tanks. Wade turned to where he kept them, under the overturned boat, out of the elements, just as he had been taught by Gill in the long summers they had spent together at the lake, and the only thing he saw was the bear. In the outline of dead reeds marking where the boat had lain, the bear had died on top of the gas tanks. Wade stared at the carcass as if he had forgotten that the bear was his whole problem: the reason he had dropped the goddamn boat on his ankle and the reason he might not make it out to the island. He almost laughed out loud. If his co-workers could see him now, not standing in front of a client doing a presentation or working on a report for his manager, but hobbling on a swelling ankle and staring at a dead bear. To get the gas tanks he would have to move the carcass.

Wade felt the wind blow in off the water, and the knowledge that he could die out here in the bush and not be found for many days chilled him. The situation now presented itself with cold immediacy. His money and reputation, his personal accomplishments, goals and ideas about living the good life, making junior executive at head office in the next five years, getting Gary to keep his eye out for good income properties, getting to drive to work every day in the new Lexus, meant nothing.

Wade grabbed a log of driftwood. With a couple of jerks the log went in under the carcass quick and painless. He started to wedge the log further under the bear and it started to move like he knew it would work, simple mechanics. The bear's back rose from the ground, one of the gas tanks was uncovered, and Wade had it moving off the other one in an arc at the end of the log. Then the carcass bent in half, ripping and spilling maggots like seeds from a ruptured sack. Dead reeds and rotting matter bound it to the ground as it rolled back to where it started. Wade lost his footing and fell and pain shot out from his ankle.

Only one thing was going to get this done. If he wanted the gas tanks to start the motor to get to his island he would have to move the bear. No maggots, beetles, no stench, just the carcass; no choice. He walked slowly over to the carcass, breathing deeply with his hands open at his sides. He set his feet and clenched his teeth and made his mind a blank. On either side of the bear's broken spine he worked his hands under the carcass until the coat was up to his elbows. He bent at the knees, like a power-lifter, rocked onto his heels, forward, coil back again, hold, then heave. The spine bent over Wade's arms like it had over the drift-wood lever. Maggots and beetles and dead shit spilled onto his arms and he pushed. Hot air and decay heaved out of the dead bear into his face. Wade grunted, reset his feet, clawed at the bear for a grip and leverage. The carcass began to tear again over his forearms where he held it and kept pushing. The blood pound-ed in his head and his legs burned. He was getting it. The carcass lifted and tilted, the white bone rising into the air and the spine bending, the head rolling. He screamed into the fur and twisted the moving carcass, tipping the bulk of the tearing body over its head so it rolled off the tanks. Bones popped as the carcass col-lapsed onto itself and pulled Wade down into it, crackling again, breaking under his weight. He screamed, took a breath, tried to push himself up, pushed his hand through the ribcage and screamed again. He pressed himself up and his fists sunk between the ribs of the carcass. He pulled them out and flailed backward, grabbing a stick he fell back on and swinging it down, breaking it over the carcass. He reached around him again and found a thicker stick, the size of his arm around, and swung it at the bear. He scrambled to his knees and battered at the blank eye socket scoured bare down to the bone. He swung again, again, again; the skull bouncing and then pounded into the marshy mud. He drew the stick back and was done. A long canine tooth stuck out of the stick where it had bit in. He dropped the stick and col-lapsed and it was over. He sat still and stiff and trembling.

The sun continued to drop to the horizon and the shadows stretched out over the water. The scraping of the metal gas tanks that Wade dropped into the bottom of the boat lit a kingfisher to flight along the shore. A low mist began to rise in the bottom of the bay. Wade primed and choked the Merc and it started on the third pull. He let it warm up while he took a heavy jacket out of his pack and zipped it up under his chin. Stay warm and keep your head, he told himself. The clouds above heaved across the sky in receding layers of grey. The sun peaked through in the distance. Lightning flashed to the west, then four, five, six seconds later the thunder rolled in a loud press of sound over the land. Six seconds, six kilometres. The storm was not hitting yet. Wade bobbed in the waves and watched the Merc tremble and warm up. He reached back around the powerhead to the gear lever and shifted into forward. The boat started churning off a wake and his neck flexed in time to the rocking waves, keeping the brim of his hat level to the horizon. He gave the Merc more gas and watched the water rolling around him as the waves crested. The land drew away and Wade did not look back to see the black carcass on the darkening shore or the turkey vultures dropping down from above. The water rolled all around him then and the prow of the boat headed straight into the waves, cutting through the wind, aiming at the island beyond.